WILD
CRUSH

USA TODAY BESTSELLING AUTHOR

KACEY SHEA

Wild Crush

Kacey Shea

Copyright © 2024 by Kacey Shea Books LLC

Cover Design: Kim Wilson, KiWi Cover Design

Cover Photography: Jane Ashley Converse

Cover Model: Jordan Wheeler

Editing: Shauna Stevenson, Ink Machine Editing

Proofreading: Laura Martinez & Melissa Hake

DEDICATION

To LaShay,
Thank you for all the easy days.

FOREWORD

Dear Reader,

This book does not contain major triggers, however please visit my website for a complete list of possible triggers:

https://kaceysheabooks.com/trigger-warnings

I hope you enjoy Maeve & Rainer's story!

Much love,

Kacey

PROLOGUE
RAINER

Fourteen years ago

"WHERE ARE YOU GOING?" Cal straightens his spine, noticing I've ditched my work clothes for clean jeans and a new shirt. "We still have three hours till quitting time." He nods to the stack of shingles that still need to be brought to the top of the ladder.

"Not me." I attempt to hold back my grin, but it's no use. "Benito said I could leave early."

Mac puckers his lips and makes smacking sounds in my direction. "He's going to see his girlfriend."

I chuck an empty energy drink can in his direction, but he dodges it with a grin.

"She's not my girlfriend." Though, if I do things right, she will be by the end of the weekend.

"Please tell us you're finally gonna tell her how you feel?" Cal peels off his work gloves and reaches for his water bottle. "I don't think I can take much more of this pining shit."

Mac nods. "I've never seen a man so committed to a woman he's not fucking."

"You both talk a lot of shit for guys who also can't get girlfriends."

"The hell I can't." Mac frowns. "But who needs that drama anyway? Not me."

Cal laughs. "Oh, is that why you're single? Because I heard from Jessica who heard from Reya that you suck at eating pussy."

"She's a fucking liar." Mac rests his hands on his hips. "She's just mad because I didn't call her afterward."

"Dude." I narrow my gaze.

"Not cool, man." Cal shakes his head.

"What?" Mac shows no remorse. He's one of my friends, but he sure is an asshole.

"I'm out of here." I hoist my bag over my shoulder and jingle my keys.

Cal lifts his chin. "Go get your girl."

"And get laid!" Mac shouts.

I flip them both the bird as I walk away, hiding my laughter. After leaving the worksite, I gas up my truck and run inside the convenience store to buy Maeve's favorite snacks before I shoot her a text to let her know I'm on my way. It'll take a good hour to drive to Flagstaff, but my overnight bag is packed and there's no place I'd rather be than with her.

Maeve Wilder has been my best friend since we met in first grade. Growing up in Wilder Valley, I spent as much time playing with Maeve on her family's ranch as I did at my own house, and we've been close ever since.

I loved her before I knew what love was. Only, when I finally figured it out, I never had the guts to tell her my feelings go beyond just friends. I should have told her in high school. I should have told her after we graduated. But more than that, I should have told her before she left for college.

I was scared.

Scared to lose her friendship.

Scared she wouldn't return my affection and I'd ruin what we have.

Those fears are still alive and well, but something I've realized since she moved away last month is that I'm more scared to live my entire life filled with regret.

This trip isn't only to see my best friend, it's for me to take a chance on love.

> **Maeve:** I can't wait to see you! Be prepared for me to tackle you with a hug!

A grin pulls at my lips and some of the nerves in my body calm as I read her text. I spend the drive listening to music in an attempt to distract my thoughts, only each and every song reminds me of Maeve. Memories of us flood my mind. The yearning I hold in my heart for this woman fills my chest, creating an ache I can't ignore. There is no doubt in my mind that Maeve loves me. But is it possible that her feelings extend to the romantic kind? There's only one way to find out.

The traffic slows as the highway meets the outer limits of the vibrant college town. I roll my window down, enjoying the breeze as I stop and go for the next mile. A train horn echoes over the rumble of the line of vehicles stopped at the light. I've only been here once before, the weekend I drove up with Maeve's family to move her in, but I've already memorized the route. I drive straight to the visitor parking lot nearest to her dorm, circling a few times before a space opens up.

My hands shake as I reach for my phone and type out a text.

> **Me:** I'm here.

> **Maeve:** Yay!! Coming down!

Shit. It's go time. I've practiced my speech over and over again, but I'm finally going to say it aloud. Nerves rattle my chest, but somehow I manage to cut the engine and gather my things before hopping out of the truck cab.

I sling the strap of my bag over one shoulder, and turn back to lock the truck.

"Rainer!"

A smile pulls my lips into a wide arc as I turn toward the joyful sound.

Maeve runs toward me, her hair wild and smile bright.

The sight of her bolsters my confidence. "Hey, gorgeous girl." I open my arms wide in anticipation and brace my center of balance for the incoming hug.

She launches herself into my embrace, wrapping her limbs around my body on a laugh. "I missed you."

My heart races at her confession. It's in moments like these I find a glimmer of hope. I bury my head in her wild curls and inhale, holding her like she's mine to keep. "Missed you more."

She pulls away all too soon, her smiling gaze traveling down my body. She spots the candy and chips clutched in my right hand. "What are those?"

"Your favorite." I grin, handing over the snacks as a squeal of approval escapes her body.

"That's so sweet. Thank you."

"You're welcome." I take a breath before opening my mouth to confess the secret I've held on to for so many years.

"Maeve?" A deep voice interrupts before I get the chance.

"Oh!" Maeve glances behind her and laughs. She practically skips over to the two people walking toward us. I didn't notice their approach; I was too consumed by her.

One person I recognize as Maeve's roommate, Liv, who I met during move-in weekend, but the guy I've never seen before. I straighten my spine.

Maeve reaches for the dude's hand, and a sour feeling spoils the joy I'd felt only a few seconds ago.

No.

No. No. No.

This can't be happening.

Maeve looks at him the way I've always hoped she'd look at me. "Alex, this is Rainer. My best friend."

I've always worn that title like a badge of honor, but not now. Now it feels like second best.

"Hey, man." Alex steps forward, his hand held out as he towers over me by a good foot. Of course he's tall and objectively good-looking. He's probably nice and treats her well too. *Fucker.* "It's good to meet you."

I instantly hate him.

"Yeah." Propriety forces my hand into his. I would never embarrass Maeve, but I have to fight back the urge to shove him. "Nice to meet you."

"I didn't know how to tell you on the phone." Maeve smiles, but I know her well enough to catch the insecurity laced in her words. "I have a boyfriend! Can you believe it?"

Alex slings an arm around her shoulders, tucking her into his side.

"I'm so glad you're here so you could meet him." Her eyes meet mine.

She wants my approval.

She wants me to befriend him.

Fuck, I don't know how I can offer her any of those things when my hopes are crushed.

But it's not her fault.

It's mine.

I'm too late.

I know how fucking perfect she is, and how any man would be a fool not to notice. What was I thinking pining for her all this time? Waiting for what? My love for Maeve has never wavered. I should have told her, but I didn't, and now I have to live with the reality that while I was on the sidelines, this Alex guy stole my spot.

1

MAEVE

Present Day

MY MOM WAS THE BEST, but she set an unrealistic standard for motherhood. She raised five children on a ranch, made breakfast and dinner for her family every day, tended a garden in her spare time, and never once lost her shit.

Growing up, I wanted to be just like her.

Now, I just want an ounce of her patience.

God, I miss her.

I wish she were here. Though, she would be appalled if she could see my home right now. The *only* benefit to her being dead is that she will never see the disaster that is my marriage and my homemaking skills, and I'll never have to witness her disappointment.

I hate the idea of disappointing the people I love, especially her.

Glancing around my home, I take in the mess of toys that clutter every surface, the sink full of dirty dishes, and the endless mountain of laundry. Collin, my fussy teething baby is not at all soothed by my rocking, though if I set him down, his cries will turn to screams. Lulu tugs at my leg, whining for more snacks even though there are plenty in the cup she's carrying. Ari sits at the table, a defiant lock to his jaw, refusing to do the worksheet his teacher sent home. It would take him all of five minutes if he would just do it, but he's as headstrong and stubborn as any of my brothers.

Four hours till bedtime.

The countdown begins. I just have to make it with my sanity intact for four more hours and then I can attempt to carve out a little bit of peace before one of my children will no doubt wake up crying. I can't remember the last time I had a full night's sleep, but I would settle for five hours of continuous, uninterrupted rest. Hell, I'd settle for an hour of time to myself where no one is complaining or touching me.

That's what I look forward to most. An hour on the sofa, with a snack I don't have to share, watching a television show that's not appropriate for children. It's my carrot to get me through these long days.

Alex won't be back until tomorrow evening, so I don't need to clean the house tonight. I probably should, but that will be tomorrow's problem.

I will never admit this to anyone, but I often look forward to the days he's on the road. It's a lot of work to run a household and raise children, but sometimes it's nice to serve cereal for dinner with no one around to judge.

Maybe it would be different if Alex were a little more helpful, but when he's home, he's exhausted. He gets frustrated with everything and everyone. Especially when he can't relax in front of the TV without someone crying or screaming or laughing—which is basically every moment of every day. He doesn't have the patience, and I get it. I struggle not to lose my shit on the daily. But he didn't grow up with a big loving family. It was just him and his mom, and it shows.

He's a good provider. He loves me, and he loves our family. But I wish he would get in the trenches with me.

I think that's why some days it's easier to do this alone even though it's not easy at all.

Plus, there's the whole sex thing.

Whenever he gets back from a trip, he expects to have sex. It's something we agreed upon early in our marriage, and in the beginning it worked. It was a way for us to connect physically and emotionally after being away from each other. A challenge when your partner is a truck driver.

But as the years passed and more children were born, it became less and less about connection and more about duty and routine. At least for me.

The thing is, I want a healthy and exciting sex life. But after parenting for an entire week on my own, the last thing I want is for anyone to touch me. Even him. It's not something I'm proud of. Hell, I should be grateful my husband wants to sleep with me, and that he finds me desirable after all these years together and after my body has carried three children.

I know I'm not the only mother who's overworked, overtaxed, and exhausted. But on the days when Alex comes home, I have to mentally prepare so I don't pull away when he reaches for me at night.

I hate myself a little for that.

He deserves so much more from his wife.

And I wish sex was more than a chore.

But that's tomorrow's problem.

The next four hours drag painfully slowly and everyone has a meltdown, including me, but by some miracle we make it to bedtime.

I'm rocking Collin in my arms, fantasizing about spending a solid hour watching television and devouring the bag of candy I hid in the back of the pantry when the faint rumble of a diesel squashes my plans.

Fuck.

Collin is not fully asleep, but I place him in his crib and quietly slip out the door.

I check my phone's calendar, thinking I must have screwed up, but instead I'm confused when I confirm Alex should be on the road another night. There's no text or missed call from him. This is so strange. He doesn't have the kind of job where he comes home early.

Well, fuck.

As I look around, the rumble of Alex's truck grows closer. The house is a disaster. There are toys everywhere. Dishes are stacked in the sink, and piles of laundry are next to the washer and dryer. There's no way I can clean this up before he walks in the door, but I try.

I race around the living room, a vain attempt to construct order, when the lock on the door twists, announcing my husband's arrival.

I don't need a mirror to know that I look more of a hot mess than the state of my house, but when Alex steps through the door and meets my eyes, I regret not taking these last few minutes to make myself presentable.

"Hey." He drops his bag on the floor. "What happened to your hair?"

"Oh." I smooth back the frazzled strands. "I didn't have time for a shower today."

He looks around the living room. "Looks like you didn't have time for anything." He frowns. "The kids aren't sick, are they?"

"No."

"Jesus, Maeve. What the hell did you do all day?"

Irritation bubbles in my chest. I almost smart back "take care of your kids," but I don't want to start a fight. He's obviously had a long day too. "You're home a day early."

"Yeah." He kicks off his shoes. "What did you make for dinner?"

"There aren't any leftovers." It's not a complete lie. We finished a box of cereal.

"Really?" His tone hardens with irritation. "I work too hard to not come home to a hot meal."

My jaw falls open. "If you would've let me know you were coming home early, I would have made sure to have something for you." I attempt to keep the annoyance out of my tone, but I'm unsuccessful.

"Let you know?" he scoffs. "This is my house. I don't need to update you on my ETA. I can come home whenever I want." He's looking for a fight, I know he is, and I should walk away.

But I don't. "Oh, I'm aware. You can come home whenever you want, and you can leave whenever you want. Do you know what I would give to be able to do either one of those things?"

"Here we go again." He rolls his eyes. "You wanted a big family, remember?"

"You wanted them too!" Aggravation ripples through my veins. I begin tossing toys into their respective baskets with more force than necessary. "It would be nice if sometimes you came home and helped clean up after them."

"Are you serious? I just drove ten hours straight so I could spend the night with my wife! And instead of showing a little gratitude, you're going to give me shit?"

I don't know what comes over me. Maybe it's the months of lack of sleep or the fact my last quality interaction with an adult was at eight this morning. But him acting like he's the only person who's had a long day pisses me the hell off. "Do you want an award for doing your job?" I meet his annoyed stare with one of my own. "I haven't slept for more than two hours at a time in days.

Your son is teething, your daughter has decided to wake up every morning before the sun, and your oldest started sleepwalking again. All that's been getting me through this day is the fact that I might have one hour to myself where I can sit down and eat junk food and watch crap TV, and instead you decided to surprise me with your shitty attitude!"

"That's real nice. What a great example you're setting for our kids. Is this what you do when I'm gone? You let the house go, forget to shower, and just take care of yourself? Because our kids deserve better than that." His digs land where they intend.

I am failing at motherhood. But at least I'm still trying. "If you think you can do this better, why don't you give it a try?"

"Sure. Right. I'll do that." His laughter is mean. "And who would put food on the table? Or pay for this house?"

Anger rises in my chest. He's got to be fucking kidding me. "We only live here because you refuse to live on my family's ranch."

"Not this again." His face screws up. "You're going to punish me because I won't be a charity case? I don't need your family's help. I can support my own fucking family."

"I didn't say you couldn't, but don't act like we need this house when there's an empty property on the ranch."

"One I can't reach with my Peterbilt!"

We've had this argument hundreds of times. "Whatever."

"Okay, sure. Whatever." He rolls his eyes. "I'm going to take a shower, and hopefully by the time I come back you're in a better mood." He stomps to the bedroom and slams the door.

Collin immediately cries.

"Fucking hell." The anger inside my chest swirls to a raging storm. I want to punch the wall. I want to cry. I want to scream. But instead, I march my ass to the baby's room and lift him into my arms. "He has no fucking clue how hard this is," I mutter under my breath as I rock my youngest in my arms. A few angry tears slip down my cheeks.

As each second passes, my resentment grows. I would love to see him try to manage this house while taking care of our children. He wouldn't last a day. In fact, I don't think he's ever juggled the three of them on his own. Most days I don't get a second to think. I don't even get to use the restroom by myself. It's not that I don't appreciate staying home to raise our children. I understand it's a privilege. But it's no cakewalk. It's not like I sit around on my ass, eating bonbons.

When Collin settles back down, I set him in his crib and walk back into the living room. The house is still a mess, but now I refuse to clean, and I sure as shit won't be making Alex dinner. I'm not doing anything until he apologizes. This mama is on strike.

I stop in the kitchen for a bag of candy and a soda, then head straight for the couch, cueing up my latest reality TV obsession. I press play and attempt to relax into the cushions though it's impossible when anger courses through my body. This moment is not as enjoyable as I had envisioned. Not after getting into it with Alex.

He emerges from the bedroom, his hair still wet from his shower and his pajama pants slung low on his hips.

I clock his movements in my periphery but maintain my focus on the TV as I pop a chocolate into my mouth and chew.

He stops and glances around the room.

I know he wants to say something, but maybe he realizes I'm at the end of my rope because instead of picking up our argument, he walks to the kitchen with nothing more than a grunt of disapproval.

The first slam of the fridge door grates on my nerves. The second time he does it, I want to scream. The clatter of silverware and rattle of a pan only add fuel to the fire in my belly.

I attempt to cool my anger by concentrating on the drama unfolding on screen, but it's impossible.

Alex is moving around the kitchen as if there aren't three children asleep one room over. The walls in this house aren't that thick.

Each time a cupboard door bangs, my anger skyrockets. He's acting like a child. And if he wakes one of ours up, it'll be me going without sleep tonight—not him. The sobering thought that he might not give a shit crosses my mind.

What are we doing? Why is this so hard? In this moment, I despise my own husband. It's not supposed to be this way. Guilt dulls my anger, but the shame left in its place feels even worse.

I feel so stuck. As if I'm suffocating in my own life and there's no way out. I don't know how to make things better. I don't know how to fix this, and part of me is exhausted to the point I don't even know if I want to. But then what? I can't leave Alex. I have three young children. I have no income, no way to support my family without full-time childcare. If I went back to teaching, I couldn't afford the daycare. So my only other option is to stay in this marriage where we're both dissatisfied.

The idea cripples my spirit.

Giving up on watching television, I turn it off and head to my bedroom. I brush my teeth and quickly slip under the covers because it'll only be a matter of minutes before Alex joins me, and right now I'll do anything to avoid further interaction. I'm too defeated to fight. I just want a few hours of rest.

When Alex's footsteps approach the door, I feign sleep and steady my breath. The bedroom door opens, and light flickers behind my eyes as he makes his way to the bathroom. A few minutes later, when he moves the blankets and slides beneath the sheets, my body stiffens.

He's a creature of habit, and despite everything that went down, I know he's going to reach for me. He still expects sex.

Anger flares in my chest. I debate my choices. Give him what he wants because I don't have the energy for another fight. Or refuse him and draw a boundary I've never set before. One that will surely piss him off and widen the schism between us.

I war within myself until the second his body presses against my back and his arms wrap around my waist.

"Don't." I think the fierceness of my command surprises us both.

His hands retreat from my body. The shuffle of fabric the only sound as he turns over, his back to mine.

I don't know what I expected. More pushback? A verbal response at the very least. But nothing . . . and it hurts.

I feel so lost. I don't know how exactly we got to this place, but I wish I could go back. Because this sucks. I'm lying next to my person and I've never felt more alone. My eyes well with tears and I let them fall silently into the night.

I don't sleep well, and for once it's not due to the kids. The disconnect from my husband and the foreboding worry that my marriage is broken beyond repair, keep me from finding any rest. I've always been strong and independent, but I'm not strong enough to raise three children on my own.

When my morning alarm pulls me from a restless sleep, I go through the motions, tugging on a sweatshirt before dragging myself from bed. I'm out of sorts, needing more than a shot of caffeine to get me through the morning routine.

Collin is whining in his crib when I step inside the bedroom. I get him changed, and before I'm done, Lulu is climbing from her bed, her wild curls and a bright smile greeting us.

"Morning, Mama!"

"Good morning, Miss Lulu." I pick Collin up and settle him on my hip, then drop a kiss on my daughter's head. "What would you like to wear today?"

"I want my princess!" Lulu tugs on the dress hanging in the closet. It's the gown we ordered for my brother's wedding in a few months. It came last week and I don't know why I haven't moved it to my closet, because each morning she demands to wear it.

"Remember, we have to save it for Aiden and Sarah's wedding? After the wedding, you can wear it every day. Deal?"

"Fine." Thankfully, she moves on quickly. I don't enjoy beginning my day arguing with a three-year-old, but most days it's inevitable.

While she's perusing her options, I walk across the hall and knock on Ari's door as I open it. "Good morning!" While my Lulu rises with the sun, my oldest son would sleep until lunchtime if I let him. I walk into the room and sit on the edge of Ari's bed to give his little body a shake. "Hey, little dude. It's time to wake up and get ready for school."

He ignores me, burrowing himself deeper under the covers.

"Mama! I wear dis?" Lulu appears in the doorway with a mismatched outfit from her dresser.

"I love it." I learned a long time ago it's easier to get looks from strangers than to suggest she pick something else. "Go get me a clean diaper and I'll help you get changed."

She furrows her brow. "I do it."

"Yes, Lulu." I bite back the urge to sigh. "You can get dressed all by yourself, but let Mama change your diaper first."

She doesn't argue, and I go back to waking Ari.

"I don't wanna go," he complains, rubbing his eyes as he finally sits up. "I hate school."

"I know you do, but it's Wednesday. And on Wednesdays we go to school." I stand up and pick out an outfit for him while he stumbles to the bathroom. Then I change Lulu's diaper, all while playing defense to Collin. His new favorite obsession is to remove all the baby wipes from the container and shove them in his mouth.

"Enough of that." I scoop Collin off the ground, then turn to Lulu. "After you get dressed, come to the kitchen. I'm going to start breakfast." On my way to the kitchen I knock on the bathroom door. "You doing okay in there?"

"I'm pooping!" Ari calls.

"Good job." I can't help but smile. "Okay, when you're done, please get dressed. I'm making breakfast."

I deposit Collin in his highchair with some cereal and begin whipping up a batch of pancakes. My mom used to make a hot breakfast each morning and it's the one tradition I continue, no matter how messy the kitchen is or how far we're running behind in the mornings.

Soon, all three kiddos are in their seats, chowing down on breakfast while I finish up the rest of the batter.

I try not to think about Alex still asleep in our bedroom. We're not exactly quiet in the mornings, and I can't decide if I'm disappointed or relieved he hasn't emerged to join us. After our argument last night, it's probably for the best.

My phone rings from where it sits on the counter. I frown at the caller ID as worry fills my gut. It's the memory care facility where my father lives.

"Hello?"

"Maeve. Is your television giving you trouble?" My father has never been one for small talk and his question eases my concern.

"I don't think so. Why? What's going on with yours?"

"I can't find the damn championship." He huffs his frustration. "We pay too much for this cable not to work."

I'm almost certain the facility he lives doesn't use cable, but I don't correct him. "What game are you trying to get?"

"Not a game. Don't tell me you've forgotten."

"I'm sorry, I don't keep up like I used to."

Collin starts to fuss for more food and I cradle the phone against my shoulder and ear while I cut up another pancake.

"The rodeo nationals." Pops's irritation grows. "I'd think you'd care considering this is the first year you aren't competing."

I pause, pain hitting me square in the chest. I haven't competed in a rodeo since my early twenties, and nationals take place each December. It's August. Sometimes his dementia catches me off guard.

"Mama!" Lulu shouts from her spot at the table. Her mouth is full as she tells me something I can't understand.

I pull the phone away from my mouth. "Chew your food."

"Maeve? Who's there with you?" Pops asks.

Lulu repeats what she said before, only louder. I still don't understand her.

"Stop whining!" Ari complains.

"Sorry, Pops. I need to go. Why don't you have one of the staff help you find a baseball game?" Thankfully, there's a slew of channels that play games on repeat. "Can you do that?"

"Fine. I'll let you go." His sigh reaches my ear despite the elevating voices of my children. "Sorry to bother you."

"You're no bother, Pops." Guilt compounds with overwhelm. I wish he were closer. That I could stop by in a little while to check on him, but he's over an hour away now. "Call me anytime. I love you."

"Love you," he says in his gruff voice before the call ends.

"Mama!" Lulu shouts.

"What?" I say, harsher than I should.

Her eyes well with tears. "Smoke." She points over my shoulder.

"Shit!" I spin around to find a billow of smoke swirling above the pan. The pancakes are completely burnt. I swear under my breath, cutting the gas to the burner and reaching for a towel to dump the ruined food into the trash while Lulu cries. "It's fine. Everything's fine." I use my most convincing voice, but it only makes her cry harder.

"Stop crying like a baby." Ari shoots a glare at his sister.

"I'm no baby!" she screams.

"What the hell is going on in here?" Alex shouts, the bang of our bedroom door drawing everyone's attention. Alex stomps over to the kitchen. Only he stumbles on one of the toys left out from last night, "Son of a—!" He kicks the toy clear across the room, and Lulu immediately starts crying louder. "Jesus Christ, Maeve! I'm trying to sleep. Can you keep them down? Or are you doing this on purpose?"

"You think I have any control over this?" I yell above the chaos.

Alex stalks forward. His hand whips out and catches my wrist. "Don't you dare sass me in front of the kids." He lowers his voice and squeezes his hold on my arm. "I won't tolerate disrespect. Not in my house. You hear me?" There's a hardness in his stare that I've never witnessed before.

Tears prick my eyes, both from the pain of his fingers wrapped tightly around my wrist, but also from what he's doing to my heart. I yank my arm away. Free of his hold, something inside me snaps. I no longer care about saving face or keeping the peace, even in front of our children. "You want respect?" My tone is controlled. My voice low. "Then how about you show me some? Or get the fuck out."

Alex is speechless, shock written in his wide eyes. But when it fades, only revulsion remains. "You want me to leave?"

I hold his stare but say nothing.

Do I want him to leave? No. I want him to stay and fight for us, for our family.

More than anything, I want him to treat me the way he used to. As if he values my worth more than anyone else in the world. But Alex hasn't looked at me that way in years, and I am a shell of the woman I was before having three children.

"We can't keep doing this." My voice is barely above a whisper. "Do I even make you happy?"

His eyes close, as if my question causes him pain, but when

they open, I barely recognize the man standing before me. "So, what?" He shrugs. "This is it? You want me to leave? You quit?"

I do want to quit. But I can't bring myself to say it aloud. "Would you consider marriage therapy?" I've only asked this once before, right before Lulu was born, and the suggestion goes over just as well as the first time I suggested we get help.

"I'm not paying to talk to some stranger."

I dig deep and find the strength to say what needs to be said. "Then maybe some time apart is what we both need."

"You're joking, right?" He laughs, but the sound is mean. He presses his lips together and glances around. The judgment in his eyes is clear, but I don't make any excuses or explain away the current status of our home. I'm done apologizing for not being superwoman.

"Say what you want to say."

I may have been the one to light the fuse, but he detonates an entire minefield.

"I don't want a wife who thinks this is an acceptable way to keep her house. One who cusses. Who can't make breakfast without setting a fire to the pan. And I especially don't want a wife who refuses to let me touch her or talks back to me in front of our kids."

A calmness settles over me. I feel myself detaching from this moment. From him. Maybe if I do, it'll hurt less. "I guess you've made your decision, then."

"If that's what you want, fine." He shakes his head, turning away and stomping back to the bedroom.

Lulu whimpers, Ari's eyes are wide with concern, and Collin resumes shoving bites of pancake into his greedy mouth. I feel like I'm stuck in a haze. Did I just tell my husband to leave? Is this it? The end of my marriage?

The door to my bedroom slams and Alex emerges, dressed with a duffle bag over one shoulder. He grabs the bag at the door, the one he left there last night, and reaches for his keys. He doesn't meet my stare until he opens the front door. "Try this on your own and call me when you realize how much you underappreciate me and everything I do for this family."

The daze I'm in clears. Is he fucking kidding? "You're not the only person in this relationship who is underappreciated." I don't know how I manage to speak so coolly when there's a hurricane around us.

"Grow up, Maeve." The slam of the door as Alex leaves, rattles the whole house.

He's gone, and I don't know if I'm relieved or destroyed.

"Mama? Is Daddy coming back?" I can't bring myself to look at Ari.

"Mo! Mo!" Collin demands, banging his fists on his empty food tray.

"I want more too." Lulu begins crying because there aren't any more pancakes.

I burnt them. Because I ruin everything. Even my marriage.

2

RAINER

AS I PULL onto Maeve's street, I clock Alex's rig parked along the road. A tinge of disappointment works its way into my mind, the same as it always does when Maeve's husband is around.

He's not a horrible person, but a friendship between us never stood a chance. But I decided a long time ago I would rather be best friends with Maeve than not have her in my life at all. So, I tolerate Alex.

Sure, the first few years they were together I secretly prayed for their downfall, and if he broke her heart, I would be first in line to pick up the pieces. But he never did. When they got engaged, I lost a little more hope. But once they were married and Ari came along, I had to make peace with the fact that I would never be more than friends with Maeve Wilder.

I park behind Maeve's minivan and retrieve the coffee from my drink holder before exiting the truck. If I knew Alex was coming home a day early, I probably wouldn't have made this stop on my way to work. But now that I'm here, I'm not about to let good coffee go to waste. That's practically a cardinal sin.

Besides, it's not like I'm doing anything wrong or inappropri-

ate. It's coffee with my best friend. Her husband doesn't need to
know it's my favorite way to start the day or that she's the only
woman I've ever been in love with.

She might not return the sentiment, but I think she looks
forward to our morning chats too. Parenting is hard work, and
when Alex is on the road, Maeve's home by herself a lot. Even
more now that her brother, Wild, is back in L.A.

I like being her confidant; the person she can vent to and
unload whatever's playing on her mind. She does the same for me.
She's a generous person and she takes care of everyone, but who
takes care of her? Bringing her a blessed hit of caffeine in the
mornings and making her smile is no grand gesture, but it is one
way I can help take care of her.

I'm halfway up the drive when the front door swings open. I
expect Maeve to step outside, but it's Alex.

His brow is furrowed and he pulls the door shut with a slam.

I stop walking, taking in the anger of his posture as he practically stomps in my direction with two bags balanced over his
shoulder.

"Hey, Alex." I don't know if he even sees me.

Alex bumps my shoulder as he passes me on the drive. "Fuck
off."

I'm thankful there's a lid on the coffee in my hand, otherwise I'd be wearing it right now. I turn to watch Alex stomp
down the driveway. We might not be best buddies, but he
doesn't speak to me like that. And I have no idea what would
have him this angry at seven o'clock in the morning. "Is everything okay?"

"No, it's not." He turns around and scoffs. "But she's all
yours."

All mine? I fucking wish. Surely that's not what he means.
"I'm sorry, man, I don't know what's going on here."

"Do you enjoy being her errand boy? Getting her coffee?

Taking my place when I'm gone?" He laughs, but it's filled with anger, not joy. "Tell me, does she refuse to fuck you too?"

My jaw falls open. "Alex, I don't know what happened, but Maeve and I are just friends." Regrettably.

He huffs, running a hand over the scruff of his beard. "Yeah. I know. And I don't know how you put up with her shit. I'm out of here."

I watch him stride over to his rig and yank open the door. A few seconds later the engine roars to life. And a minute later he drives away.

I have witnessed more arguments than I've ever wanted to over the years, but I have never seen Alex that angry.

Concern fills my chest as I jog the rest of the way up the driveway. Usually Maeve meets me outside, but not today. No doubt it has to do with whatever went down between her and Alex.

I don't waste time knocking at the door, instead pushing it open and stepping inside. "Maeve?"

She sits in the kitchen on one of the chairs, Collin fussing in her lap as tears stream down her cheeks.

My footsteps slow as I approach. I fight off the urge to pull her into my arms.

"What happened?" I set down the coffee and take the little guy from her arms, bouncing him in an attempt to soothe his complaining. The smell of burnt food permeates the air.

Maeve doesn't say a thing. She stares forward, almost as if she's looking through me, and the alarm in the pit of my stomach grows with concern.

"Daddy make Mama sad," Lulu says from her seat at the table.

I hate that she witnessed her parents argue. It isn't like Maeve to have it out with Alex in front of the kids. Hell, in all the years I've known her, I've never seen her like this.

"Honey." I touch her shoulder gently, and her chin lifts to

meet my gaze. "Why don't you take a minute? I've got the kids, and I can take Ari to school. Is he up yet?"

I expect her to argue with me. At the very least refuse my help, but she must be in a very bad place because all she does is nod.

"Have you eaten anything yet?"

She shakes her head. "I'm not hungry."

"You want this?" I reach for the coffee I brought and slide it closer to her.

She nods. "I have a headache."

"Let me get you some water and some pain reliever."

"You don't have to . . ."

But I'm already digging through her cabinets. I bring her a glass of water and two tablets. "Take these."

"Don't you have to work?"

"Work can wait." She's more important, and I won't leave her like this. I'm dying to know what the hell happened. What did Alex do? I swear to God, if he hurt her . . . I will hurt him too.

"Mama, I hungry. More." Lulu pounds her little fists on the counter for attention.

"Just a minute." Maeve sighs.

I level her with a stare. "I've got this."

"But you said you'd get Ari to school."

"I've got it all. Promise."

Thankfully, Collin isn't fussy anymore, his chubby little hands occupied with attempting to remove the buttons from the front of my shirt. I walk over to the counter and grab a banana from the bowl of fruit. I peel it halfway, breaking off the end and popping it into my mouth before handing the banana to Lulu. I don't know why, but she refuses to eat the ends. "Here you go, little mama."

She takes the banana, studying the end to make sure I removed it. "Mo pancakes?"

"If you're still hungry after you eat that banana, we can make some more once we get your brother off to school."

I walk down the hall to Ari's bedroom. I knock on the door and stop short, surprised when I see Ari fully dressed. He sits on the floor at the foot of his bed, a stuffed animal clutched tight to his chest.

"Hey, cowboy." I sit across from him, leaning against the wall, and allow Collin to crawl between us.

Ari burrows his face into the top of his stuffed animal, but his wide eyes meet mine.

"Are you okay?"

"Daddy yelled at Mama."

"Do you want to tell me about it?"

He shakes his head no.

"How did that make you feel?"

"Scared."

My heart breaks for him as much as it does for Maeve. "You know, sometimes I get scared too."

"You do?" His gaze widens. He loosens his hold on the stuffed animal as Collin tugs it out of his arms.

"I do. It's okay to feel scared. It's okay to feel all your feelings. Everyone feels scared sometimes."

"I don't like it when Mama cries."

"I know you don't. That's because you love her and you don't want to see her feeling sad, but I promise you, your mama is one of the strongest people I know, and she's going to be just fine. Sometimes we just have to cry. There's too much feeling inside and it has to come out."

"Do I have to go to school today?"

If it were up to me, I'd let him skip, but it's not my call. Besides, it's probably best he's not here today to observe his mom. The younger two aren't old enough to get it, but Ari notices everything. "Yeah, but I'm gonna drive you. And if you get your shoes on all by yourself, I'll let you pick the music we listen to on the way. That fair?"

"Okay." He offers me the hint of a smile.

"Good man." I scoop Collin off the floor and make my way back to the kitchen. Maeve hasn't moved, and I wonder if she's sipped any of the coffee yet. Her despondent state twists my gut with worry. I check the clock. Shit. We're gonna have to hustle to make it to school on time.

"Do you mind if I go lie down?"

"No, not at all."

While Maeve slips out of the room, I busy myself with packing Ari's lunch and filling his water bottle. I leave the dishes to clean later but take a wet cloth to Lulu's face and fingers.

Ari walks into the room.

Lulu giggles, pointing at her brother's hair. "You silly."

Ari's frown deepens. "I'm not silly."

Lulu points again, but I interrupt her train of thought before she continues. "Hey, sweetheart, will you do me a big favor? Can you put your shoes on like a big girl?"

Her eyes light up. "Sparkle ones?"

"You can wear whatever you want."

"Mama doesn't let her wear the sparkle boots outside," Ari grumbles.

"Sparkle boots!" Lulu narrows her gaze at her brother, then looks up at me with those big brown eyes.

I have a hard time telling her no. "If you let me carry you to the car, you can wear them." I faintly remember Maeve complaining about how difficult it is to get mud off of the sequin shoes. "Is that a good compromise?"

"Yes! Compomise!" Lulu climbs down from her chair and runs into the other room.

"Can I bring a toy to school?"

I wet my hands at the faucet and brush them through Ari's hair. "What would your mama say?"

"She doesn't let Lulu wear sequin boots."

I chuckle at the idea I'm getting shaken down by a five-year-old. "If you keep it inside your backpack all day, that's fine."

"Yes!" He runs off.

I look at Collin. "You want to break the rules too, buddy?"

He grins.

"That's what I thought."

I wrangle the kids out to the minivan, exchanging my keys for Maeve's, and drive Ari to school. I drop him off with his backpack, lunchbox, and water bottle, hoping I haven't forgotten anything else. At the very least he has the essentials. Besides it's kindergarten, the most challenging thing is getting him here every day.

On the drive back, I call Mac, one of my best friends and the only person I trust to run my company on the rare occasion I take a day off.

"Hey, motherfucker, where you at?" he answers. "Don't tell me you're late."

I glance in the rearview mirror at my precious cargo, and wince. "You're on speaker and there are little ears around."

"You playing babysitter at Maeve's?" My friend laughs. "Should've guessed. I don't think you'd miss work for anyone else."

"Yeah, about that. I'm going to be out for the day."

"Everything okay?"

I appreciate his concern. Especially when I know he would prefer to give me crap about it. "Yeah, everything's fine." It's a big lie, but I'm not about to fill him in on all the details when Lulu and Collin are listening.

"Fill me in later. I've got everything here covered."

"Thanks, Mac. I appreciate it."

We say goodbye and I end the call just as I'm pulling back into the driveway. I turn in my seat as I cut the engine and then smile at Lulu. Her sparkle boots kick the air from where her legs dangle off the edge of her booster seat. "Girly, you look so cute in those boots.

I think we should have a tea party when we go inside. What do you think about that?"

"Tea party?" Her eyes light up.

"Won't that be fun?"

"Fun!" she cheers, and her delight causes Collin to smile.

God, I love these kids. I want to make everything in their world right, and to do that I'm going to need to figure out what the hell happened between Maeve and Alex, and what that means for the future.

3

MAEVE

SOMETHING inside me breaks when Alex leaves.

I don't feel like myself. The idea of eating turns my stomach. I don't want to do anything.

I'm not one to mope around, even when the world is falling apart, but the idea of doing anything exhausts me, so I curl up in bed and wrap myself in the covers to cry.

It wasn't that long ago that Alex was my whole world. And I was his. How did we get here?

In all our fights, he has never threatened to leave, and divorce has always been off the table. My sadness mixes with anger as I think about our interactions last night and this morning. Is this how my marriage ends? Seven years down the drain because of crying kids and one refusal of sex?

No.

That's not true. I've been ignoring the reality for years. Things haven't been good for a while. We both wanted a big family, at least I thought we both did, but it's hard work and money is tight. The stress of everything eats away at the connection we once had.

But I thought it was normal. I thought once the kids were

older, things would get better and we would find our way back to each other.

I was willing to wait it out. To put in the work and be patient. All I've ever wanted is to be a good mother and raise a family with the man I love. I never once considered he would stop loving me.

A fresh wave of tears fills my eyes, and I reach for my phone. I don't know what I hope to see, maybe a missed phone call or a text apologizing for the way he laughed cruelly or asking for another chance. But there's nothing.

The joyful sound of laughter and chatter bleeds through the thin walls. Part of me longs to join Rainer, but I don't want my children to see me right now. I know they're safe with him, and I need this moment to process.

I don't know what to do next. The idea of having to provide for my children is so far off from the worries I had yesterday, I almost laugh. They would hire me back at the high school in a heartbeat, but who would raise my babies? The idea of leaving them with anyone breaks my heart.

I should call my brothers, but selfishly, I pray that Alex will realize he made a mistake and I won't have to. I hope he calls soon. I hope we can repair what's been broken. Because if I do tell my brothers what happened and I give Alex a second chance afterward, they'll never be kind to him again.

I don't know what to do.

I wish I could ask my mom. Losing her was excruciating, but there have been so many moments in recent years where I would give anything for one more conversation. One more bit of advice. She would know what to do. She always did. I wish I were more like her. I wish I could go back in time and treasure the moments we did have.

But all I'm left with are my memories of her and the faded recollection of her voice. "Mama, what do I do? How do we get through this?" I whisper aloud, but no one answers, and I cry myself to sleep.

The rattle of dishes along with the opening of cabinets, pulls me from my daze. My eyes burn and the skin around them is puffy from crying. I don't know what time it is or how long I've slept. I reach for my phone to check the time and practically leap from my bed. School ended over an hour ago! I need to get Ari! Stumbling from my room, I pause at the doorway and take in the view.

Ari sits at the table, his little head bent in concentration over his homework. His pencil moves across the paper, and he pauses to reach for one of the chocolates lined up in the center of the table. Collin sits in his high chair, shoveling bits of food into his mouth and making a mess. But it's the sight of Rainer wearing one of my aprons and twirling Lulu with one hand while he stirs something on the burner with the other that brings a smile to my face.

"Mama!" Lulu spots me first and comes running.

I drop to my knees and catch her in my arms. "Hey, munchkin. How was your day?"

"Sparkle boots." She points to her left toe and taps it for me to see.

"Hey there." Rainer walks over to us. "I was wondering when you would join us."

"Yeah, sorry." I stand up but feel a little lightheaded.

Rainer is at my side, wrapping his arm around my waist to catch me. "Don't apologize."

I use his body to steady myself.

"Dinner will be ready in a few minutes. Why don't you sit down." He walks me over to an open chair.

Ari looks at him and then me and then the chocolates, concern in his wide eyes.

If I didn't feel so bad about my life right now, I would laugh.

"Ari and I made a deal. Dessert before dinner *if* he could finish his homework in less than ten minutes." Rainer glances at the clock. "And I think he's gonna make it. Aren't you, cowboy?"

"Yeah, I am!" To my complete and utter shock, my son goes back to his homework without any crying or complaining.

Rainer is a freaking miracle worker. More like a child whisperer. He catches my gaze and winks.

I hardly know what to do with myself, Rainer refuses to let me help him with dinner, and there are no meltdowns or crying. It's as if I've stepped into an alternate universe.

"Here you go." He brings me a plate of food after serving the older kids.

"Aren't you going to eat?" I ask when he doesn't make himself a plate and instead takes a wet washcloth to wipe Collin's hands and face.

"I will. But I'm going to give this guy his bath first."

"Oh." I'm stunned. He's doing everything I normally do, and making it look much easier. "Uh, can you do this every night?" I tease.

Rainer glances at me, a look in his eyes I can't quite decipher. "If you want me to."

I laugh, not sure if he's joking. But he doesn't smile. Surely, he's not serious. There's no way in hell an attractive single man in his thirties would subject himself to this life. Even if he's my best friend.

"We'll talk more tonight." He lifts Collin from his high chair. "Ari. Lulu. Make sure you eat all your dinner and help your mom clear the table when you're done."

"We will!" Lulu chimes.

Ari gives a nod.

Wow. If I weren't starving, I'd sit here with my jaw open. I don't know what he did while I was sleeping, but everyone is entirely too agreeable. Maybe I'm still asleep and this is a dream.

After Collin is down for the night and the older two are in

their room, Rainer leaves. He promises he'll be back in less than an hour. I should tell him not to bother coming back, but I can't stomach being alone, so I nod.

I've been warring with my thoughts all day and they're driving me mad. I consider packing all of Alex's clothes into trash bags and hauling them to the carport, but I can't muster up the anger to fuel me. I want him to come back, right? Throwing all his shit out of the house isn't the most welcoming return.

Normally, I would love a glass of wine to help me unwind, but I'm too keyed up to enjoy that. Instead, I make a hot tea and grab an old quilt from the closet to settle on the porch. The two rocking chairs outside belonged to my grandparents, and there's something about sitting out here, listening to the chirp of crickets and the faint passing of cars on the highway that begins to calm my thoughts.

Without the highway noise, this could be the ranch.

It's weird to consider, but if Alex and I are done, I could move there. There's an empty cabin on my family's property with more than enough space for the children and me. We could get chickens. I could teach them how to garden. They could play in the dirt and I could show them all the things I love about growing up in Wilder Valley.

Alex never wanted to live on the ranch. He claimed it was too difficult to drive his Peterbilt in and out of the road there, and that it added too much time to an already long drive. He didn't want my father and my brothers to view him as a man who couldn't provide for his own family, so we rented this place to be closer to the highway.

But I always suspected it was more.

I don't think he understood the appeal of being tucked away from shops and stores. He doesn't love animals like I do. He never even wanted to get a cat or a dog, but our landlords always had a strict no pets policy, so I never pushed the matter. I made so many concessions in our relationship—tiny little things that added up to more than I want to admit.

If it were up to him, we would have moved somewhere bigger like Flagstaff or even Phoenix. I'd considered it when we first married, but I couldn't bring myself to leave my family or the town I loved. This was home. It always would be.

The headlights of Rainer's truck flash my way as he turns onto the street. I shield my eyes from their brightness as I take another sip of tea.

Rainer parks in the driveway and exits his truck with two large duffle bags. He walks up the driveway and places them on the steps, walking over to join me in the empty rocker. We sit, rocking, not saying anything for several minutes before he breaks the silence.

"Are you ready to talk about what happened today? You don't have to tell me. But I've never seen Alex like that, and I'm drawing my own conclusions here."

He deserves an explanation. But I don't know that I can give him an answer when I don't know myself. "I've never seen him like that either."

"Did he hurt you?"

"No." My free hand goes to my wrist. The skin isn't bruised, but it's sore. "I'm fine." I don't know who I'm trying to convince, Rainer or myself.

"Is he coming back?"

My eyes well with tears. "I don't know."

Rainer nods. "Okay then. Until you figure that out, I'm going to stay here."

It's a generous offer—more than generous—but completely unnecessary. I'm on my own with the kids most of the time, and this isn't any different. "Rainer, I can't ask you to do that."

"Good. Because I'm insisting. I'm not letting you do this alone."

"I'm fine." But I'm not. I'm incredibly proud. And while Rainer is my best friend, his offer is too much.

"Don't insult me by lying. I know you better than anyone. And I know how much you love him." His eyes close and he swallows hard before meeting my gaze again. "Whatever this is between you two, a break, or more, I will not let you do this on your own. You're my best friend, Maeve, and I would do anything for you. Which includes sleeping on your couch."

I shake my head. "You're not sleeping on the couch."

"Why not? You let your brother sleep there for a month and he's almost a foot taller than me."

My brother had nowhere else to go. Rainer has his own house fifteen minutes away. "What does height have to do with it?" I can't help but smile.

"Your sofa is kind of short."

I roll my eyes as the burst of laughter shakes my chest. "Hey, don't pick on my furniture. It can't help its size. It's the way it was made. I happen to like it a lot."

He grins. "I'm glad you like short things."

My amusement fades as I think about why he'd be sleeping on my couch in the first place. "Thank you."

"For what?"

The list is so long, if I started to count the ways, we'd be here all night. "Everything."

4

RAINER

IT'S BEEN a week since Alex left and my concern for Maeve grows each day. She rarely smiles, and when she does, her eyes don't hold the same light they used to. She sleeps a lot and her appetite isn't what it used to be. She embodies the classic signs of depression, and yet I feel so helpless because I can't fix this for her.

Maeve loves with her whole heart, and I'm worried Alex has broken a part of her that no amount of time or space can heal.

Not that I don't try.

I care for the kids. I cook. I clean. In all the moments I'm not working, I attempt to lighten her load. She needs time to process and space to feel, which is incredibly challenging with three tiny humans who are dependent on her for everything. I don't want her to feel alone, because she isn't. I will sleep on her couch for the rest of my life if that helps her get through this.

She won't talk about Alex, and I get the feeling he's completely dropped off the face of the earth. Which only further pisses me off. What kind of man leaves his family and doesn't check in? I don't care about whatever is going on between him and Maeve, it doesn't give him the right to abandon his children.

I never liked Alex. Though, it wouldn't matter if he were a fucking saint, the fact that Maeve fell in love with him, and not me, secured my distaste for the man from the second we met.

But watching him walk out on her, and the family they created together, boils my blood.

I hate him more than ever. The asshole has no clue how good his life is. That he has everything I've ever wanted.

These are the thoughts that run through my mind as I drive out to assess a new job for a client at the end of my workday. As I pull into the driveway, I smile, realizing I've been to this place before.

"Hey, Rainer." Liv waves from the front porch. She's surrounded by stacks of papers and several textbooks.

"Hey! I didn't realize you were my client today."

She grins. "Yeah. When I made the appointment I thought I'd mess with you by giving your secretary a fake name."

"Alotto Dix." I read aloud the note on my phone and then chuckle. "Good one."

"Right? One of my students came up with that. Perks to teaching high school."

"Better you than me." She's a freaking saint. "I don't know how you do it."

"Eh. Teenagers get a bad rap." She shrugs. "Most days I prefer their company to adults. Adults are fucking assholes."

I lift the brim of my hat and wipe away the sweat on my forehead before bringing the bill low again. "Now that, I can relate to."

"Except for when it comes to Maeve, right?" Liv studies my face with a somber expression. "How's she doing? She skipped book club last week, and she's been unusually quiet in the group chat."

It surprises me that Maeve hasn't talked to her friends about Alex. But I feel protective over her. "Oh, you know how some weeks are. The kids keep her very busy."

"That all?" Liv cocks her head to the side. "Because you know how this town loves to talk."

"I do."

"And everyone's used to you driving over there daily." She raises her brows. "But rumor has it you've been parked in the driveway every night for a week."

"I didn't take you for a gossip."

"I don't know what's going on, but if Maeve is going through something, I want to show up for her. We all do."

I release a sigh and squint as I look up to the sky. Maeve hasn't been herself. And while I don't want to betray her confidence, what she's going through is bigger than what I can handle on my own. "Alex left."

Liv's brow furrows as she shakes her head. "Like he's on a big job?"

"No." I lean back on my heels. "Like they had a fight and he left."

Liv's jaw falls open. "For good?"

"I don't know. Maeve doesn't want to talk about it, but that's the assumption I'm making."

"Oh no. Poor Maeve."

"So that's why I've been staying there."

"You're a good friend to her." Liv meets my gaze. But there's something in her stare that causes me to look away. If I don't, she might see the truth. She might realize I want to be a whole lot more than friends with Maeve.

"She'd do the same for me." It's true. There is no one more generous and self-sacrificing than my best friend.

"What can I do?"

"Honestly? I think she needs to get out of the house. Some company besides me and the kids might lift her spirits."

Liv nods. "I'll pick her up tomorrow for book club. I'll swing by after I leave school. Will that work?"

"Yeah, I'll make sure she's ready." I glance around the property. "Now, do you have a job for me to quote, or was this an elaborate ruse to pull the truth out of me?"

"Oh, there's a job." She grins and waves for me to follow her. We walk around the back and she points at two Ponderosas near the detached garage. "I think these big boys need grounding wire."

"Sure do." I nod, walking over to the tall trees to examine their bases. "Have they been wired before?" I'm pretty much the go-to for this sort of job, and I would've remembered running these.

"I don't think so. I've had this place for six years now, but the prior owners were on a limited budget. Hell, I've been putting this off to funnel my extra cash into more exciting home improvements."

"I get it." Most people do the same. It's not fun to spend money on stuff like this, but they tend to regret it when a lightning strike takes down one of their gorgeous trees, or worse, starts a fire that takes out the entire property. "Should've called me sooner. I would've hooked you up with the friends and family rate."

"Thanks." She grins. "Hopefully, you'll still hook me up?"

We work out a price and schedule a day for me to come back with my crew and the needed supplies. It's not until I'm back in my vehicle, that I notice a missed text from Maeve.

> Maeve: Do you have time to stop at the store on the way home?

Not wanting to waste time texting, I put my truck into drive and dial her cell phone.

"Hey." The sound of Maeve's voice warms me from the inside. Collin babbles in the background, and I pick up a few words of Lulu's chatter. It's loud and chaotic, but it doesn't sound like anyone is having a meltdown, including Maeve.

"I got your text and I'm done for the day, what do we need from the store?"

"I'll send you a list if that's okay? I started to make dinner but I'm missing a few ingredients."

"You're cooking?" I don't mask the surprise in my voice.

"Yes. Are you shocked?" Maeve hasn't done much of anything in a week.

I'm not shocked, I'm relieved. "No, I'm excited. We both know you're a better cook than I am."

"You don't give yourself enough credit. I like it when you cook."

I grin, because I like cooking for her. "Shoot over the list and I'll have everything on your doorstep within the hour."

"My personal shopper. You should add it to your website."

I chuckle at the idea. "Nope, my concierge services only extend to you."

"Lucky me."

I'm the lucky one.

"Okay, I sent you the list. Diapers and wipes are on there. I'm sorry." I wish I could erase the worry in her voice. "I promise I will pay you back. I'm just not sure when."

"Good thing I know where you live."

"I should ask my brothers for money." She sighs. "I just don't want to hear their opinion about Alex right now."

I'm not interested in protecting Alex, but I would do anything for Maeve. This is an easy fix. "Don't ask them. I've got you."

"Rainer, you can't pay for everything forever."

The hell I can't. "Maeve, I promise you I'm not hurting for money." I apprenticed as a roofer for Benito for over a decade, and when he retired, he sold his business to me. In the years since, I've added other types of services to the company, from cleaning gutters to running grounding wires and downing trees. Anything that involves repairs and heights . . . I'm the person to call.

When I was a kid, my dad said I couldn't climb trees for a living, but now I like to remind him I do exactly that. It's hard, honest work, and most days it keeps me close to home in Wilder Valley. I couldn't ask for more. "Business is good. I promise, Maeve."

"I don't want to be a burden. We aren't your responsibility."

I beg to differ, but I know she won't accept that argument, so I take a different approach. "If I needed anything, you would be there for me in a heartbeat. Right?"

"Of course."

"Then I've got you, okay? End of discussion."

"Thank you, Rainer. I don't know what I would do without you."

"I feel the same." And I pray to God we never have to find out.

THE HOUSE IS in a frenzy when I step through the door an hour later, my arms loaded with grocery bags. Music plays over a speaker. Collin is fussing and Lulu is singing. From around the corner, I spot Maeve cooking in the kitchen. Ari's set up an entire battlefield in the living room with what seems to be every single toy from his room. From the intense sound effects leaving his mouth, shit's about to go down.

It's loud.

It's messy.

It's real.

I feel honored to be welcomed into this space, and into their lives. It's silly, but for a second, I make believe these are *my* children and I'm coming home to *my* wife. God, I wish. But as much as I might want that, there's no promise that Maeve will ever see me as more than a best friend.

Most days I'm okay with that.

But there are moments, like this one, where I get a glimpse of what life could be if she were mine. I'd never want for anything else.

An ache of longing takes root in my heart. I can't quite shake it off as I head into the kitchen.

"Rain-Rain!" Lulu calls at my approach. I love that she can't quite say my name. I'll be sad when she finally learns to pronounce it properly.

"Hey, girlie. Those are quite the dance moves."

She grins.

"Smells good in here." The simmer of something in the big pot on the burner causes my stomach to groan.

"Hey." Maeve glances over her shoulder and flashes me a grin. "Thanks for stopping at the store."

"No problem." I hand her the celery and onion she requested.

Maybe I imagine it, but she doesn't seem as despondent as she's been the last week. The light in her eyes isn't totally back, but it's progress.

I set the bags on the empty corner of the kitchen table and begin unloading everything except the one box I don't want her to see. I slip it behind my back as she turns to face me.

She raises her brow in question.

"It's a surprise."

"Oh!" There's a twinkle in her eye as she steps closer. "What is it?"

"No peeking." I laugh, shaking my head. "It's for after dinner."

"Oooh! I hope it's dessert."

"It's not."

"I'm already disappointed." She pretends to pout and turns back to chop the vegetables.

"You'll like it. I promise." I open a cupboard and slip the box inside before she catches a glimpse. "Now, what can I do? Entertain the monsters or finish cooking?

"Can you wrangle them? I'm touched out."

"On it." I wash my hands at the sink, then wet a cloth to clean Collin's hands and face before pulling him out of his highchair. "Hey, mister. What do you say we give you a bath?"

"Rainer." Maeve calls before I walk out of the room.

"Yeah?"

"Thank you."

"You don't have to thank me. I want to be here." There's nowhere else I'd rather be.

The next hour passes in a busy routine. I bathe Collin and convince Ari to pick up his toys before dinner. I bribe Lulu to help. We eat and there are more baths, hair brushing, teeth brushing, diaper changes, potty breaks, and thankfully, not too many tears. By some miracle, we get it all done. I honestly don't know how Maeve managed all this on her own. Alex was on the road for more nights than he was home, and I don't recall her ever complaining about how much work it is to care for three little ones.

While Maeve puts Collin to sleep, I read stories to the older two, then finish cleaning up the kitchen and clear the table for her surprise.

"Hey." Maeve's voice holds the exhaustion of an entire year.

"Hey." I glance at the clock on the microwave to find it's already half past nine before meeting her gaze. "He go down okay?"

"Finally." She smiles, but it's strained. "Let's hope he stays asleep. I think he's working on cutting a few teeth. He was a bear all day." She's tired.

"If you'd rather sleep, we can do the surprise tomorrow." My idea for tonight can wait.

"Oh! I almost forgot." Delight transforms her expression. "Let's do this."

"Okay." I point to the chairs around the table and grin. "Sit. And close your eyes."

Her smile radiates with anticipation as she follows my orders. Mostly. Her fingers covering her face part enough for me to spot the glint of her eyeballs.

"Hey. No peeking," I warn as I turn my back and retrieve the board game. I take the seat across from her and slide the box between us. "Okay. Open."

She does and, to my satisfaction, her smile widens, taking over her entire face. "A murder mystery!"

"Surprise!"

"I've always wanted to play one of these!"

I know. I remember the first time she said so.

"Where did you find this?" She opens the box and begins to unpack the contents.

"I'll never tell," I tease. "I was sworn to secrecy." More, it's borderline embarrassing. I ordered the game when she first told me how much she wanted to play it. I stashed it in my bedroom closet along with other trinkets and small items I keep with the intent to give them to her. Most of them stockpile until I have an excuse to spoil her, like her birthday or Christmas. She is my best friend, after all. But I always have to be careful not to upstage Alex. Not anymore. It's a relief not to worry that my kindness will spark a conflict.

Maeve pours over the instructions for the game, just like I knew she would. She loves games, but she's a stickler for the rules. This could be awhile.

"What do you want to drink?" I slide out of my chair and head to the fridge to retrieve a beer.

"Do you even need to ask?" She grins over the pamphlet.

This woman could survive on coffee alone. "Iced or hot?"

"Ohh . . . let's go iced."

I set to making her a glass, adding her preferred amount of creamer and sugar, before heading back to the table.

"Thank you." She takes a sip and moans, drawing my gaze to her mouth.

I try not to stare. But it's impossible not to imagine how her lips would look wrapped around my cock.

Fuck.

I shake the image out of my head and take a long pull from my beer. I never allow myself to daydream of a future with Maeve, especially in her presence. But with Alex out of the picture, it's as if that filter in my brain is broken.

There's no partner or marriage to disrespect.

At least, I think. *Fuck.* Even if Alex is out for good, I can't bridge the gap between friendship and more. Maeve's in a vulnerable place. She doesn't need a lover, she needs a best friend, and I need to get my intrusive thoughts under control.

It feels forbidden to lust after her, not because she's married, but because I tell Maeve everything, and I can't tell her about these thoughts or feelings. The last thing I want is to create a divide in our relationship.

"So, how do we play this game?" I listen to her explanation, focusing on the rules of the game and how beautiful she looks right now, her hair coming loose from its messy bun and falling around her face as she talks.

"Make sense?"

"I think so." I bite back a grin, knowing she'll correct me if I misstep. "Who rolls first?"

"Obviously you."

"Me?" My brows rise. "What about ladies first?"

"I'm going to win. You need all the help you can get."

"Oh!" A bark of laughter shakes my chest. "Is that it?"

Her cell phone on the edge of the table pulses with the vibration of an incoming call. We both glance at the screen, and I don't miss the flash of worry that steals her joyful expression. "Sorry, I need to take this."

"Of course." By the caller ID, it's the facility where her dad lives. I know how much she feels torn by the decision to move him there. It's best for his dementia, but it's too far away for daily visits.

"Hello?"

From where I sit, I can't make out the exact words on the other end of the phone, but the panic in her dad's demanding voice is clear.

"Pops. Take a breath." Her posture straightens with alarm. "Tell me what's wrong." She nods, her expression somber as it meets mine across the table. A few seconds later, her shoulders drop. "Pops. They didn't steal your clothes."

His voice escalates in volume.

"Dad. I promise."

I mouth the words *"Is everything okay?"*

She nods before speaking to her dad again. "Can you do me a favor?" She pauses, a deep sigh leaving her chest. "Okay, do you see the closet doors? The ones behind your bed? Yeah. I want you to go over and open them. Yeah, I'll wait."

It's only a few more seconds before he breaks the silence through the line. She holds back a chuckle. "You're welcome, Pops. No, it's okay. I know. Maybe they weren't there before, but they're back now. Yes, call me if anything else goes missing." She bites her lower lip. "No. I understand. I'm not making fun. I won't worry Ryan. Promise. Love you, Pops. Bye." She ends the call and sets the phone down on the table.

"Everything okay?"

"Besides the fact he believes the staff are stealing his clothes? *All* of his clothes? Each and every article?" Maeve shakes her head, a smile cracking as a burst of laughter escapes her lips. "He said, 'they took my drawers!'" She mimics his no-bullshit attitude. "'Who the hell wants an old man's drawers!'"

I can't help it. Laughter works its way out and shakes my chest. It's only funny because we know he's safe, but picturing her father going on about his undergarments is enough to make anyone laugh. Mr. Wilder is no jokester, and I can only imagine his exasperation.

"I can't." Maeve laughs harder, covering her mouth to stifle the sound. Her giggles are contagious, and soon we're both gasping for breath and wiping tears from our eyes.

Only, in a split second, the energy shifts and Maeve's laughter turns to sobs.

"Oh, honey." My stomach sinks with worry as I move to her side. I open my arms, pulling her to my chest as she cries. "I've got you." I rub her back, feeling helpless to do anything other than hold her for as long as she'll let me.

Her tears stain my shirt. Her sobs shake her body. I feel her pain as if it's my own, and it's an honor to help her carry just a fraction of the emotion she's bottled up. The entire week she's been detached. She's been depressed. But I haven't seen her let go and let everything out. I think she needs this. She doesn't pull away or make excuses, she just continues to cry until all her tears have been shed.

After several minutes, she finally pulls back, holding a hand over her face.

"Here." I reach across the table to the small stack of napkins and hand her a few.

"Thanks." She wipes her nose and blots the remaining wetness from her face. "Fuck. Talk about a hot mess."

"Feel better now?"

She inhales a shaky breath and considers my question before answering. "Yeah, actually, I do."

"Good." I reach out and brush a few hairs back from her face, tucking them behind her ear. *Fuck.* I don't know why I did that. I glance down at my lap, disguising the waves of self-consciousness that roll through my body.

"Can we pretend that didn't happen and play the game now?"

Does she mean pretend I didn't reach out and touch her as if I'd done it a million times or pretend she didn't cry? The answer is the same either way. "Yeah, let's play."

5

MAEVE

I HATE CRYING, but last night I couldn't hold it in. Rainer was probably right, I needed to release the emotion and stress of the last week. I only wish it made me feel better. It's as if I'm coming out of a fog that hasn't quite lifted. The hurt of Alex's abandonment hits hard in the strangest of moments, like when Collin babbles the word "Dada" for the first time, or when I put Ari's laundry away and find a doodle of a semi-truck taped to the side of his dresser.

I don't know how I'm going to move forward.

Hell, I don't know how I'm going to pay the electric bill next month.

Or rent.

Or fill my gas tank.

Worry after worry compounds as my mind races. The feeling is suffocating. The idea of food turns my stomach, but I force myself to eat a little something at each meal. If I don't, I won't be able to keep up with my children, and they are my reason for getting out of bed. They're my everything.

As my sadness fades, it's replaced with anger. I'm not sure that's much better.

Fuck the man I married.

Fuck the man I built a life with.

Fuck the father of my children.

Fuck. Him.

This is my new mantra.

I'm not an idiot. Things in my marriage have been bad for a while, but I expected so much more from the man I promised to love and hold forever. We've been together my entire adult life. I knew him as well as I knew myself, and this wasn't our first argument. I expected he would leave for a few days at most, to lick the wounds of his damaged ego, before coming home. I expected Alex to put up more of a fight. At the very least, I expected a fucking phone call.

If not for me, for our children. What we built isn't something a person can just walk away from.

But for him, I guess it is.

I realize no one gets married expecting anything other than till death do us part, but never once did I expect to be a single mother. I'm trying to accept a future I didn't plan for, and as each day passes, any hope for a chance of reconciliation lessens.

If I'm being honest, a tiny piece of me is relieved. Because I don't want to pretend everything is fine when it's not. I don't want to bandage up a relationship when I'm the only one who seems to ever do the mending.

I just want some fucking peace.

I want to find a way to move forward, even if the future scares me.

I glance up to see Rainer's truck coming down the road. Strange. It's just after noon. He doesn't wrap up until three or four most afternoons.

He runs a successful roofing company, though he would never brag or boast. But he doesn't have to. Everyone in this town loves him. He's the guy you call if you have issues with your roof, or a tree, or anything really. If he can't help, he knows someone who can. He's fair in his pricing and he treats his employees well, which is more than most do. He must pay well too, because no one ever quits, and his full-time employees own homes and drive nice trucks.

Once I suggested Alex ask Rainer for a job so he could be home every night. It was after Ari was born and I was completely overwhelmed by motherhood, made worse by the fact Alex was always on the road. He completely overacted, and we fought to the point I was in tears. He punished me with the silent treatment for the next week. We were both sleep deprived—having an infant will do that—but I could never understand why the idea made him livid. I never suggested it again, though it would have solved so many problems. Alex could have been home every night, he'd get more time with me and the children, and he'd make the same money, if not more.

Rainer would have hired him if I asked, but Alex hated the idea of nepotism getting him anything. It was the main reason why he wouldn't accept living on the ranch in one of my family's cabins too.

Maybe it was naïve, but I didn't view life that way. Family takes care of family, and Rainer was as much my family as my own blood relatives.

Even now, I don't understand why the suggestion offended him. What was so wrong with learning a trade and accepting a job from my best friend?

"Rain-Rain!" Lulu shouts from where she plays in the yard. She drops her toy and runs toward the gravel driveway to greet him.

"Lulu, stay!" I shout the command as if she's more a pet than a small human.

She stops short, waving and jumping in place to get his attention. It's adorable and puts a genuine smile on my lips for the first time today.

Rainer grins and waves out the window as he pulls behind my minivan and puts his vehicle in park. After he hops down from his truck, he walks toward her and scoops her into his arms. "How's my favorite girlie?"

For the hundredth time this week, I ruminate on how lost I would be without Rainer. His friendship has always been steadfast, but he's stepped up in ways he shouldn't have to. Since Alex left, I've been scared, sad, angry, and depressed, but not once have I felt alone. Rainer makes sure everyone is taken care of, including me.

"Where's Collin?" Rainer asks as he deposits Lulu on the top step of the porch, just for her to run back down and resume her play in the yard.

"He's napping." I rock back in my seat and take a sip of my coffee.

Rainer sits in the rocker next to mine. "Nice. Easy day, then?" The hope in his eyes is sweet, even if it's a little delusional.

I huff out a laugh. "I don't think anyone would classify a day spent with my children as easy."

"Definitely not." He grins. "Maybe today wasn't easy, but you're stronger than you were yesterday. Stronger than you were last week. And you'll be stronger tomorrow. So, by that account, today was an easy day, right?"

"Are you gaslighting me?"

"Never." He chuckles. "I am fucking amazed by you. You know that?"

His compliment warms me from the inside out, even if it's misguided. "Nothing about me is amazing." I press a hand to my cheek, feeling flushed. "I'm a hot mess."

"No." His gaze meets mine. "You aren't."

I look down at my feet, unable to hold his stare. "Easy day, huh?"

"Easy day." I hear the grin in his voice.

"Mama! Rain-Rain! Watch dis!" Lulu twirls in the yard, tossing her doll up in the air and catching it right on her face. "Ooof."

I bite back the urge to giggle.

Rainer turns his face to cover his laugh.

For the next few minutes we sit in comfortable silence, watching Lulu play and enjoying the breeze. The sky is full of clouds, moving and swirling quickly above the pines. If we're lucky, we'll get an afternoon shower.

Rainer clears his throat. "I'm going to ask something, but you don't have to answer."

"Okay?" My stomach twists as I drag the word out.

"Have you talked to Alex? Since he left."

"No." I shake my head. "He hasn't called." I bite at the bottom of my lip. "He texted me once the day after we fought, but since then he's been radio silent."

"I'm sorry, it's none of my business."

"No. It's okay. I'd be wondering the same." I appreciate that he allowed me to avoid the topic as long as he did. We can't avoid reality forever.

"You want to talk about it?"

Do I? A heavy sigh pushes out of my lungs, along with a week's worth of frustration. "Should I call him? Because I don't want to. He's the one who left. But how do I move forward when I don't know where we stand? Everything feels so incomplete."

Rainer stops rocking, leaning forward to rest his elbows on his knees. "What do you want?"

"What do you mean?"

Rainer removes his hat to run a hand through his hair. "The way I see it, your future shouldn't rely on whether he comes back or not. You're gonna be just fine, either way. But it's your choice to invite him back or not. Not his."

He makes it sound so simple. "I don't know who I am without him." I whisper the confession that haunts me each night.

Rainer shrugs. "Maybe you should find out."

Yeah, maybe I should. "I don't even know where to start."

"You're a smart woman. You'll figure it out." Rainer waits for my gaze to find his. "And I'll be here every step of the way. No matter what. Oh, and, Liv is picking you up for book club."

"What?" This is why he's here and not at work? I already feel enough guilt for how he's completely upended his life to be here for me. "Rainer, I can miss book club." I probably can't avoid telling my friends about Alex leaving forever, but another week won't hurt. "You didn't have to cut out of work early for this."

"But since I already did, you should go."

"Really?"

"Yeah. I'll pick Ari up from school and hold things down here."

"You're spoiling me."

"Good."

No. Not good. I am going to be a mess when he goes back to living at his own place.

"Did you read the book?"

"For book club?"

He nods.

"No. I didn't finish it." I grimace. I don't like abandoning books. "I read ten chapters before I quit. Does that count?"

"More than I read." He chuckles. "What happened after chapter ten?"

"The couple was too happy." I crinkle my nose. I don't know what it says about me, but once the couple got together, I couldn't enjoy the story. I wanted an escape from my current real-life problems, but watching two characters fall in love? Reading about a man who was so fucking perfect? It only added salt to my wounds. "I think I need a palate cleanser."

He considers my words. "Maybe try mafia romance?"

I sit straight and turn in my seat. "How do you know about mafia romance?"

"I've been to the library." He grins with a shrug. "And Rosalie's displays can be very informative. If not a little risqué for the general public."

"Ugh." I roll my eyes. "Don't tell me you're jumping on the book banning wagon. Because that might ruin our friendship."

"No way. Fuck book bans. People deserve access to diverse books, especially in public spaces. But you best believe some of the more conservative townies had something to say about the 'Praise Kink' display next to the children's section." He chuckles. "It's brilliant, really. Everyone in town is talking."

"Yeah, Rosalie texted the group chat. They've had a record number of new card sign-ups this month and digital downloads are up fifty percent."

"Damn." He nods, clearly impressed. "Book club at her place tonight?"

"Yeah." I swallow back a wave of nerves. "I should start getting ready. You sure you don't mind? Because I can stay home."

"Go. You've earned a night out."

I don't know if that's entirely true, but I haven't left my house in over a week and I can't remember the last time I did that. It will be good to see my friends, even if my stomach twists at facing a fact I've been trying to ignore all week. My marriage is over and I don't know how to deal with that.

"Oh, and I think you and I should get out of here for a few hours on Sunday."

"I don't want to run into anyone." More like, I'm not ready to deal with whispers, gossip, and prying questions.

"Which is why we're going a few towns over."

His assertiveness, and obvious planning, pique my interest. "Oh? Where are we going?"

"It's a surprise."

I fucking love surprises, but they aren't always practical. "What about the kids?"

"Already taken care of."

Okay. Excitement gathers in my belly. "Are they coming with?"

"Your nieces are babysitting. I hope that's okay I asked. They seemed pretty excited to make some cash."

"I bet they are." I can't help but smile. Knowing Rainer, he offered them more than the going rate. "You've really taken care of everything."

"I try." He winks. "Now, go get ready for book club. Liv will be leaving school as soon as that bell rings."

"LOOK WHO I BROUGHT," Liv announces as we step inside Rosalie's.

"There's our girl!" Ash cheers.

Val walks forward, greeting me with open arms. "I thought maybe you had enough of our bullshit."

"Never." I relax into her embrace.

"It's so good to see you." Sarah hugs me next.

"How are you?" Rosalie squeezes my hand.

I promised myself I would not cry tonight, but my eyes well with tears at the concern reflected in everyone's gazes as they gather around. "I'm here."

Asher hands me a drink. "And thank fuck for that."

They deserve more of an explanation, though it's likely unnecessary. Knowing this town and the way news travels, they already have some idea of the truth. Might as well address the elephant in the room. "So, Alex left." I manage to say the words with my head held high.

"Do you want to talk about it?" Jamie asks.

I shake my head no.

"Does this mean we can talk about the book?" Rosalie presses her hands together, and I could hug her for pulling the conversation away from me.

"Uh, I didn't read it." Bernadette shrugs. "But I did bring a killer desert."

"Another one of your complicated casseroles?" Liv teases.

"You know it."

"Did anyone read the book?" Rosalie's exaggerated huff is full of disappointment.

"Sorry." Jamie sighs. "You know how the start of the school year goes. I didn't have time to read."

Val raises her hand. "Me either."

"I never read the books y'all pick," Asher says in his usual dry humor that causes everyone to laugh. Well, everyone but Rosalie.

"I read until chapter ten," I volunteer.

"This is why you're my favorite." Rosalie meets my stare with a smile, then rolls her eyes at the rest of the group. "Fine. I guess we'll just drink and eat."

For the rest of the night we do just that. No one pries into what went down with Alex. No one makes me feel bad or judged. I am lucky to have such wonderful friends. The warmth of their conversation along with lots of laughter is exactly what I need, and for that I'm grateful.

6

RAINER

IT'S COMPLETELY dark outside as Maeve and I get ready to leave on Sunday morning. We move about the house quietly, careful not to wake any sleeping children.

I'm brewing coffee when the flash of headlights shines through the kitchen window. Checking to make sure it's Riley and Tess, I quickly fill the travel mugs, then softly knock on Maeve's door. "You almost ready? They're here."

Maeve's gorgeous smile greets me a second later as she opens the door. "Ready."

Witnessing her excitement makes the plan of this surprise outing well worth the effort and coordination. I wasn't sure how she'd feel leaving the kids. Hell, I wasn't sure how she would feel leaving at all. Since Alex left she's become a homebody, and while she isn't back to her normal, carefree self, she's getting back to good.

I just want to sprinkle a little sunshine on these dark days.

With everything already packed in my truck, including snacks and drinks for the road, Maeve and I step out onto the front porch as Riley and Tess walk up the driveway.

"Morning." I lift my hand in a wave.

"Hey, Rainer!" Tess grins, passing me to give her aunt a hug. "Hi, Aunt Maeve."

"Hey, Tess."

"Right on time." I had my doubts when making plans for Riley to babysit. She was initially appalled at the five o'clock start time, but when I incentivized her with a bonus, she was all in.

"Y'all are crazy, but I like getting paid."

"That's fair." I chuckle. "We should be back by two, but if anything comes up, don't hesitate to call us."

"We'll be fine." Riley yawns, then slings an arm around her sister. "Enjoy whatever it is you're doing at the ass crack of dawn."

"We will." I nod.

"I left instructions on the counter," Maeve says to her oldest niece. "Help yourself to anything in the pantry or fridge."

"We've got this." Riley smiles.

"Okay then." Maeve looks at me. "Shall we?"

"Let's go." I dangle the keys. The girls head inside while Maeve and I walk to my truck. I open her door, then walk around the front to hop into the cab. I settle our travel mugs into the cupholders and place my phone on the console. Reaching for the charging cord, I offer it to her. "Would you like aux?"

"I was hoping you would say that." She accepts the cord, our fingers brushing in the exchange and sending a thrill through my body.

I glance away, pretending to concentrate on the road and not how one simple touch from her lights me up from the inside. A few seconds later music begins to fill the cab.

"Are you going to tell me where we're going?"

The excited energy in her voice brings a smile to my lips. "Nope."

"No? How about a hint?"

"Hmm . . ." I run a hand down my beard. "Okay. You haven't done this before, but you want to."

"I haven't done it, but I want to . . ."

"Any guesses?"

"Win the lottery."

"Nope."

A few minutes pass in silence.

"Oh! Achieve my lifelong dream of appearing in the background of a music video or movie?"

"Damn." I shake my head. "Maybe next week."

She giggles and it's the best sound.

"I need another hint."

I turn the truck onto the highway that takes us toward Ember Ridge. "It's something more practical."

"More practical?" She scoffs. "Wake up ten pounds lighter."

"No, and that's completely unnecessary." I frown.

"Oh my God." She practically gasps.

My hands tighten on the wheel instinctively, but there's nothing on the road. "What is it?"

"I'm going to be single." Her eyes are wide as they meet mine. "Shit. I *am* single."

"Hey." I glance between her and the road as worry claws at my chest. "Breathe."

"You don't understand." Her hands rake through her hair and she groans. "If I ever want to have sex again, that means someone is going to see me naked."

Despite her obvious distress, I can't stop the smirk that works its way onto my face. "I don't think that'll be a problem."

She motions her hands down her body. "I don't think you are aware of the optical illusion I've mastered, but underneath these clothes it's nothing but loose skin and stretch marks."

My brows knit with my furrow. "Stop it." The demand comes out harder than I intend.

"What?"

"Don't talk about yourself like that." I turn down the volume on the speakers and glance away from the road to meet her stare so she understands how serious I am. "You are fucking beautiful, not to mention how incredible of a person you are. Any man would be damn lucky to earn the privilege of seeing your body."

Her eyes widen. "Oh."

"Yeah." I look away, but only because I have to in order to drive.

"Thank you." Her voice is small, but her words go straight to my heart. "You always know what to say. What I need to hear."

I wish she believed what I know. She's fucking gorgeous. She's perfect exactly the way she is, and I hate that anyone or anything in life has made her think otherwise. "It's the truth, you know that?"

"I don't know if I believe you."

"Maybe if I remind you enough times, one day you'll see what I see." *Maybe you'll see that I'm wildly in love with you. And maybe, if I'm lucky, someday you'll love me back.*

7

MAEVE

ON THE OUTSIDE, I smile and sing along to the 90s mix playing through the speakers, but in my mind, Rainer's words echo with each passing mile. *"Don't talk about yourself like that."*

I'm not a woman who tears others down, but I've allowed myself to nitpick at every imperfection and weakness my body carries. Unfortunately, as a woman, we're taught to compare ourselves at a very young age. We're told by society's standards that our value is inherently tied to our appearance or how agreeable we are.

I've intentionally parented my children in a way that bucks these social norms, and yet, somehow, I lost track of those things when it comes to my own self-worth. If I've learned anything since Alex left, it's that I deserve better.

Rainer is right. I know my worth, or at least I'm working to remember it. At the end of the day, I'm a good human, and I try my damn best to show up for my kids. I might not be the most attractive person, and age has taken its toll on my body, but I've fucking earned every last stretch mark, wrinkle, and scar. I don't want to be with a partner who values physical traits more than my heart or my personality anyway.

While it might take me a little time to find the confidence to be intimate with someone new, I'm certain I don't want to be single forever. I crave the kind of partnership my parents had. The kind where you show up for each other. Where you work hard and build something beautiful together. The kind I thought I could share with Alex.

The truck jostles my focus back to the present as Rainer turns off the main highway onto a dirt road. It's familiar, though still dark, and I try to remember what we passed along the way to discern the location.

A few minutes later I gasp as soon as I spot the sign near the trailhead. "Sunrise yoga!"

Rainer pulls his truck into an open parking spot and cuts the engine. "Are you excited?"

"I've always wanted to do this."

"I know." He reaches into the back seat and pulls out two yoga mats.

My jaw falls open. "How did you...?"

"You said something about it once." He shrugs, but I catch the smile on his lips as he turns away.

I open my door and climb out, meeting him at the front of the truck. "You have a good memory because I don't even remember mentioning that to you."

"I remember everything." He hands me a water bottle, then produces a flashlight and flicks a beam of light toward the sign. "Come on. We don't want to be late."

The hike to the class is less than ten minutes. The instructor, Phoenix, walks over to introduce himself and give us a few pointers. Rainer and I roll out our mats onto the red dirt and take a seat.

The clearing opens to the dramatic backdrop of Ember Ridge. In the dusky morning air, the outline of the sky as it meets the red rocked cliffs only teases the breathtaking view we're about to experience.

I cross my legs and sit straight, closing my eyes and inhaling deeply, while ambient music plays through a speaker. My heart rate slows and the stillness wraps around my body as the tightness in my chest loosens. It doesn't matter that I haven't practiced in years, my mind remembers what to do as soon as I'm on the mat.

Breathe.

Settle.

Be.

In college, I attended the free yoga classes at the rec center. What started as a way to stay fit, became an activity I needed in order to get through a hard week. As life evolved and my days became busier, my yoga practice became a distant memory. My mat is stuffed in the back of a closet collecting dust.

"Welcome to Sunrise yoga. I'll be leading you through today's practice, but before we get started, I want to invite you to set an intention. What do you need? Is there something you want to release? What kind of energy are you inviting into your life?"

Inhale. I want peace.

Exhale. I want moments like these.

Inhale. I want to move on. *Exhale.* Without Alex.

The realization drifts into my thoughts of its own accord, catching me by surprise. I don't think I've been brave enough to fully admit that's what I want until this moment. Maybe it's the space. Maybe it's the fact he left and never even bothered to check in on me or the kids. But it's the brutal truth.

Maybe, with a little courage, I can trust the universe and discover my way in the world again.

Phoenix leads us through the practice, and I surprise myself in a good way. My body, a lot older and less agile than it was the last time I did this, struggles to bend and flex into more challenging poses. But I'm stronger than I think.

The flow of the practice keeps my mind focused. The sky lightens before the sun finally breaks over the mountain ridge. My breath catches at the sight, my heart full of wonder and awe. How lucky am I to be alive, at this moment and in this place?

I turn my head to catch Rainer staring at me instead of the sunrise, his smile breaking through his full beard when our eyes meet. I want to hug him. I want to thank him.

"We're going to move through that flow once more," Phoenix says, drawing our gazes to him. "This time at your own pace. Connect with your breath. Connect with the earth. Give up the idea of perfection and let yourself go."

I used to schedule my classes around the yoga schedule.

This feeling right here is why.

As we lie on our mats to stretch before the final resting pose, there is nothing but gratitude in my heart. Maybe it's silly, but tears fill my eyes.

The last week and a half I wallowed in my mourning of a future I thought I'd have forever. One in which my husband, the father of my children, would be by my side until the day one of us took our last breath.

I mourned the end of my marriage and the life I built with Alex.

But I can't stay in that place forever. As sad as I am, I have to move forward, if not for myself, for my children.

My marriage is over.

But maybe my life isn't over. Maybe if I allow myself to be open to possibility, there's a life waiting for me that exceeds my expectations. One full of promise. Of hope. Of something better.

"As we settle in for savasana, I invite you to lie on your back, close your eyes, comfortably spread your legs and let them relax deeper into the earth. Do the same with your arms, and as you relax your hands, decide what you need most today. If you are open to receiving from the universe, place your palms up. If you seek grounding, place your palms down."

I reach my hands out to my sides, my palms up, ready for what comes next, even if the idea scares me a little. As I relax, my right hand brushes against Rainer's. The normal instinct to pull away and put space between us doesn't draw my hand away. He must feel the same because instead of moving his hand away, he slides it closer.

It's the barest of touches. Nothing intimate or sexual, and yet my body crackles with awareness at the connection.

His thumb ghosts against my skin in the gentlest of caresses. I don't even know if he realizes he's doing it. In my mind, a vision of his hands touching me all over sends a shiver up my spine.

Am I . . . *turned on?*

Maybe it's the fact I haven't been touched this tenderly in longer than I can remember. Maybe it's that he's been there for me every day and my mind is crossing signals it shouldn't. I miss the connectedness that comes from regular sexual activities, and because I'm so raw, so open, I'm feeling things for him that I shouldn't.

Or maybe, it's more.

Emotion stirs inside my belly.

Longing.

Aching.

A desire for more.

Which is so fucking crazy.

This is Rainer! My best friend. Not a lover. We've touched a thousand times before today. He hugs me all the damn time. Yet, there's something about the way my hand rests against his, just shy of holding hands, that feels more intimate than any of those times.

On my next exhale I move my hand closer to his, delighting in the sensation of his rough calluses as they brush against the back of my fingers.

Desire pools in my lower belly. My breath catches in my chest. But I refuse to open my eyes or fully reach for his hand, because if I do, I just know it will break this spell. And for a moment, I don't want to be practical. I want to pretend. I want to believe a man like Rainer could want me.

"Slowly bring movement back into your limbs." Phoenix's voice pops the bubble of my imagination. Following his instructions, I shove the foreign feeling of attraction for my best friend to the farthest corner of my mind. Seconds later, when Phoenix invites everyone to sit up, I decide I will deny it ever happened.

I focus instead on Phoenix and the words coming from his mouth. "Thank you for showing up this morning, not only for me and each other, but most importantly for yourself."

Yes. I am showing up for myself. I don't know why I stopped.

"The light in me, sees the light in you." Phoenix steeples his hands at his chest and bows. "Namaste."

"Namaste," I whisper back, mirroring his movements and allowing my eyes to drift shut. Everyone begins to stand, rolling up their mats and chatting quietly. I open my eyes and turn to Rainer.

His gaze is almost too much.

"That was incredible." I blink back the sudden urge to cry.

"I'm glad you liked it." His eyes see through me in a way no one else does. He sees everything, and maybe that should be terrifying, to expose the raw parts of my soul. But he is a soft place to land. He's safe and secure, and steadfast. "Come on." He nods his head toward the way we hiked in. "Let me feed you."

I don't argue with that.

Thankfully, nothing is weird or changed between us as we drive into Ember Ridge to have breakfast at The Spot. I've been here a couple of times, and on each visit it's as crowded as it is today.

Rainer puts our name on a list and after we join the patrons outside to wait for an open table.

We've only been standing for a few minutes when my phone rings with an incoming call. I pull it from my bag. It's my brother, Wild. He rarely calls. I hope everything is okay.

"Do you mind if I take this?"

"Of course not."

"Thanks." I slide my finger across the screen. "Hey, stranger." I stroll away from the waiting crowd so I can hear him better.

"Hey, little sis." The smile in his voice chases away my momentary worry. "How are my favorite little monsters? How are things with you?"

"Um, that's kind of a loaded question." I laugh though it's not funny at all. There's no good way to sugarcoat it, so I just say it. "Alex left me."

"Shit."

"Yeah."

"I'm sorry."

"Yeah, me too." My gaze lifts to study the community board on the wall of the building. Scattered across the space are a plethora of flyers. "I haven't told the rest of the family yet, but Sarah and Val know."

"So, our brothers will be banging down your door any minute."

"Yeah." I smile in spite of the subject matter. "I made Val and Sarah promise to give me a week. The protective hovering shall commence soon enough."

"Do you want to talk about it? Do you need anything? What can I do?"

The last thing I want to do is ruin the positive energy from today's yoga class. Besides, saying the truth out loud this time didn't hurt as much. It almost felt like a relief. If everyone knows, it will no longer be a shameful secret I have to keep.

"Tell me something good."

He doesn't answer, and I wonder for a moment if we've been disconnected. "Simone and I are together again."

"What?" My jaw falls open. "How?"

"It's a crazy story, but there's even more news. I've been keeping it to myself until everything was official."

"Well, don't keep me waiting!"

"I signed with a record label. I'm on tour Maeve, and I'm going to be flying back and forth over the next few months to record my album."

"Your album?" My eyes well with tears. After all the years he's worked for this dream . . . I can't believe it. "Wild, that's amazing."

"I couldn't have done any of this without you."

"Me?" I laugh through my happy tears. "What did I do?"

"You never made me feel bad that I was bumming it on your couch for most of the summer. If I hadn't felt so welcome there, I might not have stuck around for as long as I did, and I might never have crossed paths with Simone. She wouldn't have given my music to this label, and I wouldn't be in a good place." He inhales a long breath. "It's why I wanted to call you first."

I don't know why, but that makes me even more emotional. I was never exceptionally close with my oldest brother. He left town and stayed away so long that we didn't bond the same way I did with Ryan, Aiden, and Jackson. "You called me first?"

He chuckles. "You can rub it in later, just don't tell our brothers yet. Give me a few hours to catch them up on the news."

"I am so fucking proud of you."

"It's kinda hard to believe. You know? I had this vision for how my life would go, and when it didn't happen the way I planned, I kinda lost hope. Now it's better than I ever imagined and I'm just so damn grateful."

I hope I can say the same about my own life someday. Because I am done living in the space where I hope Alex comes back. I need closure. I need to be able to move forward, even if the unknown terrifies me.

"I should let you go."

"Thanks for sharing that with me. I am so happy for you."

"I'll see you in a few months. At Aiden and Sarah's wedding."

"Yeah." My heart squeezes with a bittersweet sensation. I'm happy for my brothers and that they've found love, but it's hard to not feel a tinge of jealousy. I want to be happy too. I want a relationship where the other person doesn't up and leave when things get hard. "I love you, Wild."

"Love you too, Maeve."

Ending the call, my stare catches on one of the flyers stapled to the board. The bold headline, FREE DIGITAL ART CLASS, practically calls my name, but the description is what encourages me to save the info with my phone.

Learn valuable skills that allow you to work from home.

That would be a freaking dream. I wouldn't have to worry about feeding my babies or leaving them with someone else.

"Maeve?" Rainer calls my name as he approaches. "Our table's ready. Everything okay?"

"Yeah." I nod, walking with him to the restaurant entrance, excited to tell him everything Wild told me, after I swear him to secrecy. Because why have a best friend if you can't tell them everything? There's a lightness in my step, and whether it's real or not, I believe everything is going to be okay, even if it's not how I planned.

8

RAINER

OVER THE NEXT MONTH, Maeve's energy begins to come back, along with the light in her eyes. She attends book club every Friday, and with my encouragement and support, she enrolls in an art class, driving to Ember Ridge once a week.

She isn't over Alex, but she's finding herself, and it's the most beautiful thing to witness.

I feel honored to support her, and yes, that still includes sleeping on her couch. But I don't mind. The best parts of my day, I spend with Maeve and her children. Making her smile and caring for the kids adds a purpose to my life that was always missing. On nights when I have to work late, like I'm doing tonight, I wish I were with them.

"Hey, motherfucker." A knock at my office door pulls my gaze away from the quarterly tax forms to where Mac leans against the frame. "Has anyone ever told you that you work too much?"

"You tell me that all the time."

"You almost done? Want to grab dinner?"

"Can't." I lean back in my chair and stretch my arms over my head as I blow out a breath. "These are due in a few days." I

usually don't wait until so close to the deadline, but with everything going on, meeting the needs of my business is more of a challenge. "Maybe next week?" I'll have to check with Maeve, because
I've already made a few commitments to watch the kids.

"Don't worry about it." He waves me off.

I actually feel bad. It's been over a month since I've met up for
dinner or drinks with Mac. "We're overdue. I'm sorry, man. That's
on me. Thanks for pitching in extra this month. I really appreciate
you."

"No problem. Anything I can do before I take off?"

"How do you feel about spreadsheets?"

"Fuck no." He laughs.

"That's probably good." I flash him a teasing grin. "We both
know I have control issues." And I refuse to allow anyone else to
carry the responsibility when it comes to taxes or filing paperwork
for my business.

"This is why you make the big bucks, my friend."

"Right." I scrub a hand down my beard and chuckle.

"Oh, wait. I do have one question before I clock out." He
walks into my office and leans against the filing cabinet.

"What's up?"

"How long are you going to sleep on Maeve's couch?"

Not this again. "As long as it takes."

"I see what you're doing, you know." He waggles his brows.
"And I respect the hell out of you, even if it's risky."

I shake my head and laugh. "What are you talking about?"

"Putting in your time . . . until you get upgraded to the big
bed."

"It's not like that." I would sleep on Maeve's couch forever if
that's as close as she wanted me to be.

The humor in his smile fades. "Look. I just don't want to see
you get hurt."

"Hurt? How would I get hurt?"

"I see how happy you are playing house. Playing daddy. But you aren't her husband and those are not your kids. What if Alex comes back? Or what happens when Maeve decides to move on and starts dating someone else? You're a good person, and I hate seeing you being taken advantage of."

"Maeve would never." She appreciates me. She would never even ask me to do the things I'm doing for her. I see how hard it is for her to accept help. If I weren't so insistent, she would do it all on her own.

"Not on purpose. But she's always been completely clueless when it comes to you. She doesn't see how much you care about her. And she might not ever feel for you in the way you feel for her."

"I know that." I cross my arms over my chest. It's not as if his concerns haven't passed through my mind before. But even if he's right, and Maeve never sees me as more than a friend, it won't stop me from being there for her. I'm not in this for a reward. I do what I do because I love her.

"Hey." He straightens and walks over to clap me on the back. "I didn't say that to hurt your feelings or bring you down. I care about you, that's all. Gotta look out for my boy."

"We're good." His concern comes from a good place, and his worries are the same ones I hold for Maeve. I don't want to see her hurt again.

"See you tomorrow, boss."

"See you in the morning."

A few hours later, I swing by my house to check on the place and grab some clothes. As we head into fall, the mornings have been cold and I don't have long-sleeved shirts or jackets at Maeve's.

The silence in my house makes it feel empty. I've already grown so accustomed to the sounds of Maeve's children. The laughter, babbling, crying, all of it bringing a fullness I've been missing.

I gave up the likelihood of fatherhood years ago. Sure, when I was younger, I dreamt about what it would be like to marry my best friend, to watch her belly grow full with our child, and to build a family with her. But when she married Alex, that dream died.

However, these last few weeks have shown me that maybe a tiny part of my hope for the future remains. It might not look exactly how I wanted, and hell, this new path for our future still might lead to disappointment. I can't replace Alex. Nor would I want to. Ari, Collin, and Lulu are his. But they are equally Maeve's, and anything or anyone that holds a piece of her is inherently good. It's a privilege to play any role in their development, and I don't take that honor lightly.

I'm tossing a few shirts in my bag as my phone pings from my back pocket with the alert of an incoming text.

> **Maeve:** Are you done with work yet?

> **Me:** Heading back to your place now. Do you need anything?

> **Maeve:** Just you!

I know she doesn't mean it in a romantic connotation, but my heart skips a beat anyway.

> **Maeve:** I have a surprise to show you.

> **Me:** A surprise? For me?

> **Maeve:** Be prepared to be amazed!

Me: You always amaze me.

Maeve: Yeah, yeah. Enough with the compliments. Get your ass home.

Home. As I stand in my house and glance around at the structure I've spent improving and fixing up, I have to smile. Because I'm starting to realize home isn't where I sleep at night, or a building I own, it's with Maeve. Even if I'm sleeping on her couch.

MUSIC BLARES from inside the house as I walk up Maeve's driveway. I smile, recognizing the familiar hip-hop beat—a popular song from our teenage years. I unlock the door and step inside. My presence goes unnoticed by the three littles dancing and laughing with their mama in the kitchen. My heart squeezes at the joyful simplicity of the moment.

Maeve is strikingly attractive, her hair falling in wispy curls around her face. It doesn't matter that she's wearing an oversized T-shirt or the same leggings she wore yesterday; it's impossible not to notice the beauty of this moment or the smile on her face.

"Rain-Rain!" Lulu catches me staring. "I twirl! I twirl!" she demands, running over to grab my hand and pull me in at my approach.

"Hey." Maeve's face is flushed pink. "You caught us having a dance party." She continues to dance, but her movements are more reserved.

I don't want her to feel self-conscious, especially around me.

"Then I got here just in time. Right, Lulu?" I take Lulu's hand and boogie around the makeshift dance floor.

"Yay!" Lulu giggles, but after a second she yanks her hand free and narrows her eyes with her demand. "Twirl!"

"Please," Maeve interjects to her daughter. "Remember you need to say please when you're asking for something."

"Twirl! Please!" Lulu demands.

"I think you better spin her before she explodes," Ari says earnestly.

I fight back the urge to chuckle. "I think you're right, cowboy." I deposit my hat on Ari's head, then spin Lulu until the song ends. It's such a simple thing. Dancing in the kitchen. But the moment imprints on my heart. The laughter. The love. Something special and scared and fleeting. At the last bar of music, I lift her into my arms so she doesn't fall over from dizziness. "You are quite the dancer, ma'am."

"More twirl! More twirl!"

Maeve turns the music down and shakes her head. "No more. Remember, I said that was the last song."

"Fine." Lulu scrambles out of my arms and pouts, crossing her arms over her chest.

"There's a plate for you in the microwave," Maeve says to me. "I wasn't sure if you ate."

Most nights I cut out of work early enough to help with the evening chaos, but tonight I couldn't. Even though I let her know ahead of time, I still feel bad. "Thank you. You didn't have to do that."

"I know." She grins. "I wanted to." She reaches for Lulu's hand. "Why don't we let Rainer enjoy his dinner in peace, and we'll go read some stories."

Lulu doesn't accept her mom's hand. "No bedtime."

"Not yet." Maeve smirks. "But after stories, yes."

Lulu pouts her lower lip. She is one conversation gone wrong from a meltdown.

"What book are you going to read tonight?" I ask, in hopes to distract her.

"The princess one!"

"Not the princess one again," Ari complains.

"You know the rules," Maeve explains. "You each get to pick one story for me to read. If you don't like the story she picks, you can look at your book while I'm reading it."

"Fine. Then I'm picking the scary dragon one." Ari takes off down the hall.

"Not the scary one!" Lulu runs after her brother, screaming.

"That's not going to end well." I wince.

"She did not nap today, and it shows." Maeve hoists Collin higher on her hip.

"Do you want me to put him down?"

"No. Enjoy your meal. I've got this. But when I get them all down, don't forget I have a surprise to show you." She flashes me a grin before heading toward the kids' rooms.

I haven't forgotten. How could I?

I picture us in an alternate reality, one in which we do life together, full partnership, but spend the evenings wrapped in each other's arms. I'm certain her surprise is not of the sexy variety, but it doesn't stop my brain from imagining a fantasy in which she drags me into her room and we both strip off each other's clothes.

By the time I'm done with my meal I'm in desperate need of a cold shower. Maeve is still working on getting the kids to bed, so I take my bag into her en suite bathroom. My gaze lingers over the empty shelf and counter space Maeve must have cleaned off. They no longer hold Alex's things. My heart beats with pride. I know that wasn't easy for her. But it's forward progress.

Under the shower spray, my fantasies from earlier morph into a vivid reality. When I rub soap all over my body, I imagine it's Maeve's hands caressing my skin. My dick lengthens, hard with need.

There aren't many moments where I allow myself to drown in the desire I feel for Maeve, but this is one of them.

Reaching for her body wash, I squirt a little on my hands and rub them together, inhaling the scent I associate as only hers. I wrap my hand around my aching cock and begin to stroke. My eyes drift closed as I imagine her stepping into the shower and taking over. I would give anything to feel her hands on me this way. Stroking. Touching. Teasing.

Desire courses through my veins with each inhalation, and I work my hand faster, gripping my dick harder. I bite my lip so I won't moan her name, but the pain does nothing to dampen my arousal. My breaths come quickly. My balls tighten. Then I'm coming, spilling my seed across my stomach and over my hands.

"Fuck." I lean forward, resting a hand on the tile wall to help steady my trembling body as I catch my breath.

The creek of a door disturbs my solitude. I cover my dick with my hands and glance over my shoulder, but no one is there.

Thank fuck.

I'm almost positive I locked the door, but maybe I forgot. I definitely don't want one of the kids stumbling upon me masturbating in the shower. I would be mortified, and they would be scarred. They're a bit young for that biology lesson.

I quickly wash myself and rinse off before cutting the water.

The house is quiet, and I'm sure to keep it that way as I towel off and dress in my pajamas.

When I step back out into the living area, Maeve is curled up on one end of the couch with her laptop open and resting on her legs.

"They went down easy tonight?" I whisper as I tuck my bag into the corner of the room and join her on the couch.

"Yeah. Easy day. Right?"

"That's right." I grin.

"So . . ." She bites her lower lip and doesn't quite meet my eyes. Almost as if she's nervous.

My muscles tighten, my body on alert. "What's wrong?"

"Nothing's wrong." She laughs softly, shaking her head. "I just wanted to show you something, and now I feel stupid."

"Well, now you have to show me." I level her with a stare. "Best friend rules and all."

"Fine." She exhales in a rush and turns the laptop toward me. "So you know I've been taking that digital art class online?"

"Yeah." I lean closer. "What about it?"

"I've been playing around with some designs, and it sort of gave me an idea. Well, that and my book club besties." She opens a document on the computer.

My eyes scan the designs as she scrolls through several images. Funny sayings, mostly about reading, adorn several illustrations. "Are these stickers?"

She nods. "Yeah, I was thinking I could dip my toes in with stickers because the overhead is less. There are several sites that host storefronts, and depending on how well they sell, I could branch out to other items like bookmarks and sweatshirts. I won't make a lot of money, but it would be a good side hustle, and something of my own. Plus, I could package orders when the kids are napping or after they go to bed at night. I wouldn't have to find a babysitter or leave them."

"I think this is great."

"Really?" Her nervous smile breaks away and a genuine one takes its place. "I probably won't make much out the gate, but there's a small business loan I can apply for to get started, and—"

"How much do you need?"

"What do you mean?"

"To get started. How much do you need?"

She shakes her head. "You are not going to give me money for this."

"Why not? I've invested in other local small businesses. Why can't I invest in you?"

"Because you've already done so much!" She closes the laptop with a snap and sets it to the side. "I couldn't have survived these last weeks without you, but I can't let you help with everything. I need to do this on my own. I want to prove to myself that I can be successful without the help of a man."

"Then at least let me front you the money. Until the loan comes through. That way you can get started now."

"You really love to save the day."

"Your five-foot-seven knight in shining armor, reporting for duty."

She shoves at my shoulder with a laugh. "Stop."

"You don't have to give me an answer tonight, but consider my offer. It doesn't come with strings and I won't meddle in your business."

"I know you won't."

"It's a fantastic idea, and I know how smart you are and how hard you work. It's going to be successful."

"I'm not the only stay-at-home mom making stickers. We'll see."

"It doesn't matter that other people are doing it, because you bring something special that no one else has."

Her eyes are wide and her stare is serious. "What's that?"

"You."

"Thanks, Rainer."

"Want to play a game tonight?"

"Do you mind if I turn in early? I want to work on a few more designs before I go to bed."

My body is exhausted from the long day, so it's probably a smart idea, even if I hate giving up any time with her. "Of course. Do what you need to do."

"Thanks, you're the best." She takes her laptop and stands. "Are you going to stay up?"

I resist the urge to yawn. "Nah. I should turn in." I'd sacrifice sleep for more moments with her, but I'm exhausted. I reach for the pile of blankets and pillows behind the sofa and start making my bed for the night.

"Night, Rainer." She flips the lights off as she walks into her room.

"Night, Maeve." I wait until the door closes before moving my pillow to the end of the couch where she sat moments ago. The scent of her lavender lotion lingers, and the aroma wraps itself around me. The cushions are still warm from her body as I snuggle in, and when my eyes drift shut, I pretend she's right here. It's a poor substitute for the real thing, but it's all I can have. At least for now.

9

MAEVE

AT THE END of the week, I sip on one of Asher's signature cocktails and stuff my face with good food while I watch my friends converse.

I've always loved Fridays. Not because it's the end of the week —as a mom of three, there is no rest, even on the weekend. The reason I look forward to Fridays is because of this book club; the overindulging of food, drinks, and laughter with some of my best friends.

But if I'm being honest, one of the main reasons I loved book club in the past is that it provided me a weekly escape from reality.

Maybe that makes me sound ungrateful. I know I have a good life. My health. My family. And I love my children. I really do. But at the end of most days I'm touched out, sleep-deprived, and exhausted from the monotony of life.

Or rather, I was.

I don't feel that same exhaustion now that Alex is gone. I couldn't see it before, but he added to my daily stress by not being a full partner. He was my husband, yet he watched me struggle to balance everything, and when he was home, he was just another person who took a piece of what little was left of me. My time, my energy, my body.

But it's difficult to grasp you're drowning when the person who is supposed to love you is the one standing by, watching you slip beneath the surface.

Not Rainer, though.

Rainer is my lifeline. With him, I don't drown. Fuck, he hasn't even allowed me to tread water. He's given me a hand, pulled me out of the depths, and forced me to rest, all while picking up the slack.

Without him I'd still be drowning.

Now, Friday book club meet-ups aren't so much an escape. They're just one of many times throughout the week where I get to fill up my cup—doing things with people who energize my mind and bring me joy and laughter.

I'm not stupid. Rainer won't live with me forever. There are harder days ahead, I'm sure, but I can conquer them when I'm surrounded by such a supportive village.

"You're quiet tonight," Bernadette leans over, whispering in my ear. "Is everything okay?"

Is everything okay? No. Not really. But I feel better than I have in months, maybe even years. "I'm good. Promise," I whisper back. "Just thinking."

"Hey!" Asher points from across the room. "No secrets. If you have tea, don't be greedy, share it with the group."

I can't help but laugh. "Nothing juicy to share."

"Juicy." Jamie blanches. "That's almost as bad as moist."

"The only thing that should be moist is cake." Rosalie nods.

"Speak for yourself," Liv deadpans. "I would do questionable things for a juicy, moist encounter."

"Amen, sister." Asher holds up his hand, and Liv slaps it with a smile.

"That reminds me!" Val claps her hands together. "Are you

ready for my book pick? It's a mafia romance . . . but they're vampires!"

"Yes!" Asher presses his hands together, steepling them in front of his chest. "Biting and sucking are two of my favorite things."

The entire room cackles with laughter. Even Rosalie breaks into a smile.

"So before we pretend to talk about last week's book . . ." I reach for my bag and dig inside. "I brought gifts."

"Wait?" Liv leans over to Val. "Did I forget someone's birthday?"

"No." I stand up to hand out my first go at creating a product. "I'm starting a side hustle. Nothing big. Just some stickers I'm going to sell online. These are only prototypes, so please be kind." I shuffle through the designs. I don't know why I'm so nervous. I had so much fun creating them, but now I'm worried they aren't as good or as funny as I hoped.

"Come on." Asher motions with his fingers. "Show us what you got."

"Okay." I hand the top sticker to him.

"'Call me daddy.'" He bursts into laughter. "Yes, please."

I hand another to Val. "This one is for you."

"'Spicy books pair well with wine.'" She reads it aloud before showing the group. "Um, this is perfect." Her smile bolsters my confidence.

I continue handing stickers out, my heart swelling with joy at their genuine delight.

"'I like my men fictional.'" Jamie laughs. "Yeah, I do."

"'Complicated casserole?'" Bernadette beams. "Oh my God. I love it."

"'I put out!'" Sarah laughs, showing everyone an image of a fire extinguisher.

"What does yours say, Val?"

"'Fuck.'" The words are surrounded by flowers. She laughs. "It's my favorite word."

"Mine too." I grin, then hand the next to Liv.

"'I'm silently judging your grammar.'" She shows off the minimalist design before meeting my stare. "It's true, and this is totally going on my laptop."

"Mine is going on the fridge." Jamie nods. "Oh! You should make magnets too!"

"Really?" I hand the last one to Rosalie.

"'If she writes it, I will read it.'" She takes in the design I spent more than a few hours perfecting. "Are these the Brontë sisters?"

I play it off, when in reality I'm ecstatic she understood what I was going for. "Of course."

"I love this! Thank you, Maeve." She looks from the design to me. "Could you do bookmarks? I have a small budget to work with, but I'd love to have some custom ones done for the library."

I'm a novice. I barely have my feet wet, but her confidence and support mean everything. "Of course. I would be honored to." If I didn't need the money, I would offer to do it for free.

"We'll connect this week."

Returning to my seat, I can't hold back my smile. Their reactions are energizing, and I'm excited to pursue this venture of mine.

"Oh shit!" Liv exclaims when a dribble of sauce drops from her fork to her shirt.

"Here." I hand her the extra napkin near my plate. In doing so, I rest my left hand on the small side table for balance.

As I sit back, Sarah's gaze catches on my hand.

My ring finger is no longer adorned with its usual solitaire diamond. In its place is an indent from the ring I wore for over seven years. The circle of skin a shade lighter than the rest of my hand still holds proof, my decision to remove my wedding band this morning remaining like a ghost.

I don't know why exactly today was the day. The flicker of the diamond every time it caught the light had pissed me off. I don't need a daily reminder of Alex when he couldn't even be bothered to return my calls.

"I'm proud of you," Sarah says. "When things blew up with my ex, I was a mess."

"Same." Val nods.

"You look amazing, you know that?" Asher comes by with a pitcher, filling my glass even though it's mostly full. "Single Maeve is working for you. You're practically glowing."

Embarrassment warms my body. I have no hesitation in giving compliments, but receiving them is somehow harder to accept. "I think I probably just put on too much blush."

"No. It's more than that. And I know how much work it takes to get to that point." His gaze is earnest. "You're doing great, and if you need anything, please don't hesitate to ask."

"Yeah. What can we do?" Jamie says. "Do you need us to help with meals? Bedtime?"

I have that covered, thanks to Rainer. "I'm good. Well, there's one thing. I'm just not sure when."

"Anything." Bernadette nods.

"I want to move." More like I *need* to. Rent is overdue, and while my landlord is a friend of my father, I won't ask for another extension. I hoped Alex would have the decency to support his kids. But if Alex is getting paid, he isn't depositing a dime into our shared checking account. I sent him several texts over the last month asking to discuss finances or if he wanted to see his children. His reply was he was working and to give him some time. Each response somehow made me feel as if I were the one inconveniencing him, which is fucking crazy. As much as I didn't want to, this week I swallowed my pride and called him. He sent me to voicemail.

"Absolutely." Val meets my stare. "Tell us when and we'll all help."

"I don't have any hard plans yet."

"Do you need to borrow money?" Rosalie's tone is as hard as her jaw. "It's bad enough he skipped town. He better be supporting you and the kids."

He's not. But I don't want to admit that part. It makes me feel so weak and helpless. As if things are beyond my control.

"Maeve will tell us if she needs anything." Asher draws the attention of the room. "Right, babe?"

I'm so grateful for his intervention. "Right."

"So does that mean we can finally discuss the book?" Rosalie levels her stare around the room.

The collection of groans that meet her question brings a smile to my lips.

She meets my gaze with the rise of my brow.

"Sorry," I mouth more than say.

She rolls her eyes with a laugh. "You are the best humans I know in this town, and you all suck."

10

RAINER

IT'S DIFFICULT BALANCING EVERYTHING, especially relationships, when you're also caring for three children under the age of six. It's also a lot of coordination and work to leave the house with the little rascals. But my parents insist they have us over for dinner while Maeve's at book club. It's been too long since I've stopped in or visited with my parents, so I agree.

I'm starting to regret that now.

"Okay, that doesn't go in your mouth." I scoop Collin up from the floor and pull the crystal lid from his fingers.

"Sorry. I thought we put everything up." My mother takes the lid, and the container of candies, and places them on a higher shelf.

"It's okay, Mom. I appreciate you having us over for dinner." It was delicious, and thankfully, all of the kids seemed to enjoy it too. Even if the house is far from baby-proof.

"It's been so long since we've had little ones around." She tickles Collin under his chubby chin, earning a smile. "Kinda forgot how much of a handful they can be."

"Not this one." My dad huffs from the screened-in porch. He

took Ari out there a few minutes ago while I changed Collin's diaper. "He's quite the cool dude. Aren't 'cha?"

I venture out to the porch with Collin on my hip while Mom entertains Lulu with some of my old toys.

"You doing okay, cowboy?" I ask.

"We're playing cards."

"Dad." I level my father with a stare.

Ari ignores our conversation, his brow knit with concentration as he barely manages to hold his cards without dropping them.

"It's never too early to learn blackjack. It helps boost those math skills!"

I suppose he's right. "Just no placing bets."

"It's fine." My dad slides a foil-wrapped candy across the table. "We're using chocolates."

I shake my head. Not sure Maeve wants an early introduction to gambling for her son, but there's no use arguing once my father decides something.

"Ah, come on. I used to do the same with you, and look how you turned out."

I check my phone for the time and cringe when I see how late it is. Bedtime could be brutal if we don't head home soon. "Five more minutes. Okay, Ari?"

"Okay." He nods.

I head back inside and glance at my mom tidying the kitchen. "What can I do to help?"

"Nothing." She sets down a dishtowel and motions to the table. "Come sit and visit with me before you have to go."

I snag a cup of snacks from the diaper bag before pulling out a chair. Collin is content to sit on my lap, as long as there's food.

"They're really good children." My mom smiles, glancing across the room at Lulu.

"They are." I can't help but beam with pride.

"And you've been helping for a while now."

Five weeks and two days. I know because I've been counting. "Do your observations come with a question?" I tease her, guessing she has more to say. She's just not sure how to do it without over-stepping.

"I just want to make sure your head is in the right place."

"What does that mean?"

"I don't want to see you get too attached. That's all."

Impossible. I'm already attached to Maeve and her children. "Mom. It's fine. I'm a grown man. You don't have to worry about me."

"I always worry. That never stops, you know? Just wait. You'll see."

"Yeah."

"Is she open to having more?"

I don't have to clarify to know what she's asking, or to whom she's referring. "Maeve and I are friends."

"I'm only asking if she's discussed having more."

She's asking if Maeve would have a child with me, and I can't completely fault her. But the idea is so far from reality, I can't even allow myself to hope. "I don't know."

"Those are important conversations. That's all I'm saying."

"You're saying a lot."

"Oh, you!" She waves me off. "It's just that family is important. I love you, and I thank God every day for you. But I wish I could have given you a brother or sister. I'm sorry that wasn't in the cards." Mom dabs beneath her eyes. My mother struggled with fertility issues. I was their rainbow baby.

"Mom, you and Dad gave me everything I needed."

"Always felt like we barely had enough."

It's true we weren't the wealthiest in town, but I never went without. "But it was enough. And this town, all the people here, I never felt like I was an only child."

"I guess with as much time as you spent at the Wilders', that makes sense."

I reach across the table to squeeze her hand. "Sometimes life doesn't go exactly as we plan, but it's still beautiful."

"You really have grown up to be a good man. Your dad and I are proud of you. Of everything you've accomplished, and how you're stepping up with these kids. They need a role model like you."

I stand as Collin begins to fuss. "Yeah, well, I think I need them too."

"I did it!" Lulu exclaims.

I glance over to see the tower of blocks she's assembled.

"Good job, girlie."

"Kitty!" she shouts and then springs off the floor, her attention lasering in on my parents' cat, who has just summoned the courage to come out. Lulu runs, catching her foot on the end of the coffee table, her forward motion knocking the tower of blocks and sending her face-first to the floor.

I move to stop her from crashing, but I'm not quick enough.

Her blood-curdling screams fill the room.

My heart plummets. *Shit!*

"Here." I practically shove Collin into my mom's arms and slide to Lulu on my knees just as she lifts her face off the floor. There's blood smeared across her chin. The pit of my stomach contracts with dread as she screams so loud my own ears ring.

Please be okay. Please be okay. I chant in my mind as I carefully scoop her off the floor and assess her injury. Tears spring from her eyes and snot bubbles in her nostrils as I search out the source of the blood. Her small hands clutch the fabric of my t-shirt.

"It's okay." I stand and walk her to the kitchen, depositing her on the counter and then wetting a clean towel at the sink to wipe her face. The gash on her chin is small and thankfully slows with a little pressure, along with her tears. The entire ordeal lasts less than five minutes, but I swear I age about five years.

"My blocks," she sobs, pointing to the mess. "Kitty." She's more upset over those two things, which gives me some relief her pain isn't too bad.

"Let's get you cleaned up so we can head home," I say as Mom hands us a box of bandages.

"No home!" she wails, her tears returning with her distress. It's late. I pushed it staying those five extra minutes.

"Now, now," my mom soothes, Collin on her hip as she shuffles through one of the cabinets. She produces a sleeve of cookies. "No need to cry. I've got treats."

"Treats?" Lulu blinks back her tears, smiling as Mom hands her not one, but two cookies.

"Really?" I level my mother with a stare.

"What?" She shrugs. "You didn't give me grandkids to spoil. I'm making up for lost time."

Despite her dig, I smile, loving how attentive she is toward Maeve's children. The way I know Maeve's own mother would be, if she were still alive. "Thank you."

"Come around with these kiddos more often. Any time. Does your father good to have a new student."

"Blackjack!" Ari exclaims from the deck.

Mom and I chuckle.

Gathering our things, we head out to the porch.

"Time to go, cowboy." I tap Ari on the shoulder.

"And here's a cookie for the road." Mom hands him the treat.

"Thank you, Mrs. Anderson." His politeness is too cute, especially paired with those big brown eyes.

Mom eats it up. "What good manners you have."

My parents walk us out to the van, talking to the kids as I buckle each one in and double-check to make sure we have everything.

"Thanks again for dinner." I hug Mom. "Love you."

"Love you more."

"Night, Dad." I open my arms and step toward him.

He pats my back as we embrace. "You're doing the right thing, son." He drops his voice low so only I can hear. "I'm sure proud of you."

"Love you, Dad."

There's another round of goodbyes as I situate myself inside the van and start the vehicle. The kids wave at my parents as we back out of the gravel driveway.

"That was fun," Ari says. "I like playing cards with your dad."

"Yeah?" I meet his satisfied grin in the rearview mirror. "Maybe we can play sometime."

"Can we bet chocolate?"

I chuckle, suspecting he enjoyed the chocolate more than the game itself. "I think we can do that."

"Yes!" He pumps his little fist in the air.

"I want chocolate." Lulu pouts, crossing her arms.

"Everyone has had enough sweets for tonight. It's jammies and stories when we get back."

Thankfully, there aren't any more tears or spills before bedtime. Collin goes down fairly easy and so does Lulu.

I check on Ari as I pass his room in the hallway, but when I notice he's still awake, I move inside and sit on the edge of the bed. "Hey, cowboy. What's keeping you up?"

His eyes tear up as they meet mine. "Is my daddy in trouble?" His earnest question catches me off guard.

"Why do you think that?"

"Because when I'm in trouble, I lose my privileges. Did Daddy lose his privileges? Is that why he isn't here?" His chin trembles. "For making Mama cry?"

Fuck.

I don't know how to answer this. I don't want to overstep, but Maeve isn't here and I don't want Ari to feel like he can't come to me with hard questions, about his dad or anything. Anger rises in my chest, all of it directed at Alex, but I force myself to calm down.

Brushing Ari's hair back from his face, I meet his wide-eyed stare. "Sometimes grown-ups make mistakes. And your daddy made a mistake by making your mom cry. I bet if he could, he would take that back."

"Sometimes I get angry and make Lulu cry." He fiddles with his blanket. "Do I have to go away too?"

"Oh, buddy." I shake my head, picking my words carefully. "You aren't going away. Ever. Everyone makes mistakes, but the important thing is learning how to take accountability for your actions. That's a big word, I know, but that's why it's so important to always tell the truth, even when you do something that hurts someone, and it's why you need to apologize. This is your home, and even when you make a mistake, you will always be welcome in your home."

"So why isn't Daddy here?" Ari picks at the edge of his blanket. "Does he not like us anymore?"

Fuck.

"Ari, I am going to tell you the truth. Okay? Man to man. This is important." I wait for him to nod. "Your daddy loves you. No matter what choices he makes, he loves you, and I want you to remember that." I can't imagine walking away from these kids. They're not even mine and my heart fucking breaks at the very idea.

"Is he working? Sometimes he has to go away for a lot of days."

"Yeah, he's working." I nod.

"When is he coming back?"

"I don't know." I wish I knew. I wish I could give Ari an answer. But the honest truth? There's a selfish part of me that wishes Alex stays gone forever. He doesn't deserve Maeve, and he doesn't deserve to be a part of his children's lives. Not after the hurt he's caused. Not when I can give them so much better.

11

MAEVE

THERE'S ONLY a few of us left at Asher's and I'm the only sober one in the group. Not that I'm complaining. It's my choice to nurse one cocktail while others have their fill.

I haven't officially given up alcohol or anything, it's just my nerves were so bad when Alex first left, that the idea of drinking anything other than coffee or water turned my stomach. Now, it's more that I feel responsible to always be on call. If something happens with one of the kids, or someone else in my family, I want to be able to get in the car and drive without relying on anyone. Maybe I'll get back to letting loose on Friday nights, but for now it's entertaining enough to watch them do it without me.

"So." Asher leans forward on the kitchen island. "Rainer's been sleeping at your place since Alex left? Every night?"

I press my lips together at his insinuation. "It's not like that."

"We wouldn't judge you if it was." Liv sighs before taking a sip from her glass.

"Leave our girl alone." Bernadette levels them both with a glare. "She's apparently too broken to notice that fine specimen of a man in her home."

"We're best friends." I roll my eyes. "And he's great, honestly. I don't know what I would do without him. My house has never looked so clean."

Liv's jaw falls open. "He cleans?"

"He vacuums, does laundry, cooks, and changes diapers, and he even gets up with Collin so I can sleep." Yes, I am a little smug recounting all the things he does.

"If I had a man cooking for me, taking care of my kids, and making my life easier every damn day . . . and he looked like Rainer, I might want him to do more than my dishes." Asher meets my stare across the island counter. "Tell me I'm wrong."

I've never thought about Rainer that way. Okay, that's not entirely true. But that was a blip. An errant thought in a vulnerable moment. I blame it on the perfect sunrise and yoga.

"I think you just put an idea in her head." Liv grins between Asher and me.

"No." I wave her off. Even if she might be a little right. "I'm done with men."

"I've said the same thing." Asher sighs knowingly. "Doesn't make it true."

"You're allowed to be attracted to him. And anyone else. You know that, right?" Liv says.

"It's just really soon." I can't meet their inquisitive stares. "Alex and I haven't even discussed divorce yet."

"Hey." Bernadette rests her arm around my shoulders. "There is no timeline for this. Okay? No rules of waiting so many months before seeing someone else. It's perfectly okay if you aren't ready or . . . fuck, if you just want to be alone. But don't worry about how it looks or what people will say. Because you gotta do you. Unless someone is paying your bills or sleeping in your bed, they don't get to have an opinion."

"Thanks." I think I needed to hear that.

"Now. Are you going to file for divorce?" Bernadette bangs a fist on the counter. "Because I can help you with that."

"Hey." Asher pouts. "How come you wouldn't help me with my trust?"

"Because I no longer practice law." She grins, raising her glass.

"So then you can't help Maeve."

"Fuck that." Bernadette shoots me a wink. "It'll be off the record. But you think I'm letting our girl navigate that system alone? Never."

My eyes water as emotion tightens my chest. It's not the first time tonight, and I'm normally not so weepy, but her kindness is overwhelming. I feel so loved. So cared for. So protected.

"Shit. It's almost eleven o'clock." Asher groans. "I'm kicking y'all out. My first appointment is at six."

"On a Saturday?" Liv's eyes bug out. "That should be illegal."

"I don't know what I was thinking when I agreed to that."

We all hug and say our final goodbyes, then I drive Liv and Bernadette to their homes before heading to mine. Tonight was a lot, but it was a good kind of a lot.

The house is quiet when I slip inside. I set my bag near the door, then tip-toe to the kitchen for a glass of water. I take note of the clean counters, everything in its place. Before, I'd always come home to a mess. Sure, Alex would stay with the kids—it wasn't really a choice—but I'd return to a sink full of dirty dishes, crumbs on the counter, and dropped food beneath the high chair.

The difference between Alex and Rainer is like night and day.

I don't want to constantly compare them, but it's impossible not to.

After I drink some water, I walk into the living room and catch sight of Rainer sleeping on the sofa.

There's a basket of folded laundry next to him. Kids clothes. When did he even have time to do that?

But that's not what has emotion clawing its way up my throat. Or why my heart skips a beat.

It's the fact that Collin is cuddled into his chest, his little arms looped around Rainer's neck.

Alex never did this. Any sleepless nights with the kids were my problem. I always thought it was fair because he worked outside of the house and I didn't. But Rainer doesn't discriminate. He doesn't remind me that childcare does not pay the bills. Or that I wanted to stay home. He never asks what needs to be done, he just assesses the situation and does it and then gets up and goes to work in the morning.

He takes care of me. He takes care of my kids.

Fuck me.

He's never been more attractive.

Tears leak from the corners of my eyes, streaking down my cheeks, as I reflect on all the little things Rainer has done for me and my family. All the ways he's supported me, encouraged me, and loved me. How he was the one who held me after my mom died. That he played with my kids at Will's funeral so I could be with my brothers. He shows up, again and again and again. *Fuck.* I don't know what I did to deserve him. In fact, I know I *don't* deserve him.

Yet, here he is, cradling my youngest in his strong, capable arms, reducing me to a puddle of tears. Fucking hell. I bite back a sob and furiously wipe away the evidence of my emotion, but it's no use. It's as if a damn has broken, and I can't hold them back.

12

RAINER

I'M in a deep sleep when a sound disturbs my slumber. In the back of my mind I register a muffled cry, but it doesn't compute. Collin's breaths fan little puffs of air across my neck, and his warm body pressed against my chest attempts to lull me back to sleep.

But I hear it again.

My eyes blink open, and it takes a moment to make out the form standing at the end of the couch. It's Maeve, and she's crying.

A surge of panic races through my body. "What's wrong?" I whisper, wrapping my arms around Collin and sitting upright.

"You're sleeping on the couch," she says through sobs.

"What?" I've been sleeping on this sofa for over five weeks. I don't understand why it's making her sad now. Obviously, it's something more. "Wait right here. Okay?" I stand and walk away, but only for a second. I go into Collin's room and lay him in his crib. He nestles himself into the mattress and continues to sleep while I slip out the door and return to Maeve.

"Come here." I open my arms to reach for her at the same time she leans into my embrace. I rub her back, hating that her sobs gain force instead of ease. "I've got you. Let it all out. I'm here." Worry grows at her continued tears, but I don't ask any questions. Not yet. It's obvious she needs this, and in some demented way, I'm happy I get to be the one to hold her as she cries.

I can't see the clock, but I'd guess ten full minutes pass before her tears subside. I hate that she's hurting. I wish I could take it away. My palms move across her back and over her shoulders, soothing whatever she's feeling.

She doesn't pull away, so I don't stop. Which wouldn't be a problem, except for my body's reaction. The scent of her body wash fills my lungs with each inhale, reminding me of how I took my cock into my hands in the shower and pretended it was her getting me off. The warmth of her body pressed against mine makes me wish for things I shouldn't. Her soft skin beneath my fingertips each time I reach the hem of her sleeves and that barest of touches sends a wave of desire straight to my dick.

Longing courses through my veins and fuels my desire.

I want her.

I've always wanted her.

And somehow, standing here in the dark, holding her to me, makes me believe for a second that maybe she wants me too.

It's the most inopportune time to get a boner. She was crying a few minutes ago, for fuck's sake! But that message doesn't make its way to my brain, and if we stand here much longer, she's going to feel exactly what I'm thinking.

"Rainer." She whispers my name.

Maybe I imagine it, but her breath grows as shallow as mine. "Yeah?"

"My snot is all over your shirt."

My chest shakes with the urge to laugh. Okay, maybe she's not thinking the same as me. "That's okay, honey." I try to step back, but she wraps her arms around my waist, keeping me close.

"I need a tissue," she mumbles against my shoulder.

"Here." I reach an arm up and between my shoulder blades,

gathering the cotton fabric in a fist and pulling the t-shirt off. I hand it to her. "You've already cried on it."

"Oh." She presses the fabric to her nose as her gaze rakes over my chest. Appreciation flares in her eyes. "Damn." She sighs, her lips parting as she drops the t-shirt.

Damn is right.

Maeve has never looked at me the way she's looking at me now, and that's probably why all propriety and good sense leaves my body. "Your turn." The words leave my lips so softly, I'm not sure if she hears them.

Then my heart stops. My breath catches. Maybe I've died and gone to heaven.

Because Maeve lifts her shirt, exposing her skin and her pale pink bra, before tossing it to the floor.

I don't know who reaches for who first. Our lips crash together. Our teeth clash. Kissing, tasting, touching. We come together like a whirlwind of explosive energy. My hands wrap around her waist, my fingers digging into her flesh and holding her to me. I'm greedy for her touch. Dying for her kiss. I don't take my time or slow down. Hell, I barely breathe. I'm scared that if we stop, this moment will cease to exist.

Her touch glides over my back, through my hair, and down my beard. "Rainer." Her palms come between our bodies and she presses forcefully against my chest. She shoves, pushing me down to the sofa, but before I can question why, she straddles my waist, capturing my lips in another earth-shattering kiss. In this position there's no doubt she feels every inch of my erection straining beneath my sweatpants.

She rocks her hips forward, finding a rhythm as we ride this feeling higher and higher. I capture her moans with my kisses. I run my fingers over her skin and dip them beneath the clasp of her bra.

A cry halts my movement before I can unfasten it.

Maeve freezes.

We both wait, suspended in time, and I swear I can hear my own heart beating in my ears.

The cry sounds again. *Collin.* I love that kid, but he's being a royal cockblock.

Maeve's groan of frustration as her body sags in defeat matches the way I feel.

"I'll go," I volunteer.

"No." She glances down between us. "You need to calm down."

It's not funny, yet something about the way she says the words causes a smile to take over my face. "Good call. I'll wait here."

"Give me a minute." She stands up, a little flustered as she yanks her shirt off the floor and tugs it on. She hurries toward the kids' rooms but stops at the entry of the hallway to look back. There's something in her gaze that causes my amusement to fade. Is she relieved? Is she disappointed?

She disappears down the hall without a word. I wish I could read her mind. To know what she's thinking. But that will have to wait for her return.

Collin's cries settle soon after she reaches his room.

My heart still beats wildly in my chest and my cock aches for relief. But there's only one thing on my mind. I kissed Maeve. She kissed me. And if her kid wouldn't have woken up, we might have gotten completely naked.

I don't know if I should cheer or cry.

I have waited my entire life to know what it would feel like to be with Maeve, and to have her desire centered on me. I thought I knew how incredible it would be, but I was wrong. All the daydreams and fantasies don't hold a candle to the real thing.

In one second, everything I knew changed.

A future I had all but given up on is now a possibility.

If Maeve feels for me even a fraction of the way I feel for her, we could be together.

Fuck.

I'm already getting ahead of myself.

We kissed, and just because she wanted me tonight doesn't mean she'll want me again.

We need to talk.

With my erection under control and no more cries coming from the bedroom, I walk down the hall to check on Maeve. Inside the room, Collin sleeps soundly in his mother's arms. She's sleeping too, her head bowed to his as they snuggle in the small recliner.

Oh, Maeve. She's exhausted.

As much as I want to know where I stand with her, tonight's not the time to have that conversation.

Lifting Collin from her arms, I place him in his crib, thankful he stays asleep. Hopefully, for the rest of the night. Then I walk to Maeve and scoop her into my arms, cradling her against my chest. Her eyes open at the movement, surprise in their depths.

We don't speak as I carry her the short distance to her bedroom.

"Rainer." Her body stiffens, apprehension in her tone as I walk toward the bed.

"Get some rest, okay?" I lay her worries to rest, setting her at the edge of the bed. I know she's not ready for that. Even if things between us got carried away earlier, there's too much history between us to just jump into bed. Too much at stake. I press a kiss against her forehead, then step back. "We'll talk more tomorrow. Okay? We don't have to figure out anything tonight. I'm not going anywhere."

13

MAEVE

THE AROMA of freshly brewed coffee pulls me from sleep. Bird chatter outside the window signaling dawn is about to break. It's Saturday, and for that I'm grateful. There are no children to rouse from sleep or get ready for school. By all accounts, this would be the perfect morning to sleep in, at least until Lulu or Collin wakes. But I can't. Not when I practically mauled my best friend last night and then fell asleep before we could talk.

I pause to listen for small voices or chatter, but there are none. Only a quiet clank of an occasional dish comes from the kitchen. Rainer's emptying the dishwasher. *Of course he is.* That man never ceases to impress me. I don't think he knows how to be lazy. He sees something that needs to be done and just does it.

Like last night.

He saw the longing in my eyes and kissed me.

Or maybe I kissed him first?

I replay the moment in my mind, my body warming with arousal. My pulse races at the memory. Embarrassment heats my cheeks.

I kissed my best friend.

The very idea sends me reeling, and yet nothing about last night felt weird or awkward or bad.

I kissed Rainer Anderson.

And I liked it.

I did *not* have this on my bingo card.

In the light of day, I worry it was an unwise decision. We're best friends, and we crossed a line. What does that mean for us? I'm not in a place to pursue a relationship or start dating, but this isn't just anyone. This is Rainer. We know each other better than we know ourselves sometimes. I need to know where his head is. At the very least, I owe him a conversation.

Self-consciousness blooms in my chest as I toss the covers off my body and get out of bed to use the restroom. I catch sight of my reflection as I reach for my toothbrush. My hair is a mess. I'm not wearing makeup, and my skin shows every single imperfection on my face. My baggy sleep pants and oversized shirt do nothing for my figure. I look more unhoused than I do attractive, and I consider changing.

Only, that's stupid. Rainer has seen me like this before. It's practically been my uniform since Alex left. "Fuck it," I mutter as I glance away from my reflection. I need to have this conversation without my children as an audience. I don't have time to play dress up. If we're going to get a moment alone, it needs to be now. With my head held high, I swallow back my nerves and march my butt to the kitchen.

My feet stutter at the sight of Rainer as I come around the corner. His jeans are slug low on his hips and his simple white cotton tee pulls up as he reaches to return a dish to its place in the upper cabinet. A few inches of his skin are exposed by the movement.

My mouth is parched, but the thirst that runs through my veins can't be quenched by a drink. In the light of this new day, I see him differently. Almost as if my mind now has permission to appreciate him fully. I'm not blind. I've always been aware of his looks. But I've always been with Alex, and lusting after someone other than my husband is just not something that my brain does.

Or at least it didn't used to.

Fuck.

My fingers ache to reach for the hem of his shirt and lift it up over his body so I can appreciate him more.

"Morning." Rainer flashes his warm smile when he notices me standing a few feet away. "Coffee?"

"Yeah." I nod, praying I'm able to mask the yearning in my voice.

Rainer retrieves two mugs and makes our drinks. I clear the clutter off the table and take a seat, waiting as he brings them over.

"Thank you." I bring the offered mug to my lips and blow softly across the hot liquid. It calms my nerves and gives me something other than his incredible body to focus on.

"Sleep okay?" he asks, the same as he does every morning, but everything about this interaction feels as if we're both tiptoeing around the land mine we both notice but neither wants to point out.

"We should talk."

He nods, his gaze slipping from mine. He studies his coffee as if it's the most interesting thing in the room. "Do you want to finish your coffee first? Or should we talk now?"

"Now is good." I exhale the nerves tightening in my chest.

"So . . ." He drags out the word and meets my stare. I can't read his expression, which is the most unnerving thing. I thought I knew them all.

"Yeah." I bite the inside of my cheek.

"About last night." His lips pull up with the start of a smile.

I can't help but grin. "Yeah?"

He blows out a soft chuckle and scrubs a hand down his beard. "I, um, well. I guess I want to know how it all made you feel."

Good. Hungry. Desired. "Um . . ." My body warms at the memory. "I was a willing participant, if that's what you are asking."

"I'm aware." He flashes me a wicked smile. "But that's not what I asked. How did it make you *feel*?"

"Like maybe I should have been kissing you a lot sooner."

"Jesus, Maeve." He looks up at the ceiling and groans.

"Am I alone in feeling that?" I need to know, even if his answer hurts.

"No." He meets my stare. A soft chuckle shakes his chest. "Definitely, not."

"Okay then." Possibilities race through my mind, but they're shut down with a healthy dose of practicality. "But I'm not sure it's a good idea."

"Why do you say that?"

"Well, for one thing, I refuse to let one momentary lapse in judgment ruin decades of friendship."

"It won't." He shakes his head, determination in his stare. "Nothing could."

I want to believe him. I do. But how can he be so certain?

"The other thing, which is kind of an obvious one . . ." I glance down at my hand, the absence of my wedding band still so strange to observe. "I'm still married."

"Right."

"And I don't know that I have anything to offer right now. I don't know if you've noticed, but I'm kind of a hot mess."

"You're fucking gorgeous. And you are one of the best people I know. So if you think the technicality of you being married is an issue for me, you would be wrong."

He deserves so much better. He deserves someone who is certain about their future, and who isn't going through a huge life transition. But selfishly, I want more of last night. The one thing I'm certain of is him.

"Can I tell you what I'm thinking?" At my nod, he leans forward and rests his elbows on the table. "From where I sit, we have two options. One, we leave it alone. We pretend it never happened and shove all those feelings away in the hopes it won't change things between us. Though, if I'm being honest, I don't see that working out since I sure as shit can't think of anything else but kissing you again."

"What's the second option?" I whisper.

"We explore this. We find our way through these feelings. No pressure. No expectations. We can go as fast or as slow as you like. I'm in no hurry and I'm not going anywhere. Whatever we do next, we do on your terms. If you aren't ready, I'll wait until you are. I'll wait forever, if that's what you need."

"Oh."

"I really hope you pick the second option."

"I don't want to lose you."

"You aren't gonna lose me."

"What if I do? What if I hurt you? Or disappoint you? What if we try and fail?"

"And what if it works out?" He reaches across the table, his hand covering mine and his gaze sincere. "Maeve, you are my best friend. A failed attempt at more isn't going to chase me off. You're stuck with me for life."

"Good." His confession quiets that fear. "Because you're stuck with me too."

"Why don't we take things slow? No pressure. No expectations."

"I like the sound of that."

"I want to take you out." He leans back in his chair and brings his mug to his lips. "On a date."

"Okay?" I like the sound of that more than I should. But this town won't allow us to take our relationship public, not unless we want everyone to know. Though, I guess, they're used to seeing us together. As long as we keep things PG in public, I'm not sure anyone would realize our relationship has evolved.

"I can see the worry forming in your brain." He chuckles. "Is it okay if I take you on a date? I promise it'll be someplace far from Wilder Valley."

He really does know me.

"Fine. When is this date taking place?"

"As soon as I can secure a sitter."

As if on cue, Collin begins to cry.

"I can go." He offers.

"No, it's fine." I take a swallow of my coffee and push to my feet.

"Mama," Lulu calls before I start walking toward the room she shares with Collin. Well, this conversation is over, as is our alone time for the rest of the day.

Rainer stands, following me the short distance to the bedrooms.

"Good morning." I smile at my daughter and youngest son. I pull him out of his crib as Lulu scrambles over to hug my leg.

"Morning, girlie." Rainer tousles her hair before retrieving two clean diapers and wipes. He kisses the back of Collin's head. "Morning, little dude." I've always been appreciative of the affection he shows my children, but today it hits even harder. "I'll change Collin while you change Miss Lulu" He sets the diapers on the floor and motions for me to hand over Collin. "Teamwork makes the dream work."

"Teamwork. Dreamwork," Lulu parrots.

"That's right." His face lights up with a grin.

My stomach flutters. We are so lucky to have this man in our lives.

"So, I'm thinking next weekend," Rainer says casually as he unsnaps Collin's sleeper. "Does that work for you?"

"There's no rush, you know?" I bite back a smile, but it's point-less. "You're going to see me every day."

"Yeah, well, sometimes I'm impatient." He winks.

"I just don't want to tell anyone. About, well, you know." I bug out my eyes, though it's unnecessary; he knows exactly what I mean. After changing Lulu's diaper, I wait for her to pick her outfit for the day and reach over to retrieve a clean set of clothes for Collin. I hand them to Rainer, the brush of our fingers as they touch in the exchange sending a thrill down my spine. I feel like a teenager, when every simple touch holds so much excitement.

"I won't tell anyone." Rainer's gaze meets mine.

I don't want him to get the wrong impression. "It's not because I'm embarrassed. I just don't want to deal with everyone's opinions and expectations." And their meddling.

"It's fine, Maeve. I promise." He finishes dressing a wiggly Collin and sets him upright. At the first sense of freedom, Collin beelines for the toys in the living room. His little crawl is so funny to watch.

Rainer pushes to his feet and reaches out a hand, pulling me off the ground. "The only opinion I care about is yours." We're the same height, and when our eyes meet and his voice lowers, it takes all of my willpower to not lean in. "I wasn't lying when I said we can take as long as you need, go as slow as you want."

"Not too slow."

"Oh?" His brows lift. "In that case." He spares a glance at Lulu who is tugging on a pair of leggings that don't match the glittery top she's selected. He reaches for my hand, walking past me on the way out of the bedroom and tugging me along to follow. As soon as I cross the threshold, he turns to pull the door shut behind us and presses my body against the hard surface. "Hey." His grin is wide as he cups my face and leans forward.

"Hey," I whisper before his mouth covers mine, swallowing my voice and shooting pleasure down my spine. His kiss is unhurried, his tongue brushing against the seam of my mouth as if he has all the time in the world. It's so different from last night's make-out session, and yet, I like it just as much.

"Mama!" Lulu calls from the other side of the door. "Where you go?"

Rainer groans as he shifts his body back from mine, his lips the last thing to break our connection. His gaze rakes appreciatively over my body as he takes another step back. The grin on his lips is playful. "I'm calling your niece right now."

"Right now?" I almost laugh. "It's not even seven on a Saturday."

"Yeah, well, I can't wait another second to plan a date with you." He winks, turning away and leaving me in the hallway with a stupid smile on my face and a belly full of optimism I have no business owning. Could this really be so simple? Could I explore a relationship with my best friend and it not blow up in my face?

14

MAEVE

THE NEXT WEEK passes with lingering touches and stolen kisses behind closed doors. I never dreamed I would be sneaking around my own home at age thirty-two, but here we are. I'm getting ready for our first date while Rainer watches the kids, and while there are some anxious nerves, I'm mostly filled with excitement.

Dating a stranger wouldn't hold this allure. My hurt is still fresh, and I'm insecure about a lot of things. But this is Rainer. I feel safe with him. I trust him. I always have. I wouldn't be doing this if it were anyone else.

"You almost ready?" Rainer knocks on my bedroom door. "Riley's on her way."

"Yeah, give me a few minutes." I put the final touches on my makeup, evening out my eyeliner and then adding more than I intend because it's impossible to get it just right. Shaking out my hair and ditching my robe, I go to the closet to pick out my clothes.

Rainer wouldn't give me any hints about where we're going today, but he did tell me to dress casually and comfortably. And while I truly believe he'll like whatever I wear, I want to impress him. This is our first date. The first date I've been on in longer than I can recall. I want to feel confident and cute.

I reach for my favorite pair of jeans, the ones that make my ass look the best, and tug them on. Only, it's been a while since I've worn them and I can barely pull the zipper closed. *Oooff.* I move around, bending and squatting to try and loosen the stiff fabric, but it digs uncomfortably into my waist. *Shit.*

These pants make me feel anything but sexy.

Staring at my wardrobe, I rethink my outfit choice. I spot my white eyelet sundress in the back corner of the closet. I haven't worn the dress in years, mostly because white and toddlers don't mix. Praying it still fits, I switch to a different bra before changing into the dress, then tug on my nicest pair of boots and select bold statement jewelry to go with it. When I assess my look in the mirror, I can't help but smile at my reflection.

Hey, there she is. I've missed her, this version of myself.

I look pretty damn good for a mom of three.

No. Fuck that.

I look good. Full stop. My confidence blooms and giddy anticipation runs through my body. I can't wait to witness Rainer's reaction. Grabbing a jean jacket from my closet and a small leather purse to hold my phone and wallet, I step out of the bedroom.

"Mama!" Lulu exclaims. "You a princess!"

I can't wipe the smile off my face as I take in Rainer as he turns to look. His brows lift. His jaw falls open. But it's his gaze as it travels over my body from across the room that lights me up inside. "Maeve." He shakes his head. "You are so beautiful."

"You are beautiful, Mama," Ari agrees.

Rainer looks good too. In a pair of faded blue Levi's, a button-down twill shirt, and boots, he looks like he belongs on the cover of a spicy romance novel and not my living room. He's styled his hair and trimmed his beard too. The little extra effort doing funny things to my insides. This date is important to both of us.

The sound of a vehicle pulling up the drive causes us both to look out the front window.

"Riley!" Lulu cheers, racing to meet her older cousin at the front door.

Rainer walks to my side and rests the palm of his hand at my back for the split second the kids' attention is pulled away from us. He leans close, whispering low at my ear. "I wish I could kiss you right now."

I wish he could do that too. "Maybe if you play your cards right, I'll let you do that later."

"Do what later?" Ari asks.

Shit.

"Eat dessert." Rainer winks.

Oh God. My thighs press together.

"You have to eat all your dinner and behave." Ari nods in earnest. "Only good boys get dessert."

"Then I guess I'll have to be a good boy."

I bite my lower lip as I pass Rainer to open the front door. "Not too good, I hope."

His playful chuckle sends shivers down my spine. I'm glad we're leaving, because it's hard not to flirt. My children are young enough not to understand innuendos, but they're old enough to repeat them.

I open the door. "Hey, Riley."

"Aunt Maeve! You look amazing."

"Thanks." I hug my niece. "And thanks again for babysitting."

"I want to dress as cool as you when I'm old," she says as we step apart.

"Old?" I gasp, pressing a palm to my chest.

"You know what I mean." She laughs, rolling her eyes. Only a teenager can get away with an insult and compliment, and still be endearing. "Where are y'all going?"

"It's a surprise," Rainer cuts in. "And we should get going, or we're gonna miss the main event."

"Event?" I cock my head. "Is that a clue?"

"No." He levels me with a stern look, but it's more playful than intimidating. He hands Collin to Riley. "I just changed him, so his diaper should be good for a few hours."

I turn to Riley. "I left instructions on the counter, but call if you need anything."

"I will. Y'all have fun."

I press a kiss to Collin's cheek, then do the same to Lulu and Ari. "Bye, my loves. Have a good time. I'll be home later."

They follow us out to the porch, waving and saying their good-byes until we drive away.

"You look incredible, Maeve." Rainer shoots me a side glance before focusing back on the road.

"Thanks." I have to press my lips together to keep from smiling. I feel like my cheeks are going to hurt by the end of the date if I don't. "Can you tell me where we're going now?"

"No." He shakes his head. "But you might figure it out as we get close. For now, you'll have to settle with playing DJ." He pulls out his phone, unlocking the screen before handing it to me.

"What are you in the mood for?" Pulling up the music app, I flip through his playlists.

"Whatever makes you happy."

"Really?" I challenge. "You know, it doesn't always have to be what makes me happy. Sometimes it can be what you want."

"But what if all I want is for you to be happy?" His answer stuns me to silence. Though isn't that how it's been these last weeks? I've never met such a selfless man. I've never been so cared for. Has it always been this way and I was too unobservant to notice?

How long has Rainer felt an attraction to me?

I assumed it was recent, the same as it is for me. But I wonder if that's not true for him. If he has romantic feelings for me, how long has he been harboring them?

I'm too chicken to ask. Besides, this is a fucking first date, not a proposal. We're exploring this. Taking it slow. No pressure. No expectations. Today's goal is to have a good time, and I'm ready for that. Fun is something my life has been lacking.

When Rainer takes the highway toward Flagstaff, I wonder if we're going to one of my favorite restaurants near my alma mater, but that guess is quickly erased as we slow with the traffic at the edge of town. *He didn't.* Signs for today's rodeo direct us toward the grounds. Excitement races through my veins and nostalgia hits me harder than the old country tune playing through the speakers. There was a time in my life when I had the rodeo circuit schedule memorized. Competing was my entire world. At least, until I went away to college.

It was the one thing I did with Pops where my brothers didn't monopolize his attention.

My eyes sting as I think of my father.

He would love this.

Growing up the only daughter with four brothers, I rarely spent time one-on-one with my father. Until I started competing. He was so proud of my determination and hard work, and looking back, the main reason I threw myself into the sport was because it was the only activity we shared together, just the two of us.

God, I wish I could go back, for just a day, and appreciate it more. Appreciate *him.* I always dreamed that someday he would help me pass down the love of horses and competing to one of my own children. At the very least we'd be able to share stories with them, laughing about how stubborn I was, or how one time Pops was so loud cheering and yelling from his place in the stands that he was asked by security to leave the venue.

But that'll never happen now.

Dementia steals so much more than time from a person. It

steals opportunities for grandchildren to know their history, and trips down memory lane with their only daughter. Emotion gathers in my body until I can't hold it back. Tears escape from the edges of my eyes. I wipe at my face, hoping Rainer doesn't notice and that I don't mess up my makeup.

"What's wrong?" Rainer asks. Of course I can't get anything past him. "We can do something else. I just thought this could be fun since it was such a big part of your life."

"No. It's so thoughtful. But being here makes me think of Pops."

"Oh, honey." He reaches for my hand, threading our fingers together and pressing a kiss to the back of my palm. "I'm sorry. I know how much you love him." He turns his truck into the lot, following the cars ahead of us to the parking area.

I sniffle back the urge to cry. "This is wonderful."

He shakes his head, his eyes full of concern, as he releases my hand to pull into an open spot. "Wonderful things shouldn't make you cry."

"They're mostly happy tears." I reach into my purse and retrieve a tissue, then flip down the sun visor to check my face in the mirror. "I just miss my dad. His dementia has stolen so many moments from us, and this is just another thing I no longer get to share with him." I turn to meet his stare as I unbuckle my seat belt. "But I'm happy I get to share it with you."

"Come on." He cuts the engine. "I'll buy you whatever you want from the snack bar."

A bubble of laughter rises in my chest. "Okay."

We pick up our passes for the day, then order way too many snacks before heading to find our seats. The stands are full, but I hardly notice anyone around us with Rainer sitting so close. I'm acutely aware of his body and how these seats barely contain his size. Rainer isn't tall. We're the same height, actually, but he's stocky. His broad shoulder and muscular thigh press against my side. To anyone around us, it's innocent enough. But each time he leans over to say something, and every time his arm brushes against mine, my stomach flutters with delight.

But when the breakaway roping begins, my focus narrows to the competitor preparing to leave the box.

"Wow. She was great." I remember the pressure of being the first in your division, and the nerves right before they release the calf. "She'll be hard to beat."

"Kinda reminds me of someone else at that age."

I meet his smirk with a roll of my eyes. "Yeah, well, that was a lifetime ago."

"You were really good. You were phenomenal."

"Stop." I laugh, shaking my head.

"Don't try to deny it. I remember everything about your breakaway roping era."

"Okay," I tease. "Let's not forget about your short stint as a cowboy. There's video proof somewhere." I should ask Ryan where those are. It would be a kick to watch our younger selves. "I wasn't the only one practicing their roping skills every day after school."

He bumps my shoulder and grins. "Yeah, well, I knew if I showed interest, it was a surefire way to spend more time with you."

"What?" My jaw falls open.

He scrubs a hand along his jaw. "This is embarrassing."

"Well, now you have to tell me."

"You probably don't remember, but when we were thirteen and you had that big show in Vegas . . . the one your parents invited me to come along to?"

"Yeah." I do remember that. It was a big deal because most of my brothers came too.

"Well, you and some of the other girls were watching the men's competition. I was coming to find you, but you didn't see me approach. The other girls were going on and on about how hot the bull riders were, but you said, *'Those guys are crazy. I want a man who knows his way around a ranch. I'm more impressed with someone who can ride fast and rope a steer.'*"

His recollection sends the memory back into my mind, clear as day. I can't believe he remembered that. I thought he became interested in competing after that rodeo because it was the first time he'd seen everything presented in so grand a manner. Hell, some of those winners walked about with big money. But all along, I was wrong. "You wanted to learn so you could impress me?"

"And spend more time with you. I told you it was embarrassing."

"You were never interested in competing?"

"Hell no." He chuckles. "I never cared about that at all. The only interest I had was you."

It makes sense. Rainer isn't the kind of person who craves being the center of attention. But still, we were thirteen. "But you never said anything." I shake my head, trying to place the pieces.

"Yeah, well, we were young. I couldn't tell you about my wild little crush. I would have been mortified if you rejected me."

"Yeah." I sit back, watching the next competitor take her place in the box. "I mean, I get it. I had a crush on one of Aiden's friends for most of my teenage years, and I would have rather died than shoot my shot."

"Which friend?" He leans forward with interest.

"Why?" I grin. "You jealous?"

"No." He brushes his hand over my knee. "No reason to be. Not when I'm here with you now."

"Oh." Giddiness spreads through my chest as I look away. If I don't, I'll be tempted to pull him in for a kiss. While I don't think anyone we know is here, the chances of someone being in attendance who knows me or my family is great enough not to risk it.

"That was cheesy, wasn't it?" He groans and covers his face with his hands.

"No." I grin. "It's actually kind of sweet."

I can't believe Rainer had a crush on me back then. Had I known, I would have reciprocated. I wonder if that would have changed the trajectory of our lives. Would we have stayed such good friends? Or would the inevitable breakup have sent us on different paths? I ruminate on the idea as we watch the next race. "If we had dated in high school, do you think we'd still be friends?" I want to know his thoughts.

"Um, yeah. Absolutely."

"You're certain?"

"No doubt in my mind."

"Why?"

"Because if we had dated, which is a big *if*, considering you never would have gone for someone like me, but let's pretend you had, at some point you would have broken my teenage heart. But I would have gotten over it. Because I can't imagine a life in which you aren't my best friend."

"First of all, rude. Why I am the one breaking up with you?"

"You have eyes, right? And if you've forgotten what I looked like back then, I'm sure you have hundreds of pictures to remind you." Of all the things we've discussed over the years, I don't know how this isn't one of them. But I hate the way he's talking about himself.

"Rainer. You were cute."

"I was short, and awkward, and shy, and I barely had two nickels to rub together."

"I'm offended you think I care about any of that. You were and still are one of the kindest, most respectful men I know."

"Thank you, but those aren't qualities that get you noticed. At least, not beyond the friend zone."

He might be partially right. As a young woman, I was drawn

to confidence and flirty banter. I appreciate good looks as much as anyone, but looks fade. A person's character doesn't. "I am offended you think I would've broken up with you. I mean, unless you gave me a reason to, which I know you wouldn't have. Why are you making me the bad guy in this made-up scenario?"

He chuckles, shaking his head. "You're really upset about that?"

"Yeah. I mean, what the hell?"

His grin fades from his face with his next words. "The reason I know it would have been you, is because most teenage romances don't last. And if I had somehow won your heart, I never would let it go." Rainer holds my stare, the intensity of his gaze piercing my soul.

He would never let me go.

Is that true? My pulse races. My breath catches in my lungs. I can't stop myself from imagining how it would be to be fully cherished by a man like Rainer my whole life. The idea should scare me. I have no business even considering a long-term commitment. Hell, I'm still legally married. Yet, my insides melt when I think of being with Rainer.

The horn through the speakers breaks our connection. I take the opportunity to look away, focusing on the event and attempting to recenter my thoughts. Slow. We agreed to take things slow. So, why do I want to jump straight to a gallop?

The next age group is introduced. Rainer and I stick to commentary about the competitors. As the riders get older, the skill level in each heat progresses. It's exciting to watch.

"She's too far back on that saddle." I can't help myself. "And her grip is too loose. You see that?" I point out to Rainer.

As the horn signals the start of her race, we watch as the girl loses precious seconds.

"Sorry, I don't mean to intrude." Someone taps me on the

shoulder from behind. "But if you don't mind me asking, where do you coach?"

I turn in my seat to meet her gaze. "Oh, I don't."

"Really?" Her brows lift. "Sorry. I just assumed, based on everything you knew. Did you use to compete?"

"A little."

"A little?" Rainer interrupts. "You won your division for five straight years, and you competed nationally."

The woman nods, clearly impressed.

"That was a long time ago."

Rainer shoots me a look before addressing the stranger. "She's got an entire box of buckles. She knows her stuff."

"Do you live around here?" The woman asks.

"I'm in Wilder Valley."

"I run the stables just north of Payson. We're always looking for good coaches. Any chance you'd be interested?"

"Oh, no." I shake my head.

At the same time Rainer says, "Yes, she is."

I shoot him a glare. "I might be."

"Here." The woman reaches into her bag and retrieves a card. "Why don't you give me a call next week and we can talk more. Set up a time for you to come by the stables and discuss a possible partnership."

"Okay. Yeah. Thank you." I tuck her business card into my purse and turn back to watch the next event. I don't know when or how I could fit in coaching. I barely have time to sleep as it is. But energy bounces around inside my chest at the prospect. I love this sport. I miss this.

"You ready for another drink?" Rainer asks as I reach for my mostly empty lemonade.

"Yeah." I nod and stand when he does. We've been sitting for a while and I need to stretch and use the restroom. "I'll come with you."

We shuffle out of our row and then head toward the refreshment vendors.

"You should call her."

"About the coaching? I don't know."

"Why not?"

"I have three children." I laugh.

"Yeah, and you have valuable experience in tie-down roping. Plus, you're an amazing teacher. You should see the way your face lights up when you talk about it. Besides, Payson is only an hour away."

"An hour." I shake my head. "I can barely coordinate my life enough to leave the house for book club and my art class; there's no way I can do more."

"Then at your brother's ranch? You miss this, Maeve. I know you do. And you deserve to have things in your life that bring you joy."

I can't help but sigh. "Still doesn't solve my childcare issue."

"I'll watch them."

"You already do too much."

"Just think about it. Take the meeting. Or talk with Ryan. You need to be around horses again. It's a part of you."

It was a big part of my life before college. Before Alex. Before I got so busy doing life that I lost track of myself.

"You okay?" he asks.

"Yeah. This is . . ." I stop walking to look around and take it all in. The sights, the sounds, the energy. "This whole fucking day has been so damn thoughtful." Rainer's put more effort and energy into this outing than Alex put into any celebration in the last decade. "You spoil me."

"I like spoiling you." I believe him. There's no reason not to, because why else would he do so much just to try and make me happy?

"How much longer until we have to be back?" I ask him.

"We can stay another hour or two."

"What do you say we go back to your place instead?"

"Yeah?"

"Yeah."

"We don't have to. We don't have to do anything you're not ready for. I meant it when I said we can take things as slowly as you need. I'm here for the long ride. I'm not going anywhere."

I take a step forward, closing the space between us and giving in to what I want, even if it might not be the most practical or safe route. "What I need, is you." I loop my arms around his shoulders, staring at his lips as I wet my own. "I'm ready, Rainer."

"Well, fuck. Let's get out of here."

Laughter bubbles up through my chest as he grabs my hand and yanks me toward the parking lot. We trade smiles and make our way to the truck like two people who can't wait to be together. I don't remember the last time I felt so light or so free. It's intoxicating, and I want to chase this feeling forever. Is this what a life with Rainer could be like? It's almost too much to hope.

15

RAINER

I MAY or may not break a few laws driving to my house. But a speeding ticket would be a small price to pay. I've been dreaming of this moment for so long. I can't believe it's finally happening. When I planned this outing, I had no expectation it would end with hours of uninterrupted time to explore each other's bodies. I would have been perfectly content to stay at the rodeo and steal a kiss or two in my truck at the end of the night. But now that we're going to my place, I am determined not to waste a second.

Maeve's flirty teasing as she rubs along the back of my neck, and her giddy laughter as she gets out of my truck and races me to the front door, chase away any nerves I might have felt. She wants this. She wants *me*. And there is nothing better in the world.

"Is this a race?" I call after her, jogging the short distance to my front door.

"Yes." She spins and bites at her lip, her gaze traveling over my body hungrily. "Last one naked is a rotten egg."

"I don't think there's any way I lose that game." I lean forward, sliding my hand around her waist to put the key in the lock while kissing that smile off her lips. I turn the key, then the knob, and walk her backward as the door swings open.

She spins away out of my arms and levels me with a glare. "You think distraction is gonna work on me?"

I shake my head and deposit my cowboy hat on the hook near the door. "No, darlin'. What you don't understand is win or lose, I'm still a winner, because we're both naked."

She grins, taking one step back and tugging her boot off. Then she takes another step back and does the same to the other boot. "I don't know what you're waiting for, cowboy."

Stalking forward with a smile permanently affixed on my lips, I begin unfastening the buttons on my shirt. I love the way her gaze follows my fingers. Her lips parting as if she likes what she sees. I was what you'd call a late bloomer. It wasn't until my mid-twenties before my body filled out and I could grow a beard. But I'm a hairy guy, and I know not every woman appreciates that. By the lust in Maeve's stare, I have nothing to be self-conscious about. "I thought this was a race."

"I was just letting you catch up." She blinks pointedly before her gaze lifts to mine.

"Sure about that?" I chuckle, very aware my striptease is the cause of her momentary hesitation. I drop my shirt to the floor and reach for my belt buckle.

Her eyes widen and she presses her lips together. "Mmmhmm."

"Dress off, ma'am."

She arches her back, bending her arm behind her to pull down the zipper as she takes a few more steps toward my bedroom.

My belt drops to the floor with a clatter. "What happened to winning?" I tease as I work the top button open on my jeans.

She spins around, her back to me as she shrugs her shoulders. The lacy white fabric of her dress shimmies down her body with each sway of her hips, exposing bare skin inch by glorious inch until it hits the floor. I follow, like a man starved. Transfixed by her body as she struts the rest of the way to my bedroom. Her bra drops to the floor before she reaches the foot of my bed. Only her panties remain. I wish she would turn around already. I'd tackle her to my bed if I weren't still wearing boots and jeans.

It's late afternoon, but you'd never know it in this room. The walls are painted in dark shades of gray, and the thick curtains keep most of the light from the space. One long triangle of light from the open doorway casts the room in a soft glow. But greedily, I want more. I want to see all of her. I reach for the light switch.

"No," Maeve calls before I flick it on.

"No?" I question.

"I feel more comfortable with it like this." She sits on the bed, scooting back from the edge and crooking her finger. "I won. Now, come join me."

"Technically"—I use the wall for balance as I tug off my boots, then peel off my socks—"you haven't won yet."

"Is that so?" Her scoff of laughter fills my chest as much as the air we breathe.

"You're not naked." I hook my thumbs beneath the waistband of my boxer briefs and tug them down along with my jeans. I push them all the way to the ground before standing proudly. "Give me those panties."

Her jaw falls open with a gasp before a smile spreads across her lips. "Why don't you come get them?"

She doesn't need to ask twice. Strutting the rest of the way to the bed, my confidence is bolstered by her appreciative stare. I'm not under any disillusions. I don't have the biggest dick. But I do know that size doesn't matter. Not if you're in tune with your partner. My experience in the bedroom is meager, at best. But I know Maeve better than anyone, and I'm excited to learn everything about her body.

Crawling onto the mattress, I move over her and capture her

lips in a kiss. I rock my hips against her, rubbing the length of my cock against her center. Sucking and nipping, I kiss my way down her body. Each time my mouth presses against the warmth of her skin, my dick grows harder. The ache to taste every inch of her body overcomes me. By the time I make it to her hips, I'm practically panting. Sliding my fingers beneath the fabric of her waistband, I pause, waiting for her hips to lift. "I can't wait to watch you come." I can't wait to taste her pussy.

"You should know." Maeve's body stiffens. It's so subtle I wouldn't notice if I weren't settled between her legs with my face inches from her center. "I don't usually . . ." She glances up at the ceiling, not meeting my eyes.

"You don't what?" I abandon the task of removing her underwear and rub my palm along her thigh until her gaze comes back to mine.

"It's not a big deal. Which is why I want to say something."

"Tell me." I don't think I've ever witnessed this level of embarrassment from Maeve. Not in the last decade, and I'm curious about what she wants to say. I squeeze her leg and grin. "Don't go shy on me now."

She huffs out a sigh before her next words tumble out in a rush. "It's just very uncommon for me to orgasm during sex, okay?"

"Oh." That's all? "Okay."

"So, like, don't feel bad if you can't. Or rather, if *I* can't. I'm good. I enjoy the process, even if I don't get there all the way."

Fuck. I love that she's being upfront and honest with me, but I also hate how it's centered around concern of my feelings and not her needs. It makes me curious. "Do you orgasm on your own?"

"When?"

"When you pleasure yourself. Do you get there on your own?"

"Oh, um..." A blush creeps up her cheeks along with a soft smile. "Yeah."

"Every time?"

"Pretty much. Yes."

I move up the bed and lie on my side, settling in for this conversation. "So talk me through it. What's different when you're on your own?"

"I guess there's no pressure." She turns on her side to face me, then tucks one of my pillows under her head. "And no rush to catch up. My body . . . she can be a fickle bitch."

"Well, you aren't a machine, so that makes sense." I drag my fingers down her arm. "What about toys? Is there anything you use to help you reach the finish line? Any ways you prefer to be touched?"

"Um. Yeah." She glances down and grins. "Sometimes I use a vibrator."

"You don't happen to have it with you?"

She scoffs, shooting me a playful glare as she shoves at my chest. "Yeah, I packed it in my bag before we left."

"Just asking." I laugh with her. "You can tell me anything. Okay, spell it out for me. Tell me what feels good, and tell me when I'm doing something that doesn't. I promise, I only want to know so this can be better for you."

"It's hard not to get in my own head about it. And if you're doing the same thing too long, without variation or other stimulus, like your mouth, hands, talking . . . my mind gets in the way."

"You need me to distract you. Sexually." In one quick movement, I push her onto her back beneath the weight of my body. "Got it."

"Don't look at me like that."

"Like what?"

"Like all you heard was a challenge."

I chuckle against her skin, kissing my way down to her breasts. I play with her nipples, already beaded into hard points, using my mouth and hands before lifting my head. "All I heard was you giving me permission to kiss you." I scoot down lower, kissing her belly. "To touch you." I run a finger over her mound, delighting at the gasp of pleasure that escapes her lips. "To tell you all the filthy, delicious things I want us to do together." I sit back on my heels, hooking the band of her panties in my fingers and dragging them down her hips.

She presses her heels into the mattress and lifts her butt to assist. God, she's beautiful. Fully naked in my bed, I take a moment to appreciate her body. The curves. This gift. Stroking my cock in one hand and dragging my fingers up her thigh with the other, I can't decide where to begin.

"Rainer." Maeve's plea pulls my gaze to hers.

"Yeah?"

"I really want you to fuck me now."

"Oh, sweetheart." I groan as I fist my cock one more time. "I want that too."

She spreads her legs, offering herself to me. "Then why aren't you inside me?"

Because I have been waiting my whole damn life for this moment. I'm not going to rush it. "I want to touch you first. Then taste you. Then fuck you. Is that okay?"

"Yeah."

Spreading her folds with my fingers, I use my thumb to rub lazy circles above the soft flesh. Her moan as I find her clit informs me that's the spot. "And Maeve?"

"Yeah?"

"Stay with me." My thumb works a little faster, adding pressure. "If you need something else, or we need to stop, you tell me."

She nods, biting her lower lip as she meets my hungry stare. "Don't stop doing that."

"God, you are so hot. So fucking gorgeous." Still playing with her clit, I use my other hand to work two fingers into her pussy.

Pumping, gliding, moving, I wait for the cues of her body to tell me what to do next.

Her hips begin to rock, joining in the rhythm my fingers create.

I lower my mouth to her mound, dying for a taste. Spreading her lips, I continue pumping my fingers inside her and press an open-mouthed kiss over her clit. When I add my tongue into the mix, she moans louder.

"Yes. There. Keep doing that." Her fingers hold my face so I can't pull away. Not that I would dream of it. She presses her heels into the mattress, writhing, riding my face.

"Here," she breathes. "Put your hand here." She takes the hand that's currently wrapped around her thigh and brings it to her lower abdomen. "Press there." She places it where she wants. "Yeah. Harder. Just like that. Oh my God. Fuck. Yes. Don't stop fucking me with your fingers. Suck my clit." Her demands grow with her pleasure. I love following her orders, determined to give her what she deserves.

"Rainer. Wait." She tosses her head back, her fingers leaving my hair as a frustrated groan passes through her lips.

"What is it?" I pull my head away and slip my fingers from her warmth. "You can tell me."

"Nothing." She shakes her head but doesn't quite meet my eyes. "I was so close."

"Okay."

"And then I got in my own head."

"And you lost it."

"Yeah."

"That's okay." I move up her body and press a sweet kiss to her lips. "Do you want to stop?"

"No." She shakes her head. "Definitely not."

"Good." I grin. "Want me to go down on you some more? Because it doesn't matter to me if you come or not, if you're having a good time, I love it down there."

"You are too good to me." She sighs, capturing my mouth with a kiss. "But it's my turn." She presses a palm to my chest. "Lie back."

Well, damn. I do as she says, reaching for a pillow and shoving it under my neck.

Her hand wraps around my straining cock. "I've been wanting to do this for a while." She opens her mouth, saliva dripping down to the head of my cock. She uses it as lube, squeezing and rubbing along the length.

It's hard for her words to compute as her hands are stroking me, but as soon as they do, I'm overcome with curiosity. I thought I was the only one harboring a crush. "A while?"

She grins, meeting my gaze, and her hands work together, stroking me in earnest. "I have a confession to make."

"Do tell."

"The other day, I caught you in the shower touching yourself." She moves her hands up and down the length of my erection. "Like this."

A groan of pleasure escapes my parted lips.

"I didn't mean to stare. I just needed to grab something from my room," she whispers, lowering her mouth so it's only a few inches from my straining erection. "But when I saw you touching yourself, I couldn't look away."

I remember. I swore I heard a door close, but no one was there. "You know, I was thinking about you."

She chuckles. "Right."

"I was. I always think about you when I touch myself. You are the leading lady in all of my fantasies."

"How about we make those fantasies come true?" Her mouth covers the tip of my cock. Her lips wrap around it as she sucks me in slowly. Her movements are almost torturous, and it takes all my restraint not to lift my hips or hold her head in place so I can fuck her mouth in earnest.

Sucking me as I moan in pleasure, she quickly takes me to the edge. As much as I would enjoy unloading into that precious mouth, it's not how I want to come the first time we're together. "Baby, that's enough."

She pulls away. "What's wrong?" Her eyes are wide as they meet mine.

"Nothing's wrong." I roll to the side and open the drawer of my bedside table to retrieve a condom. "Everything's right."

"Oh, good." She studies me as I ditch the wrapper and roll on the condom. "I want you."

"Tell me how you want me, sweetheart."

"I want to ride you."

Fuck. I want that too. I lie back on the bed, my dick bobbing with enthusiasm. "Take me. I'm all yours."

Maeve straddles my hips, and together we line up my cock. She sinks down, slowly taking me in, working me inside until she's deeply seated on my length. Her hands go to my chest, her fingers spread wide. She moves, rolling her hips, riding me with power and precision. My hands settle on her hips, brushing along her skin with each gyration.

She throws her head back, her eyelids drifting half closed, giving in to the pleasure she finds. As she rides me harder, I join in, thrusting my hips, my pelvis pressing with hers each time our bodies meet. She doesn't say anything. She doesn't need to. The quickening of her breath and the gasps that leave her lips are clues enough.

I don't want her to lose it again. I don't want her to overthink. So I fill the room with demands, encouraging her to take what she needs. "That's it, baby. Fuck me. Fuck this cock. Ride me." I reach up and cup her tits, rubbing her nipples between my fingers and giving them a tug. "Fuck, you look incredible, riding me like this." I stave off my orgasm, determined not to come until she gives in. "Take my cock. Fucking take it. God, you turn me on. You fuck me so good. Yes, you do. Give me that pussy. Give it to me." I say the words through gritted teeth and thrust my hips harder.

"Oh God. Oh God. Yes." She whispers the chant, her muscles contracting and trembling as her orgasm rips through her. It's incredible. *She's* incredible.

"Fuuuuuck." I drag out the word and let go. Coming inside her as her body spasms with the aftershocks of pleasure. A guttural grunt leaves my parted lips, and Maeve slumps over my body, kissing my neck, as we both come down. My arms wrap around her, holding her to me and memorizing every sensation of this moment.

"Oh my God." She breathes against my skin. "That was . . . wow."

"Yeah, it was." I can't fight the grin spreading my lips.

"You're gloating, aren't you?"

"Maybe." I chuckle and hug her tight.

"Oh God." She groans, but I hear the playfulness in her tone before she pulls back and climbs off my body. "You're going to be insufferable." She glances around the room. "Can I borrow one of your shirts?"

"You can take whatever you want." I cup myself and shuffle to the edge of the bed before removing the condom. "I'm going to throw this away."

"I'm going to clean up too." She sighs, her skin still flushed from our activity. There are marks on her skin from where my beard rubbed against her. *Fuck me.* As brutish as it is, I love knowing my marks will remind her of this for days.

We each use the restroom, then meet back on the bed, curling up together. With Maeve in one of my shirts, and me in only a pair of clean boxer briefs, this almost feels as intimate as sex.

Maeve runs her fingers in lazy circles through the hair on my chest.

"What are you thinking right now?" I ask.

Her head lifts from where it rests on my shoulder. "Um, this is going to sound weird after what we just did . . . or rude, or whatever."

There's nothing she could say that would offend me right now. "Maeve, just say it."

"I don't feel comfortable sleeping together."

"Okay?" Confusion knits my brow.

"Like, actually sleeping, sleeping together."

"Oh." A chuckle shakes my chest as I'm flooded with relief.

"I'm sorry. I know it's just a bed, but I only ever shared that bedroom with Alex." She exhales a rush of air from her chest. "Besides, I don't want to confuse the kids, and I'm not sure what they would think or say if they woke up and saw us sleeping in there."

"No, I respect that. That's fine." I run a hand along her side, pulling her back down to cuddle. "I'm not here to take his place. I'm not pushing for more than you're willing to give. We can take things as slowly as you need, and I will respect whatever boundaries you put in place. I'm happy to sleep on the couch."

She snorts. "No one is happy sleeping on that couch."

"I'm happy to if it means I get to wake up and see you every morning. That I get to help with the little monsters, and I get to spend more time with you than if I were to drive back and forth between my place and yours."

"Oh." Her body relaxes against mine. Silence stretches until she breaks it by pressing a kiss to my chest and then saying, "Thank you. For the best first date I've ever had."

"You're welcome. Best first date for me too."

"Can I ask you something?"

"You can ask me anything. Always."

"How come you never got married?"

"I never met the right person." No. That's not the whole truth. "Or rather, my person met someone else."

"That's what I thought." She pulls away to meet my gaze. "Or at least, it's something I've come to realize more recently." Her smile is sad. "I hate that for you, by the way. I wish I would have known."

It's a dangerous game, wishing things were different. I need her to understand. I need her to know that whatever regrets I've had in the past, they were mine to live with, no fault to her.

"I made peace with the fact I missed my chance. I should have told you how I felt. I was young and scared you might not want to be friends if you didn't feel similarly. But, later on, even when I tried dating . . . I couldn't find the connection I was looking for in a partner. No one compares to you, and I finally accepted they never would."

"So, you were okay with staying single forever?"

"I have a good life. And an amazing best friend."

"What about being a dad? I know you always wanted that."

"I did, but it would be disingenuous to do that with someone I didn't see as a lifelong partner. Someone I'd constantly be comparing to you." Maeve's eyes mist with unshed tears. "Hey." I cradle her face in my palm. "Why are you crying, baby?"

"I just . . . I'm the reason you never got to experience father-hood. And that kind of breaks my heart."

"All those times you told me I should meet someone and start a family of my own? I couldn't. I wouldn't. Because if I did, I'd be giving up on the possibility of us, and I'd rather spend a lifetime alone than give up on you. That was my choice, Maeve. And I don't regret it." The only choice I regret is not telling her how I felt before she left for college. But even still, I can't really wish for that, because that would mean there would be no Ari, no Lulu, and no Collin. They are Maeve's world, and I could never wish for a reality in which they didn't exist. "Maybe we were meant to make those choices so they would lead us to this moment, for a reason."

"And what reason would that be?"

"To appreciate each other. To be old enough and wise enough to take a chance, even when it feels like the biggest risk in the world."

"I like that." She presses a kiss to my lips.

From the other room, a phone pings. It must be hers. Mine is on silent.

Her brow knits as she sits up. "That was weird."

"What?"

"I've never heard my phone make that sound." She gets up to retrieve her purse from the other room. She's in the living room when she shouts, "Oh my God! Rainer!"

"What?" I spring from the bed, worried something's wrong until she returns, a megawatt smile on her face.

"My first order! I got my first sticker order!" She jumps up and down, doing a little dance.

"Maeve, that's incredible."

She grins, her gaze bouncing from me to the screen of her phone.

"I'm so proud of you." I hug her.

She laughs, shaking her head. "It's only ten dollars. It's not that big of a deal."

"It is. Because you set a goal and went for it." I lift her chin with my finger so our eyes meet. "Most people never do that, you know?"

"Yeah, I guess so." She bites at the corner of her lip, her smile working its way back onto her face.

"You want to go home and package the order, don't you?"

"Yes, is that okay?" She presses her palm to my chest. "I'm sorry. I really enjoyed everything about today. The closing ceremony activities especially."

"I enjoyed those too." I chuckle. "We need to head back anyway. I told your niece there'd be a rate increase for each additional hour past the initial four." I check my watch. "At this point I'm up to fifty an hour."

"Rainer!" she gasps. "That's too much!"

"Worth it. Every fucking penny." I press a kiss to her lips and give her ass a playful smack. "She could have charged more."

16

MAEVE

IT'S FUNNY, I never imagined I could be this happy again.

I had my concerns, starting something with Rainer so soon after Alex. And if it were anyone other than my best friend, I don't think I'd be ready. But Rainer knows me, and I know him. There's a level of trust between us that's been forged over the years, and maybe that's why we're able to achieve this level of intimacy so quickly.

After our date on Saturday, we fall into a routine that works. We tackle the household responsibilities and child care the same as before. Only, after the little ones are tucked into bed, we find stolen moments to touch and taste and bring each other pleasure. We get creative too, because I don't feel comfortable bringing him into the bedroom I shared with Alex.

We fuck in the laundry room. He eats me out in the kitchen. We turn off all the lights on the front porch and I sit on his lap, riding him while he presses one of my vibrators against my clit and swallows my moans as I come.

He's working late tonight, and I'm packaging a few sticker orders so I can jump him the second he walks through the door.

Fuck. It's ridiculous how turned on I am anticipating his return. I can't remember the last time I thought about sex this much or wanted it this frequently. The last time I did, I was—

I freeze at the flutter in my belly.

The kind of flutter that has nothing to do with nerves or excitement. It's a unique feeling I've experienced before. Three times before, actually.

Fuck.

"No, no, no, no, no."

Abandoning my project, I practically race to the calendar hanging on the wall. My hands shake as I yank down. It's been stuck on the month of August since the day Alex left and Rainer moved in. I was so depressed at first, I stopped using it. And then I went to using my phone for everything so I could share schedules and appointments with Rainer. I hadn't given it any thought until now.

The flutter in my belly comes back again.

Fuck. This cannot be happening.

I flip back to July, my entire body tight with nerves as I look for a small drawn star—the kind Mama taught me to draw at the age of fourteen so I could track my cycles. My shoulders tense and my pulse races when I don't find one. "Fuck!" I swear aloud, flipping back another month. There it is, penned in blue ink in the first week of June.

I could scream right now. I could cry, but instead I do the math, confirming that I have not had a period in over three months. Panic claws at my throat. This cannot be happening. Not when things are just starting with Rainer.

Rainer.

My heart squeezes as tears prick the corners of my eyes at the sound of his truck pulling into the driveway. How do I tell him I'm pregnant with another man's child? This is going to break his fucking heart. I sink down into the chair, my heart hammering in my chest so loudly that I can't think. I can't hear. I can't breathe.

It's as if I'm being sucked into a tunnel, a bad dream I can't wake up from.

"What's wrong?" Rainer takes one look at me as he steps into the house and comes running. "Breathe, honey." His palm rubs along my back and he pulls me into his arms. I shouldn't lean into the comfort of his embrace, but I'm not strong enough to push him away.

"Maeve." Rainer pulls back to cup my cheeks. His eyes are wide as they search mine for answers. "What's happening? Is it your dad?"

I shake my head violently. I don't want to say the truth aloud. Once I do, I can't take it back. This is going to ruin everything. But he deserves to know. I can't keep this from him, and selfishly, I need to confide in my best friend. "I think I'm pregnant." The words leave my mouth in such a soft whisper that, for a second, I'm not sure he hears them.

His brow scrunches as he shakes his head. "That's impossible." I watch his expression morph from one of confusion to understanding as he makes sense of it all. He doesn't say it, but the disappointment and hurt are clear on his face.

"I'm so sorry," I whisper as tears spring into my eyes.

"No." His brow furrows. "Don't apologize."

"I didn't know. I promise." My tears come faster, my chest rattling with each word I say between sobs. "I would have told you. I promise. Rainer, I would have—"

"Hey, baby." He tugs me back into his chest. "Breathe. It's okay. I believe you. I do." He holds me as I cry, his strong and steady arms anchoring me when I feel out of control. When my tears slow, he pulls back and wipes them from my cheeks. "What do you need?"

"I need to take a pregnancy test to be sure." I need to see the double lines to confirm, even if I already know it's true. "I don't have any here."

"I'll run to the store." He nods.

"No!" I grab his arm. "You can't go!"

"Why?"

"Because someone will see you buy it."

"I don't give a fuck."

"Everyone knows you've been staying here. You buy that and everyone will know you are buying it for me." And they'll assume this baby is his.

"So?"

"What do you mean, so? I won't do that to you." Maybe that would be easier, but he doesn't deserve that. I won't put that on him.

"Do what to me?" He shakes his head. "I don't know what you want me to do here."

"I don't know either."

"Let's take this one step at a time, okay? I will track down a pregnancy test. And no one will know it's me or who it's for."

"How? That's impossible."

"I have connections." He winks. "There's a black market for everything, right?"

I laugh in spite of my nerves. "Black market pregnancy tests. Great."

"Hey, everything is going to be okay. Easy day, right?"

This is not an easy day. "Get the test. Tonight, please." I have to know. "I might not even be . . ." I can't say it. The idea of another life inside of me rattles more than my nerves. It upends the life I started to envision for myself. I barely had the chance to reclaim myself, and I've done this three times before. I know how this goes. As beautiful and precious as a child is, growing and giving birth and breastfeeding and sleepless nights . . . it all takes. It depletes. My body won't be my own in the process. My mind will be ruled by someone else and their needs. Tears prick my eyes again as I realize everything is about to change.

"Hey, come here." He draws me into his arms again and his hand rubs along my back, soothing my tears. "We don't know for sure, but if you are, we'll figure it out."

"But, Rainer." I don't know why I feel the need to spell it out. "It's not yours."

"I know, and we'll figure it out."

"I'm so sorry."

"Stop apologizing. We'll figure this out."

***

TWENTY MINUTES LATER, after Rainer calls in a favor and I've wiped away all my tears, Mac pulls into my driveway. I stand off to the side of the window and watch as Rainer goes out to greet him.

I shouldn't eavesdrop, but Rainer doesn't shut the front door all the way, and I can't help but listen in on their conversation.

Mac grins as he rolls down his window and cuts the engine. "Are congratulations in order?" He hands over a small brown paper bag.

Rainer scrubs a hand along his beard. "Fuck, man. I guess we're gonna find out."

"I don't know how you did it." Mac chuckles. "You're getting everything you wanted."

"It's not that clearcut," Rainer says, and my heart squeezes.

"What do you mean? All you've ever wanted is a future with Maeve."

"Yeah, well, it's complicated." He sighs. I've caused him pain tonight, no doubt, and while he might hide it well, I hate that he's hurting.

Mac shakes his head. "Doesn't seem all that complicated to me. If you love her, you love her. End of story."

Rainer loves me?

I hold still, straining to hear his response, but it's muffled.

"I'll feel a lot better when divorce papers get filed."

"Oh man." Mac whistles. "That is complicated."

"Thank you again, for dropping this by." Rainer lifts the bag and takes a step back.

"No problem. Your secret's safe with me." The roar of Mac's truck engine makes it impossible for me to decipher the rest of their conversation. They talk briefly, sharing a laugh before Mac backs out of the driveway.

I move from the window and take a seat on the sofa before Rainer walks back inside.

His expression is neutral as he hands me the bag. "Do you want my help?"

"Peeing on a stick? No, I think I can handle that on my own." I crack the joke just to witness his lips curve up.

"Right. Then, you do your thing, and I'll set the timer."

I go into the bathroom and open the box, familiarizing myself with the instructions even if they are mostly the same as other at-home tests I've taken. I set the test on the counter and head out to find Rainer at the kitchen table. "Five minutes," I say as anxiety grows in the pit of my belly.

"Timer is set." He taps on his phone and nods at the empty seat next to his. "Let's play a game while we wait." He reaches for the small stack of games we keep near the table.

I shake my head. "I can't concentrate on anything right now." My entire body is tight with nerves. Because in less than five minutes, anything I ever had with Rainer will be over. If I think about it too much, I might be sick.

"Maeve." Rainer opens the box to one of our favorite games and begins dealing the cards between us. "I get it. I do. But no matter what that stick says, the next five minutes are going to pass anyway. We might as well do something fun. Besides, I don't want you stressing. It's bad for the baby."

Is this man for real? Is he so unbothered by the idea of me carrying another man's child?

"I don't deserve you." I whisper.

He chuckles, picking up his cards and arranging them in order. "I think you've got that backward. *I* don't deserve *you*."

I laugh. A big belly laugh. "You think I'm the catch in this relationship?"

"I know you are." He plays his first card. "Your turn."

We play the game, and for a few minutes, I pretend this is just another normal night. I tell him funny stories about things Lulu and Collin did throughout the day, and before I know it, his phone begins to buzz. Time is up.

"Do you want to look?" He silences his phone. "Or should I?"

"Why don't we do it together?"

"I like the sound of that." He reaches for my hand and we walk to the bathroom. It's no surprise to find two clear blue lines. But I cry anyway.

His arms wrap around my waist as he pulls me tight to his chest. "Maeve, this changes nothing."

"This is going to be complicated."

"I'm not scared of complicated."

"I need to tell Alex."

"I know you do." He sighs into my shoulder and presses a kiss to my neck. "You're the kind of person who wouldn't keep a father from knowing their child. It's just another thing I love about you." There it is again, that love word. Yet, it's something he would have told me before romantic feelings came into the picture. Maybe that's why it doesn't feel weird or forced.

Do I love Rainer? I always have. Maybe those feelings have

evolved. Maybe things are more complicated than I'd like them to be. But maybe with him at my side, we can figure this out.

"Rainer," I whisper. "I'm scared."

"I will be here for you, every single step of the way." He hugs me tighter, then leans back to look into my eyes. "I love you, Maeve. You're it for me. There's nothing you could do to change the way I feel. And this baby? It's not another mouth to feed. It's another life we get to love together. I don't care that I'm not their father. I love your children with my entire heart, because they are an extension of you."

Tears prick my eyes. The stress on my shoulders lightens at his words because he is the kind of man who backs them with action. This isn't lip service. He's not saying what I want to hear. He's not attempting to manipulate my emotions. He's making a promise. "I don't deserve you."

"You do. You deserve to be loved and cherished and cared for. I will love you with my last breath, for as long as you let me."

17

RAINER

YEARS ago I made peace with the fact that I'd only ever be a friend to Maeve. Sure, it hurt like hell to watch her fall in love with someone else, but I had to decide if I could live without having just a little of her love or nothing at all. I chose to be her best friend, and I was content with that role.

But these last few weeks have caused me to hope for a reality in which I'm more than her friend.

But now she's pregnant.

The challenges to navigating our budding romance have compounded.

She's worried, and I get that. But she doesn't need to be. I will provide for her and the children. I have no qualms about paying for everything she needs. What's mine is hers. But I promised her we'd go slowly, and no one even knows we're dating. The last thing I want is for her to feel pressure. I want her to take all the time she needs to be sure about us before taking our relationship public. I want her to be with me because it's the right choice for her, not because I insist on paying for everything or because she feels trapped.

While the timing of her pregnancy is not ideal, I can't stop the excitement that fills my chest as we sit in the waiting room for her doctor's appointment. The office is about an hour from town, and maybe that's why Maeve feels comfortable enough to hold my hand. I wish the baby were mine. Only because that would be one less reason for Alex to reappear in our lives. Maeve won't hide this baby from him. She's too honest. Too good.

Which means that piece of shit is coming back.

I'm unsettled by the idea of Alex finding out about the baby. Will it change things for him? If he comes back and desires another chance to make their marriage work, will she give it to him? They have a history I can't compete with. And now that I've had a taste of what our life could be like together, I don't want to give her up. Could I go back to being the best friend after every-thing we've shared?

More accurately, could I do it without shredding my heart?

The exam with her doctor is shorter than I expected. He's nice enough, and Maeve doesn't have a lot of questions. In fact, she's quieter than usual. I can only imagine how overwhelming this is. I hope on the ride back she'll open up so she doesn't feel alone. For now, I sit and listen, taking a few notes on my phone. While she gets her bloodwork drawn, I use my phone to order her prenatal vitamins.

Because she's so far along, they want to do an ultrasound, so we head back into the lobby for even more waiting. Maeve checks in with Jamie, who is at the house watching Lulu and Collin. Her knee bounces anxiously as minutes pass. "If they don't bring us back soon, I'm going to need someone to pick up Ari."

"Ask Rosalie?" I suggest since Edward's in the same class as Ari.

She worries her bottom lip between her teeth. "Her nanny usually does pick up. I don't want to overstep, and besides, I don't know her well enough."

"Rosalie has a nanny?" This is news to me.

"Yeah." Maeve smiles for the first time all day. "You didn't know? She's loaded."

I shrug. "I kinda figured, given her home, and well, I can't imagine the county pays that well. At least, not with a library our size. But a nanny?" I lift my brows. "That's something."

"I'm glad she has the help." Maeve lifts her chin. "She doesn't have family like I do or the same support system. It's just her and Edward. She has to work." Maeve frowns. "At least I think she does. Still, it doesn't matter. If she wants to work, she should. There are too many women who judge other women for the choices they make. Parenting is hard. Staying home is relentless. Sometimes I wish I could have both. But that's not really practical."

I open my mouth to ask her what she would pick if she didn't have to be practical, but before I can, her name is called from across the room.

"Maeve?"

"Yes."

A woman in pink scrubs smiles warmly. "The ultrasound tech is ready for you."

Maeve pushes to her feet at the same time I do. She reaches for my hand and I stand a little taller, loving the feel of her palm in mine as we follow the woman to a small exam room. Maeve sits on the exam table and I take the chair at her right. We're left alone for a few minutes before another woman comes into the room and introduces herself and explains how the sonogram will go. She confirms Maeve's date of birth as well as the start of her last menstrual cycle and then pulls up several screens on her computer.

"Go ahead and lean back," the woman says, cutting the overhead lights and bathing the room in darkness. "If you can pull your shirt up to your bra, and since you're wearing leggings, I'm just going to roll them down to where I need them, if that's okay with you?"

Maeve nods as the woman helps get her situated for the sonogram.

"This is gonna be a little cold." She squirts a clear, gooey liquid onto Maeve's belly, then presses a scanner-type probe thing against her skin. "Ready to hear the baby's heartbeat?" she asks, turning a few nobs on her machine. A scratchy woosh, rhythmic and fast, fills the room.

Maeve stares at the screen, her eyes filling with unshed tears.

I stare at Maeve, completely transfixed by the sound. There's a baby inside her, heart beating strong, and I am overcome with gratitude. To be here, with her. To experience this special moment.

"So, you're right at sixteen weeks. We might be able to tell you the sex of the baby if that's something you'd like? They'll also know after your bloodwork, but this is more fun."

Maeve turns her head to meet my gaze.

"Do you want to know the sex?" I ask.

"Do you?"

I squeeze her hand. "Whatever you want."

"Yes." There's a spark in her eyes that fills me with relief.

"'Kay, give me a few minutes to take some measurements and then we'll see if the baby's being agreeable today." The tech slides the probe over Maeve's lower belly, occasionally dipping it into more of the gel. She points out different body parts throughout the appointment. Heart. Lungs. Limbs. It's incredible, that something so tiny and so perfect already exists.

"Well, she's just showing off."

Maeve's eyes widen. "She?"

"Congratulations, mom and dad." The tech flashes us a grin. "You're having a girl."

"A baby girl?" Maeve repeats.

I squeeze her hand.

"Lulu's gonna get a little sister," she whispers as tears gather in her eyes.

My own eyes mist, and I can't stand being so far away from her. Standing from my chair, I lean down and press a kiss on her temple.

"Almost done here." The tech removes the probe from Maeve's belly and taps a few buttons on her keyboard. "I'll print a few of these good ones for you to keep. The paper is heat sensitive so—"

"Can you print doubles?" Maeve asks, and that one question throws my world off kilter. She needs a second copy, because I'm not the dad. It's nice to pretend and play the role, but at the end of the day, that child is as much Alex as it is her.

I try not to let it sour my mood. I really do. But I hate that Maeve thought of him in that moment.

It's not until we're in my truck cab that Maeve breaks the silence.

"This is for you." She hands me one of the black and white prints.

"Me?" She asked for a duplicate for me. She wasn't thinking about Alex. Not the way my jealous heart assumed.

"I thought you might want to put this in your office." Her gaze drops to her lap. "Maybe that's silly."

"No." My heart swells with pride. "Not silly at all."

"Rainer." She lifts her gaze.

"Yeah?"

"Thank you for coming with me today."

"You don't have to thank me." I turn in my seat to face her. "If anything, I should be thanking you. I want to be here. For all the doctor's appointments. For sleepless nights. For everything."

"I love you."

She's never said those words to me, and it makes this moment all the sweeter. "I love you so much." I reach out, running my hand along the small swell of her belly. "I love you, and I love this baby."

"You don't have to . . . I would understand. It's a lot. It's all too much, really."

"You are never too much. Not for me. I'm all in, Maeve. I always have been."

"I don't know what to tell everyone."

"You don't owe anyone anything."

"They're going to speculate."

"Let them. Doesn't matter what anyone says or thinks, it won't change my mind."

"I want to tell my family." She blows out a long sigh. "About the baby."

"Why don't you call Jamie to see if she can pick up Ari? We can grab some food, then stop over and see your dad?"

"You don't mind?"

"Why would I mind?"

"I, um . . ." Her eyes clench shut, almost as if in pain. A few tears escape down her cheek and her chest shakes as she cries.

"Is everything okay?" Alarm races through my veins. "Do we need to go back inside?"

She shakes her head in the negative as she pulls herself together. "I always thought I had a hard time accepting help because I'm so independent. But I'm starting to realize, it's because whenever I asked for things, I was made to feel like I was being difficult. That I was too controlling. That I was nagging. So, I stopped asking. I did things myself, or I didn't do them at all. I made myself more palatable. I dismissed my own needs. I didn't go see my dad as much as I wanted. I didn't do a lot of things I wish I would have. And I lost myself in that. In parenting and in being a wife, I lost my sense of my own wants and desires."

I listen intently, hanging on her every word.

"But maybe the entire time, it wasn't my needs that were too much or inconvenient. Maybe I was never the problem at all." She laughs, but the sound holds no humor. "I don't know how to be with a partner who is fully supportive. I don't know how to react when you offer to take me to see my dad even though it's more than two hours out of the way. I don't know how to accept your love without feeling like I'm selfish."

"Oh, baby." I pull her into my arms and hold her. "Be selfish with me. Always."

I fucking hate Alex. But I am so grateful she sees it all clearly. Because now that she knows, she can learn to expect more.

WE'RE ALMOST to the memory care facility in Pinetop when my phone interrupts our music and Maeve's brother's name overtakes the display screen in my truck.

Maeve and I share a questioning gaze before I connect the call. "Hey, Ryan."

"Hey, Rainer. How are you?"

I grin at Maeve. "Never better."

"That's good to hear." He clears his throat. "Hey, so I hate to ask. And I know it's last minute, but we've got a cattle drive next week and I'm short a man. Richie, I think you've met him before, is sick and can't ride."

"He okay?"

"He will be. It's pneumonia. Doc put him on another round of antibiotics and it'll be another week before he's cleared to work. I'd push the drive out, but with Aiden's wedding in two weeks and all the shit we've got to do to host the ceremony here on the ranch, that's cutting it too close." That's right. Aiden and Sarah are getting married. I'm invited, of course, and while Maeve and I haven't discussed it, I'm hopeful we can go together—maybe even as an official couple.

"When's the drive?"

"We're leaving Tuesday and will be back late Friday. Been forever since you joined us. I know you've got your own business to run, but I really need another skilled roper on this ride, and well, you're one of the best."

"Let me check with Maeve." I meet her gaze and lift my brows in question.

"It's fine." She rolls her eyes, a grin on her lips.

"You sure?" My gaze darts to her belly.

"I'll be good. I promise." She rests her hand on my shoulder. "Hi, Ryan."

"Hey, sis. Sorry, I didn't realize you were together."

"Yeah." *Oh, we're together alright.* I bite back the urge to laugh. "We had to, uh . . . We're going to the nursery. Down in Show Low. Maeve wanted to check out some options. For the, uh, the garden she wants to grow."

She bugs her eyes at me, a silent warning to pull myself together.

"But count me in for the cattle drive. I'll double check but Mac should be able to cover things at work this week."

"Appreciate it. So much. Sorry, I'll let you two get back to it. Thanks again, Rainer."

The call ends, our music piping back into the speakers.

"My garden?" Maeve exclaims. "That's what you came up with?"

"I choked," I admit. "I'm not a great liar."

"I suppose that's a good thing. Next time, less detail. Running errands would have sufficed." She shakes her head, then points at the turn up ahead. "Right there. The facility is on the left."

Following Maeve's directions, I park in a visitor space and come around the truck to open her door. There's a somber shift in her energy as we walk inside the building. We sign in, the security staff checking our IDs against the list of approved visitors before buzzing us in to another checkpoint. No one gets in or out of this place unnoticed, though I suppose that's the point. Still, I can't imagine that's an easy adjustment for a man who lived his entire life on a ranch.

We make our way to Mr. Wilder's floor and a staff member lets us inside his private suite before leaving the three of us alone.

"Hey, Pops." Maeve's smile is too bright as she walks to where he sits in his recliner, staring at a television that's powered off.

"Hey, sweetheart." His eyes twinkle as his lips curve with his smile. "Where are the children?"

"I left them home." She bends down to give him a hug, then takes a seat on the small sofa next to his chair.

"Playing hooky? Good for you."

"Hi, Mr. Wilder." I walk forward and offer him my hand.

"Hi, Rainer." He shakes my hand. "How're your parents?"

"They're doing well, sir." I take a seat next to Maeve. "Thank you for asking."

"Good. Good." He nods. "And business?"

"Can't complain."

"That's why I always liked you." He points his finger in my direction as he looks at his daughter. "This one's not a complainer."

"Oh, I'm aware." The admiration in her tone makes me feel as if I've won a gold medal.

We sit, letting the silence stretch. But it's not uncomfortable. Mr. Wilder was never the kind of person to fill the quiet with chatter.

"Pops." Maeve leans forward, her eyes finding his.

"Yeah?"

"I came today because I wanted to share some good news."

"Oh?" His spine straightens. "What's that?"

"I'm expecting. You're gonna be a grandpop again."

"I am?"

"Yeah."

"Boy or girl?" His brow furrows. "Or do you know?"

"A little girl."

"That's wonderful, Maeve." He pushes to his feet, and she stands too. He opens his arms and they hug, holding on to each other for a long moment. "You're such a good mama." He pulls back to meet her gaze. "Your mother would be so proud. Bless her soul."

"I hope so." Maeve swallows hard and blinks back tears.

"Sure do miss her." Mr. Wilder shuffles back to his chair and takes a seat again.

"Yeah, me too." Maeve sits, and reaches for my hand.

"Rainer, how's business going these days?" It's unsettling, how perfectly healthy and lucid he is as he asks the question I've already answered.

"Good, sir. Business is good."

"That's wonderful. Give your parents my best. Haven't seen them around town in a while now."

"I will, sir," I say, squeezing Maeve's hand. This time with her Pops is precious, and I don't want to rush off even if there's not much to say. "Should we put on the game?"

"Who's playing?" Mr. Wilder asks.

"Diamondbacks, I think." Maeve flashes me a grateful smile.

"Good. Good," he agrees.

I find the remote nearby, turning on the television and toggling through the stations to find a channel where baseball games play on repeat. I return to my seat, and once again Maeve reaches for my hand, threading our fingers together and giving it a gentle squeeze.

"Thank you," she whispers, one solitary tear escaping from the corner of her eye. She wipes it away discretely before her father notices. Though even if he did, it would only be a matter of time before he'd forget her pain ever existed. My heart breaks for him, and again for Maeve. She lost her mom too soon, and in many ways, she's also lost her dad. I don't know why life is so cruel. I wish I could take away her hurt. If it were an option, I would. Instead, I sit here and bear witness to the love between a father and daughter that not even dementia can erase.

18

MAEVE

IT'S WITCHING HOUR. At least, that's how I refer to the block of time after Ari is home from school until the kids' bedtime. Everyone needs something: food, baths, diaper changes. I'm exhausted just thinking about it. Rainer's on the cattle drive with my brothers. He only left this morning and already I miss him more than ever. He's truly spoiled me. I'm not sure how I used to do all of this on my own most days. I want to cry when I think of how it will be with another baby in the mix.

The idea of it all is overwhelming and daunting, so I try not to think about it.

I try not to think about a lot of things.

Like telling Alex about the baby. Or that I want a divorce.

Telling my brothers I'm pregnant with my husband's child, but oh, hey, I kinda have a boyfriend and you already know him because he's my best friend.

That news will spread faster than wildfire in this town. I don't look forward to the judgmental looks or the advice I didn't ask for.

I won't be able to hide my pregnancy with oversized t-shirts much longer. I need a plan. I need to move out before I'm evicted.

I wanted time and space to be able to explore this new relationship with Rainer. There will be enough outside pressure as it is when we take this thing public, and now more than ever I can't lose my best friend. But this baby adds so much more. I feel like we're up against a timer, each grain of sand falling faster than I can count.

"Mama. I hun-gee." Lulu tugs on my arm, pulling me back to the present.

I glance at the clock and sigh. "I suppose we should figure out dinner."

"Dinner! Yeah!" She hops up and down, her sweet smile sweeping away my worries for a moment.

A honk from outside drags my gaze to the front window. Bernadette's car is parked behind my minivan. She and another woman walk up to the house, arms loaded down with several bags.

I go to the door and swing it open as I try to make sense of their arrival. "Hey. What are you doing here?"

"A little birdie told me you might need backup tonight." Bernadette grins, nodding to the woman beside her. "This is my friend, Mimi, she's in town for the weekend. Mimi, this is Maeve."

"It's so nice to meet you," Mimi says.

"It's nice to meet you too." I step to the side, holding the door open as they come inside. As Bernadette passes by, the aroma of home-cooked food fills my nostrils. "Did you bring dinner?"

"Of course. Can't show up empty-handed." She takes the bags to the kitchen and begins unloading two pans covered in foil, several plastic containers, and a loaf of bread. It's so much. Too much.

Her generosity brings tears to my eyes and I have to blink them back. *Damn hormones.* "Thank you."

"No worries. I can only imagine how much work it is to raise one child, let alone three."

About to be four. "Yeah."

Collin begins to fuss, crawling toward me to complain further.

I scoop him up and rock him on my hip, careful not to pull the fabric of my shirt across my belly.

"I brought you two casseroles. One for tonight and one for tomorrow. The heating instructions are taped on the top. Each will need to cook for about an hour."

"You are a godsend. I'm going to put one in the oven now."

"I've got it," Bernadette offers. "Chicken and broccoli or potatoes and sausage?

"Surprise me." My stomach rumbles loudly. "Anything you make is a treat for us."

While Bernadette preheats the oven and loads my fridge with the other items she brought, Mimi smiles at Collin. "He's adorable."

"He is." I press a kiss to the top of his head. "He's cutting teeth again. I think that's why he's so fussy."

"May I?" She holds her arms out, offering to take him.

"Sure." Collin surprises me by going to her without complaint. His wide eyes study her hazel ones as he reaches for her hair. She smooths it back over her shoulder before he gets a fist full. The light catches on the gold necklace she wears, garnering his attention.

"He loves jewelry. Which is why I hardly wear any now."

"I don't mind." Mimi laughs as his little hands attempt to pull at the tiny charms on her necklace. "My cousins' babies do the same thing."

"Can I get you something to drink?"

"Yeah, I have time for a tea, if you've got it?" Mimi says.

"Absolutely." I turn to Bernadette. "What about you?"

"I'll take a glass of water."

With dinner in the oven and each of us holding a beverage, we head out to sit on the porch so the older two can play in the yard. I bring out a few of Collin's favorite toys and set them in a small play yard so we can keep an eye on him while we converse.

"So, how do y'all know each other?"

"We actually went to law school together," Bernadette says.

"Oh, that's awesome you still keep in touch." Bernadette doesn't say much about her career as a lawyer, but I know she gave it up shortly before moving to Wilder Valley, and that's been at least six years. I turn to Mimi. "Do you practice?"

"Yeah, I specialize in family law."

I straighten at her answer. This is almost too perfect. "Are you in Arizona?"

"No. California."

"Oh, that's too bad."

She chuckles, nodding at Bernadette. "That's what this one keeps telling me."

"That's because I want you to move here."

"I just need a divorce lawyer." I shrug.

"I'm sorry, Maeve." Bernadette frowns. "He's an idiot to give this up. You deserve better."

"Yeah, I'm kind of glad he left. Because I'm beginning to realize I do deserve more." I try not to think of Rainer, but it's impossible. He's a big part of that self-discovery. "So, now I just need to figure out the easiest way to file for divorce. I'm totally clueless when it comes to this stuff." Just reading through a few articles on the internet last night hurt my head. "As soon as the legal jargon comes in, I'm lost."

"If you want to talk through a few general things, I can try to help."

"You don't mind?" I ask.

"Yeah, ask me anything. Though, I have to give the disclaimer that everything I tell you is my opinion only and should not be used in place of legal advice. If I practiced here and you were my client, I could advise you officially."

"Yeah, that's fine." I blow out a long breath. "I'm hoping we can move forward without involving lawyers."

"Have you discussed filing for divorce with him?"

"Um, no." I roll my eyes. "The only exchanges we've shared since he left are a few text messages."

"Will he fight you on it?" she inquires. "Or are you both in agreement that divorce is the best option?"

"Well, we haven't discussed it, but by his actions, I'd say yes." My gaze drifts to Bernadette. "He stopped paying bills."

"What a dick," Bernadette grumbles.

"Okay." Mimi nods. "Does he work? Are you a dual income family?"

"He's a truck driver. And he's fully supported me staying home since Ari was born."

"Do you have your own bank account?"

"No."

"Are you listed as an owner on any shared assets?"

"Everything is in his name. The lease on the house. The mini-van." A sinking fear gathers in the pit of my belly. It worsens as the baby kicks.

"Okay. That's okay."

But it doesn't seem okay at all.

"What about the children? Do you know if he'll want custody?"

"I don't think so. I mean, I won't keep him from knowing them. But he can't handle more than one of them at a time."

"You'd be surprised at how many men claim to want shared custody once they look at child support figures, and most judges lean toward a shared agreement when possible."

Anxiety tenses my muscles. "I haven't missed a day of their lives." I don't trust them to be in his care, not if I'm not present. "He travels for work a lot. Won't a judge take that into account?"

"That will help. Most judges want to maintain what's best for the children, and prioritize their current routine when possible."

"It's going to be okay, Maeve." Bernadette reaches for my hand

and gives it a squeeze. "You are so strong, and I'm here if you need anything. You know we all are."

I take a slow inhale before exhaling in a rush. "I just hate this stuff. Getting judges and lawyers involved . . . Sorry, I don't mean to offend you." I turn to Mimi.

"No offense taken. But the system is in place because most people can't agree on splitting assets or dividing child care. It doesn't always work, but it is designed for protection of those most vulnerable."

"I kind of want to stick my head in the sand. But I guess I can't do that."

"Start the conversation. See how receptive he is to working things out outside of the court system, or even using mediation."

"Yeah." I can't ignore this forever, especially with his baby on the way.

"My suggestion? Decide what you want and reach out to see if you can come to an agreement amicably. Can you fight it out in court? Absolutely. But not all divorces need to be that way."

"Thank you."

"Here's something else I tell all of my clients. Divorce can get messy. People are capable of lying and deceit, especially when money is involved. So listen to your gut. If something seems off, it probably is."

"Thank you. I really appreciate the advice."

"I wish I could do more, but you always have Bernie as a sounding board."

"Bernie?" I lift my brows.

Mimi grins. "Did that nickname not follow you to Arizona?"

"No. And we're gonna keep it that way." Bernadette levels me with a warning glare.

"I can be convinced to stay silent . . . as long as you continue to supply me with your famous casseroles."

"Bribing a former district attorney?" Bernadette laughs. "Bold move, my friend."

We share laughter and the conversation moves to lighter topics. When the timer goes off, announcing that dinner is ready, Mimi and Bernadette say their goodbyes.

I call Ari and Lulu inside to wash up, then change Collin's diaper before depositing him into his highchair. Dishing up plates for all of us, I think over everything Mimi said. Before I sit down to eat, I retrieve my phone and do the thing I've been putting off.

> Me: I will be filing for a divorce next week. Please call me when you can so we can discuss the specifics.

The text is cold and direct. I don't even know if he'll respond. It's sad that this is how our relationship ends, but I'm ready to move forward. I'm excited about a future with Rainer. I can't do either of those things while I'm still married to Alex. This is for the best. At least, I hope it is.

19

RAINER

IT'S BEEN a couple of years since I've joined the Wilder men on one of their cattle drives. The day provides hard, grueling work, but afterward we set up camp for the night and I'm overcome by a sense of gratitude. I don't like being away from Maeve and the kids, but I called in a few favors, so I know they're well cared for.

There is a peacefulness that comes from being out in the wildness, away from the hum of the highway, away from humanity. Armed with the most basic necessities and sitting under a sky bright with countless stars, it reminds a man of what's truly important.

This family has always made me feel like I belong, and I carry that pride as we gather around the campfire to feast on baked beans and cornbread while sharing stories. Ryan brews a pot of coffee after dinner and Jackson passes around a bottle of whisky.

"So." Aiden taps me on the shoulder from where he sits on my left. "You've been spending a lot of time with my sister these days."

"Yes, I have." I try to hold back the smile that comes over my face when I think of Maeve and the kids, but it's useless.

"Is there something more you need to tell us?" Ryan raises his brow.

I meet their expectant gazes. Well, shit. I'm not quite sure what to say. Not without betraying Maeve's wishes.

"Out with it." Ryan states plainly. "What's going on with you and our sister?"

"I don't wanna hear about my sister getting railed," Jackson grumbles before I have a chance to answer.

"Jackson!" Ryan chides.

"Jesus Christ." Aiden runs a hand through his hair. "I don't think that's what Ryan was asking."

"I respect your sister, which you already know." Maeve and I discussed taking things slow, but that was before we knew she was pregnant. Now everything's changed.

"So, are y'all dating?" Ryan raises his brows. "Because one of my friends said something about seeing the two of you together at the rodeo." He shrugs. "And I was gonna write that off, but then Pops's facility sends me alerts each time someone visits, and Val has this theory the two of you have some kinda secret romance going."

"Maeve is still reeling. Alex hasn't even been gone more than a few months." Aiden lifts his hands. "We just wanna make sure you realize she's in a precarious position."

"And we don't want anyone taking advantage of that." Ryan clears his throat. "Even you."

"I would never." It's the damn truth.

"People talk 'round here, and while I'm not one for gossip," Ryan leans forward, meeting my stare. "Regina Salas's neighbor saw the two of you leaving the obstetrician's office."

Hell, you really can't go anywhere, even three towns over, without someone noticing.

"Fuck." Jackson draws out the word. "Maeve's pregnant?" His

gaze darts between his brothers before settling on me. "You knocked up my sister?"

"Uh . . ." I feel the urge to protect her and her unborn child. I know she doesn't want to let everyone assume that it's mine, but I have no issues with that. Because in all the ways that matter, I will be that child's father. I will show up for her, in the same way that I plan to show up for Ari, Lulu, and Collin. "Maeve's medical care is just that. Hers. If you have questions about why she was at the doctor, you'll have to ask her yourself." I scrub a hand along my jaw, smoothing my beard. "But as for my intentions? I would do anything for your sister."

The worry on Ryan's face lessens.

"I feel the need to remind you that if you hurt her, we will have to kill you." Aiden levels me with a stare.

"Sorry, brother, you're on your own for murder." Ryan laughs at Aiden before turning his gaze back to meet mine. "I trust that y'all know what you're doing. But she's vulnerable right now, the kids too. They don't need someone who isn't in it for the long haul."

"I've always been in this for the long haul." If the sincerity of my words isn't proof enough, my actions surely are.

"I can't wait until you're officially a part of the family." Jackson lifts his bottle of whisky with a grin. "I call dibs on planning the bachelor party."

"Bro." Ryan shakes his head. "Alex has only been out of the picture a couple of months."

"And I'm pretty sure Maeve's still married," Aiden grumbles.

"I'm just saying." Jackson shrugs. "I've always liked Rainer better."

"I'm glad I have your vote." I can't help but chuckle. "But the only opinion that matters to me on this subject, is your sister's."

"You have our support." Ryan nods.

"Unless you break her heart," Aiden adds.

"That's fair." I clear my throat. "It would be an honor to marry your sister, but she's been through a lot, and I'm not about to rush her or force the decision. She's my best friend, and I can't imagine a life where she isn't a part of mine. My promise to you all is that I am fully committed, to her and raising those kids, in whatever capacity that looks like."

"You're a good man, Rainer Anderson." Jackson points his whisky bottle in my direction. "And when it's time, you will let *me* throw the bachelor party, right?"

"Don't mind him." Aiden chuckles. "He's still mad I'm not having one."

"I don't understand why." Jackson glares at his brother. "It's the only good thing about a wedding!"

"Not committing to a partner you want to spend your life with?" Aiden challenges.

Jackson sighs. "I don't know what y'alls obsession is with settling down."

Ryan chuckles. "I cannot wait for the day that some woman brings you to your knees, little brother."

"You're going to be waiting a lifetime, because it's never happening."

"The more you deny it, the harder you'll fall." Aiden grins. "Mark my words."

"You want to bet?" Jackson shakes his head. "I have the perfect life. I do what I want. I fuck who I want. I'm not letting some woman screw that up for me. Or worse, children."

"What do you have against kids?" I scoff.

"They're exhausting, and expensive, and they always cock block."

Aiden laughs. "He's not wrong."

"You talk like you weren't raised by a loving mother." Ryan

shakes his head. "Or surrounded by siblings who constantly put up with your shit."

"I just don't see the point." Jackson takes a swig of alcohol. "It's fine for you all, but I prefer my freedom and peace."

We let him have the last word, but I can't help but think he has it all wrong. I've never felt more peace than being loved by Maeve. There's no greater freedom than that.

20

MAEVE

ON WEDNESDAY NIGHT, Asher drops by with a to-go bag from a Mexican restaurant. On Thursday, Sarah brings us food from the diner. I have more food in my fridge than before the week started! While I miss Rainer, I suspect he's behind the surprise meal train, and my affection for him grows. Even when he's not here, he finds a way to take care of me. The kindness and generosity of my friends is overwhelming in a good way.

I feel secure and loved. Maybe that's why I finally tackle a task I've been putting off for weeks once the kids are settled in their beds for the night.

"Hi, Mr. McGrady." I say, when my landlord answers my call. "It's Maeve Adler. Tim Wilder's daughter."

"Maeve, dear. How are you?"

"I'm doing okay." I rub my temple. "Sorry to call at such a late hour. I needed to talk to you about the rent."

"You do?" The surprise in his tone is clear.

"Yes, I'm sorry. I should have called sooner." I'm several months behind now, and shame washes over me at the idea he assumed I continue ignoring his notices. This is a difficult decision, but putting it off doesn't make it disappear. "Quite frankly, this is embarrassing, but I need to put in our notice."

"Notice? I don't understand."

"I don't have the money for rent. I'm sorry. I truly am. And I promise I'll pay you back for what I still owe." I swallow back my pride. "As soon as I can."

"Maeve, dear." Mr. McGrady chuckles. "Your rent is paid."

"I'm sorry, could you repeat that?"

"Rent is paid. It's been paid through the end of the year."

"For the year?" My jaw falls open.

"Yes, ma'am."

"Oh. Okay then. Sorry about that."

"No need to apologize. You just take care of those babies and give your Pops my best."

"Will do. Thank you." I end the call, more than a little stunned.

Who the hell paid our rent through the end of the year?

The familiar rumble of a diesel engine growing louder interrupts my thoughts. It's a sound I haven't heard in nearly two months. My stomach instantly coils with nerves as bright headlights flash across the front window. It's Alex. I know it is before I push to my feet and head toward the door.

Why is he here? What does he want?

It's because of the text I sent. *Fuck.*

When I asked to discuss things, I never expected he'd show up on my doorstep. I should have waited until Rainer was back before I sent that message. Grabbing a jacket from its hook near the door, I pull it on as I step outside, wrapping it around my body as if it can shield me from more than the cold. Should I tell him about the baby I'm carrying? Or that I've been with Rainer? *Fuck.* What about Rainer? How will he feel when he discovers Alex is back?

Guilt floods my mind. For moving on. For being intimate with another man.

Which is ridiculous.

If anyone should feel guilty, it should be Alex.

He left.

He deserted us.

I study Alex as he exits his rig and saunters toward the house. There's apprehension in his approach. As if he's unsure if he's welcome. As if he isn't sure he should be here. Good. He looks like shit. The deep circles under his eyes and the pallor to his skin are concerning.

"Maeve." He stops at the bottom of the porch and dips his chin.

"What are you doing here?"

"I'm so sorry." His eyes are glassy in the porchlight when he meets my gaze. "I'm sorry, baby."

His apology is too little, too late. His presence snaps something inside of me, and I unleash everything I've been holding inside since he left.

"What are you sorry for, Alex?" My anger slices through the night air. "Are you sorry for leaving? For not calling? For abandoning your children? For abandoning me? Or are you sorry for not supporting your family for almost two months and having the audacity to show up on my doorstep without my fucking permission?"

"I didn't come here to fight."

"Oh? Too bad!" I want to fight. I want to yell and scream and make him witness what he's put me through. "What do you want then? What could you possibly want from me after ignoring my calls and texts?"

"I just want to talk."

"Then talk." I throw my arms out wide. "I'm listening." I don't realize my error, until it's too late.

Alex's eyes widen, his gaze transfixed on my belly.

Fuck.

"Oh, Maeve." His eyes fill with tears, only this time he doesn't blink them back. He takes the steps slowly, his shoulders slumping. "I'm sorry. I'm sorry. I'm sorry," he murmurs over and over. When he reaches me, he falls to his knees, his hands open wide as he rests them on my stomach.

I stiffen.

"When?" he sobs, lifting his head. "How long have you known?"

The anger inside my heart deflates.

Guilt seeps into my soul.

I shouldn't have kept this news from him.

"We're having another baby?" he asks, pressing a kiss to my shirt. He bows his head, his apologies coming like a prayer through his tears.

"Alex." I can count on one hand the times I've seen this man cry. Witnessing his emotion causes tiny fractures to splinter in my armor. What if I've made a mistake? What if I wrote him off too soon?

"I didn't know." He pushes to his feet, wiping at his tears with the backs of his hands. "I would have come back sooner if I would have known."

"You didn't answer my texts," I whisper, holding on to the hurt this man has caused. The worry I've grappled with. The insecurity I've felt.

"I know. I'm sorry. I screwed up." His face is pained as he whispers, "How far along?"

"Four months."

"Four?" His eyes widen with concern. "How are you feeling? Is everything okay? Are you doing okay?"

The question is so absolutely absurd I almost laugh. *Am I doing okay?* No. My husband left me. I think I'm madly in love with my best friend, but I'm having a baby with Alex. And I don't know what to do about any of that.

"You're cold." It's not until he makes the observation, that I realize I'm shaking. "Can I come inside?"

I don't know how to answer that.

I don't know what to do.

Fear holds me hostage with indecision.

The front door opens and we both turn as Ari steps outside, his eyes full of delight as he shouts, "Daddy!"

"Hey, big guy." Alex steps forward, dropping to his knees and opening his arms wide to envelop our son.

"Daddy!" Ari squeezes Alex. "Daddy, I missed you!"

"I missed you too." The pain in his muffled voice as he clutches our son to his chest slices through my defenses.

I don't know if I can be happy with Alex again. I don't even know if I want to try. But watching him hug our son reminds me that my decisions affect my children most, and they are the most important people in my life. What kind of a person refuses to allow the father of their children to make amends? My shoulders sag in defeat.

"Lulu! Daddy's home!" Ari shouts, turning to run into the house.

They should be sleeping right now, and it's going to take forever to settle them back down when he leaves, but I can't keep him from seeing them. "Come inside. It's too cold out here for them." My voice doesn't feel like my own. My body doesn't either as I lead him into the house and slump onto the sofa. The weight of everything settles on my shoulders and wraps around my heart.

Lulu wanders out of her room, following her older brother, but when her gaze lands on Alex, she slows her approach.

"Hey, Lulu. Come give Daddy a hug."

At his request, she glances at me for approval.

"You can hug your dad, then you both need to go back to your rooms. It's bedtime."

"Okay, Mama." Lulu skips to Alex, giving him a hug before running back to her room.

"Do I have to go to sleep? I want to stay up with Daddy," Ari says.

"It's okay, buddy. Get your rest and I'll take you to school in the morning." Alex's promise fills my gut with dread.

Then, I feel guilty for the thought.

"Good night, Daddy." Ari smiles.

"Good night, Ari." Alex waits until the bedroom door closes before turning to me. "What about Collin?"

"In his crib." I rub at my temple.

"Can I see him?"

"I don't know if that's a good idea." Though, it'll be a miracle if he's still asleep with all this commotion.

"Maeve, please." Alex takes the seat next to me. There's a desperation in his gaze I've never witnessed before. "I know I screwed up. I shouldn't have left."

I nod, my eyes welling with tears.

"And I should've called."

"Yeah." I cross my arms around my body protectively.

"I know I have a lot to make up for, and I don't expect to go back to the way things were, but please, please let me try. I might not deserve a chance, but those children do. They deserve parents who refuse to give up on them. After everything we've been through, I want to figure this out. To find a way we can both be happy. I don't want to become a stranger to my own children. I don't want you to move on with someone else, not without giving us a chance. We aren't quitters, Maeve. We don't give up. Please. Please, don't give up on us. Don't give up on our family."

His begging strikes the center of my heart, each word landing like a blow.

I am not a quitter. I don't fail, and leaving my marriage was never an option I gave myself before. But he's the one who left when things got hard. Not me. "I don't know if I can forgive you for what you did."

It's the truth.

"Can you try? Please. If not for me, do it for them." He glances down the hall and then to my belly. "Do it for our baby."

This would be so much simpler if he had stayed away. If he didn't want another chance. It breaks me, knowing the consequences of my decision. My own desires battle against those of my children.

I want Rainer.

I want what's best for my children.

If those two things are in opposition, I will pick my kids every single time.

Alex hurt me, and he let us all down. I don't know if a reconciliation is possible, but I can't end a marriage knowing I walked away without trying. "We would need rules."

"Anything you want." He nods eagerly. "Whatever makes you comfortable." He presses his hands to his heart. "Please, Maeve. I lost my way, but it wasn't until I left that I truly realized what I was walking away from." His eyes are rimmed in red as he holds my stare. "I have a week off before my next run. We can work this out. Figure out a way to go from here. Just give me the week. Please."

"A week?" He's never had that much time between jobs.

"I put in overtime while I was away. It's one of the reasons I didn't call. But when I got your text the other day, I asked for the week off. You and the kids are more important to me than a paycheck."

Now I feel even more obligated to give him a chance. "I can't promise you a week."

"Then how 'bout we take it day by day? It'll give us the opportunity to talk."

"You want to talk?" The question leaves my lips with a scoff.

If he's hurt, he pretends not to be. "I know we've put off hard conversations, but I'm ready now. I'm ready to listen. I'm ready to put in the work."

"Fine." I instantly regret it the moment the word passes through my lips.

"Really?"

My stomach sours. "One day at a time."

"Thank you, baby." He reaches for my hand.

I pull it back. "I'm not ready for that."

"Okay." There's disappointment knit in his features, but his next words are kind. "Take as long as you need. I'm here. I'm not going anywhere."

"You can stay here and we can try to work on things, but we're not sleeping in the same bed."

He laughs. "Where am I supposed to sleep?"

I glance at the sofa we're sitting on and raise my brows.

"Yeah, I'm not sleeping on the couch." He scrubs a hand along his jaw. "Maeve. I can't. Not with my back."

I try to be sympathetic. I do. But Rainer never once complained about sleeping on the sofa.

"Alex, I am not sleeping in the same bed with you."

"Maeve, I promise I will respect your boundaries. Sleep, nothing more. But this is my home too. I should get to sleep on my side of the bed. I'm sorry, but I am not sleeping on the couch."

Realization dawns. He paid the rent. *Fuck.* I curse myself for not asking Mr. McGrady more questions when I called. Though, I'm not sure having a heads-up about Alex's return would've changed this outcome.

"Then you can sleep in Ari's bed."

"Where's he going to sleep?"

"He can sleep with me."

Alex opens his mouth as if he wants to argue, but all that comes out is a resigned "Fine."

The impulse to apologize is on the tip of my tongue, but I bite it back. I'm done apologizing. I'm done sacrificing to make his life easier when he was never willing to do the same. He's put out about sleeping on the sofa? Too bad. Minutes ago he was begging, promising to do anything if I'd give him another chance.

Maybe I'm too angry or just plain exhausted. But part of me questions his intentions. His promises already feel a little empty. "I'm going to move Ari to my bed, then I'm going to sleep." I drag my body off the couch, the world feeling so much heavier than a few hours ago. "Lock up before you turn in." I don't spare Alex a glance. I'm done talking for the day. I'm just fucking done.

21

RAINER

AS MUCH AS I appreciate Ryan asking for my help on the cattle drive, by day four of no showers and no conversations with Maeve, I practically race away from the ranch upon our return. I'm so excited to see her, I don't even stop at my place to shower. I head straight to her house, the windows rolled down, singing along with a tune that reminds me of the love I hold for Maeve. The sunset is incredible tonight, the sky painted in hues of purples and pinks as the big ball of fire meets the horizon.

My body is sore from days of riding. I should be exhausted. But the anticipation running through my veins could keep me up for hours. I hope it does, too, because once Maeve catches me up on everything I missed this week, I'm going to pleasure her body until we both pass out.

Turning off the highway and onto the road that leads to Maeve's, all of my excitement is snatched away. Alex's Peterbilt is parked along the road. He's back.

Dread gathers in my bones as I pull my truck behind Maeve's minivan. I cut the engine and leave my bag in the back seat. I check my phone to be sure I haven't missed a text or call from

Maeve. But no. The last message sent between us was from me to her.

> Me: We're back. I'll be at your place in an hour.

I sent the message forty minutes ago, and I wasn't bothered by the fact she hadn't responded. At least, until now. I hop out of the truck at the same time Maeve comes out of the house. Her expression is unreadable, but the lines in her brow do nothing but fuel the worry taking root in the pit of my stomach.

She walks down the porch steps, meeting me halfway up the driveway.

"What's he doing here?" The question snaps from my mouth.

"Rainer."

"Maeve, what is he doing in your house?"

"It's his house too."

"No." I shake my head. This cannot be happening. "Fucking no."

"Rainer." Maeve closes her eyes, a sigh leaving her lips. Even with a pained expression on her face, she's beautiful. When her eyes open to meet mine, I know what she's going to say before she parts her lips to speak. "He's the father of my children. I have to give him another chance."

My heart, unprepared for the impact, shatters into a thousand fucking pieces.

"No, you don't," I implore. "You don't owe him anything. Not after the way he treated you."

"It's not that simple."

"So, what?" I lift my hat from my head to run my fingers through my hair, yanking on the ends. I can't believe this. I left for four fucking days. "Are y'all back together now?"

"Not exactly."

I glance at the house. Alex stands at the window, his hard stare meeting mine. "Does he know that?"

"Don't make this a pissing contest."

"I'm not." But if it were, I would win.

"I'm strong. You know?" Her chin lifts defiantly.

"I didn't say you weren't."

"I managed just fine before."

"Managed?" A bitter laugh leaves my mouth. "Is that what you want out of life? Maeve, honey, you deserve so much more."

"Rainer." She sighs.

"He doesn't make you happy. Hell, he does the opposite. He brings you down. He makes your days harder. He sucks the light right out of your beautiful eyes. How many fucking chances are you going to give him before you completely lose yourself?"

"We have children together. Rainer, I don't expect you to understand, but you can at least try."

Anger flares in my chest. "Don't you dare. This isn't about me. This isn't even about us, though I wish to fucking God it were. This is about you, Maeve. What makes you the best version of yourself. What brings you the most joy. The most peace." I wish she could see what I see. I wish she would put herself first. "For the love of God, don't trade that all for some twisted perception of obligation. Maeve, please. You don't have to pick me, but don't go back. Not to him."

"Maeve?" Alex calls her name from the front door. "Everything okay?"

"Yeah. Just give us a minute." She lifts her voice but doesn't sever the connection of our gaze.

Disappointment wraps around my chest, seeping into the cracks of my heart. She isn't going to pick me. She isn't going to choose herself.

"I can't be your friend through this," I admit.

"I know." She presses her lips together, her eyes filling with tears.

"I hope you're happy." I mean it. I really fucking do. "Goodbye, Maeve." Garnering all the strength in my body, I force myself to turn and walk away from the woman I love. Because as much as I want her, I can't stand by as a spectator and watch her destroy herself. I have too much self-respect to put myself through that.

"Rainer." She chokes out a sob before I reach my truck. "Rainer, wait." She rushes toward me, and I turn to catch her as she flings her body into mine. Her arms band around me as she buries her face into my neck and cries. Her embrace is full of desperation. It's the kind of hug that breaks my fucking heart all over again, because I know, I just know, this is the last time I'll hold her in my arms. She's made her choice, and it doesn't include me.

"I should go," I say stiffly.

"I'm sorry." Her silent sobs shake her body. "I'm so sorry, Rainer. I never meant to hurt you."

I believe her. I do. But sometimes we hurt the ones we love most. That's the risk we take when we give away our hearts. "Don't apologize." I step back and fight the urge to wipe away her tears. "Go inside. Your husband is waiting for you."

22

MAEVE

WHEN ALEX FIRST LEFT, all I wished was for him to come back.

I wanted to forget the entire thing, move forward, and try to salvage our marriage.

Well, he's back, and while I can tell he's trying to prove himself by being more involved, things are mostly the way they were, and I'm fucking miserable.

Regret settles on my chest with every day that goes by, not only for letting Alex back into my life, but for choosing him over Rainer. I made the decision I had to, for my children. But I miss game nights and evenings cuddled on the couch. I miss help with the kids without having to ask. I miss moments of peace and cups of coffee. I miss lighthearted conversations, flirty stares, and stolen kisses.

But more than anything, I miss Rainer.

I miss the version of myself I am when I'm with Rainer.

Because I've changed over the last two months.

And I feel so guilty, because I shouldn't have these feelings when I'm trying to mend a relationship with my husband. I want to give Alex a real second chance. I have to. I don't have the freedom to be selfish right now. My children, including the one growing inside of me, deserve my full devotion to repairing the tears in my marriage. But as much as I try, it's impossible not to go through the day without constantly comparing the two.

"Dinner's almost ready," Alex calls from the kitchen. He offered to cook tonight, and I accepted the offer, even if I'll be expected to clean up afterward.

"Smells great." I deposit Collin into his highchair and strap him in. "Ari, Lulu, time to eat! Please wash your hands and come to the table," I call over my shoulder. Collin begins to fuss. "You ready to eat?" I baby-talk to Collin, peppering his face with kisses until he squeals with joy.

Alex moves to the table with a pan and two pot holders. "Jesus fucking Christ. Can I get some help here?" His irritation is unnecessary and over the top.

I take a breath before acknowledging his outburst. "What do you need?" I paste on a smile. I refuse to shift my mood for him.

"The table's a mess." He motions with one hand, then turns back to the stovetop, where something's beginning to burn. "There's no room in this kitchen to cook."

I don't know what I'm supposed to do about the size of our kitchen, but I clear the table. I was fulfilling online orders before Collin woke from his afternoon nap. I didn't get a chance to box everything up.

"I don't understand why there's so many damn stickers," he mutters under his breath as he sets down the dish and moves to the stovetop.

In the days he's been home, we haven't done much talking about the time we spent apart. "I started a business designing, printing, and selling them."

His brows lift. "You sell those?"

"Yes." I smile proudly. I make a plate for Collin, cutting up his food and allowing it to cool before placing it on his high chair.

"And you came up with the designs? The sayings too?" Judgment seeps into his tone.

I bristle. "Yes."

"I wasn't going to say anything, because you have a right to your hobbies. But, Maeve, you are a mother and Ari can read. Some of those stickers, they're inappropriate. Embarrassing even. What kind of example are you setting for our children?"

I open my mouth to answer, but my sharp reply is cut off. Ari and Lulu run into the kitchen, climbing into their chairs.

"I hun-gee!" Lulu demands.

"I'm hungry too." Ari turns his nose up at the food on the table. "That smells weird, Daddy."

"Yeah, well, you're going to eat what I serve. Big boys don't complain."

"Mama lets me have a bowl of cereal if I don't like dinner," Ari grumbles.

"Well, I'm not your mother." Alex blows out a frustrated breath as he takes his seat at the table.

Dinner is painfully quiet. Ari picks at his plate, no doubt too intimidated by his father to confess he doesn't enjoy the food. I don't blame him. It's not the most appetizing meal Alex has prepared. Lulu reads the energy in the room, staying unusually quiet, and Alex stabs his food with unnecessary force, his frown unwavering.

I don't say a word. If I do, it won't be nice.

The only one to interject is Collin, who shovels food in his mouth and whines if his plate gets too low.

"May I please be excused?" Ari says once Alex has finished eating.

"That's fine." Alex eyes the half-eaten plate but doesn't point it out. "Bring your plate to the sink first."

"Thank you, Daddy."

"I be 'scused too?" Lulu blinks at him with her wide eyes.

"Yeah, baby. You can go play."

"I no baby." Her scowl cracks the ice.

Alex laughs, then Ari. I can't help but smile too.

"I no baby!" She hops off the seat and stomps out of the room.

"I'm sorry dinner wasn't my best work." Alex shakes his head before meeting my gaze. "I think the only one who loved it was Collin."

"He has questionable tastes," I deadpan.

"Yeah." Alex chuckles, standing and gathering the dirty dishes. "I'll clean up if you want to get them ready for bed."

Guilt permeates me with his offer. He's trying to be better. He's doing things he never did before. I guess I should stop expecting the worst from him.

"Hey," I say to him as I wipe off Collin's hands and face. "Do you want to play a board game later?"

"I'm kinda tired. Why don't we watch a movie?"

"Oh, okay." I should probably finish packaging today's orders anyway. At least that's something I can do while he watches TV. "Maybe tomorrow." I don't know if he hears me, but he doesn't acknowledge my bid for connection. The rejection stings, not because I'm dying to play games with Alex. But because I know if I would have made the suggestion to Rainer, we'd be ending the evening with a board game.

The worry that's been clawing at me for days, rises to the surface. I can hardly think the words. What if I've fallen out of love with my husband? What if everything he's trying to do is a little too late? What if I'm the one who can't exist in this marriage without losing herself? Because I fucking like the woman I am. I like being able to speak my mind and having my opinions be valued. I like to laugh and dance in the kitchen and drop an f-bomb in front of my children without it being the end of the world. I want a partner who is proud of my side hustle, and not too prudish to appreciate the hard work I'm putting in so there's more money in my bank account.

The things that felt so important before, like the number of anniversaries we celebrated or the vows I promised on my wedding day, no longer hold the same importance. I'm more concerned with how we speak together, the joy we can find in the normal day-to-day activities of raising children, and the kindness of a partner who is as concerned for my feelings as he is of his own.

What would happen if I stopped taking Alex's preferences into consideration or allowing his mood to dictate my own? Maybe I need to start living the way I was when he was gone. I don't think he'll like it, but what's the worst that can happen? He leaves me? He's already done that and I survived it just fine.

No. I didn't just survive. I flourished, thanks to the support of this town, my family, and Rainer.

If I'm being honest, there's a part of me that wishes Alex would leave again, this time for good. It would make everything easier. It would make the hard choice for me. But that's not fair to anyone, including Alex.

I love our family, but him leaving us gave me a perspective I never dared to dream. We would be fine without him. I'm not alone, and I wouldn't raise my children alone. My brothers would help. Rainer would help. Or, at least he would have. Now, I'm not so sure.

Maybe I could be happy.

I could find peace.

Because, as difficult as these last months have been, I didn't stop experiencing joy. The anxiety I'd been feeling every time Alex came home but never wanted to acknowledge, was no longer there. I was good without him. Fuck. Not just good. I was better.

It scares me that I've fucked that all up by letting him back in. That I've fucked up any chance of finding happiness. I don't know where to go from here, but I do know I can't exist in this space— one where I lie to myself just to keep everyone else comfortable. I'm at a crossroads, and, fuck, I wish there was a crystal ball so I could choose the right path.

23

RAINER

"I LIKE that you're free, but you're horrible company."

"Sorry, Mac." I shouldn't have agreed to meet for drinks. I should have stayed holed up in my house where I could nurse my broken heart in privacy.

"She's really got you twisted up." He sighs.

"Yeah."

"Want me to drive over there and punch him for you?"

"No." Despite my sour mood, his suggestion brings the ghost of a smile to my lips.

"Spit in his food?"

"Mac." I roll my eyes, a burst of laughter escaping my chest. "Why would you be near his food?"

"That's for me to figure out." He grins. "I would do anything for you. You're like a brother to me."

"Same, and thank you. But I think I'll just wallow in my self-pity a little longer." It's actually embarrassing how much I want to sit and feel sorry for myself. Besides work, I haven't done much else until Mac insisted we go out after work for a beer.

"I can't believe she picked him over you."

"Yeah, well, she did." I blow out an exaggerated breath.

He takes a sip of his lager. "Maybe it's time to put yourself out there. Start dating. Find someone who appreciates you and what you bring to the table."

"Maybe." Not anytime soon, but maybe.

I've spent my entire life hung up on Maeve and what our future would have been if we were together. Living that dream, even if only temporarily, was more fulfilling than I could have imagined. But I am done waiting on the sidelines for Maeve to realize what I should have been brave enough to tell her years ago. I love her. I have always loved her, and if given the chance, I would never stop showing her just how deep my love for her runs.

But I was too late. Or maybe my love for her never mattered. If the last two months weren't enough for her, then nothing ever will be. I need to move forward. I need to find a way to open myself up to the idea of loving someone else the way I love her.

"Maybe I need to start fresh." I clear my throat. "Some place new."

"You want to leave Wilder Valley?" Mac scoffs.

"No." I shake my head. I don't *want* to. "But maybe I need to."

"That's the stupidest fucking thing you've ever said."

"Excuse me?" I can't help but laugh.

"Your livelihood is here. All your friends. Your parents. If you left, who the hell would run your business?"

I lift my brows and meet his stare.

"Oh no." He shakes his head. "You better not be looking at me. We've already established my retinas self-combust at the sight of an accounting book."

"Then I guess you aren't my guy."

"Look, I get it. I do. And I'm not trying to tell you how to live your life. But running away won't make you love her any less."

God, ain't that the truth.

My mouth presses together in a grimace. I take another swig from my beer glass. "I don't think I can stomach seeing them together."

"Now, maybe. But give yourself time." He leans forward, resting his elbows on the table. "I take it you're no longer attending Aiden and Sarah's nuptials."

"Yeah, no." I shake my head. The wedding is this weekend. It's hard to believe I was hoping that day might be my and Maeve's first official outing as a couple. How quickly life can change.

"I guess I won't go either." He shrugs.

I roll my eyes. "You can go without me."

"Nah. Gotta stand in solidarity with my man. Besides, there's a good chance you're going to get shitfaced that night. Someone's gonna need to watch over you."

"I don't need looking after." I chuckle. "I'm fine." Rather, I will be. After I lick my wounds.

"Yeah, well, no matter how fucking independent you are, it's okay to lean on your friends when you need them."

"Thanks, man, I really appreciate that."

"Besides, if you get drunk, I want to be there to join you in the endeavor. It's a rare sighting, Rainer Anderson, unhinged."

"Get your telescope ready."

"I will. Happens like once a lifetime."

We spend the next hour trading jokes and sipping on beer before we call it a night. I might not have been in the best head-space, but I'm glad I said yes when Mac invited me out. Sharing conversation and drinks with a friend was just what I needed. It doesn't erase my pain, but it validates my experience. Sometimes the best medicine is finding someone who understands.

My heart aches as I climb into my truck and plug my phone into the charger. The impulse to unlock my screen and text Maeve is automatic, same as always. It fills me with sadness that we no longer have that relationship.

Last week I lost more than the love of my life, I lost my best friend. Those are big shoes to fill, and it's going to take time, but I won't spend the rest of my life hung up on someone who didn't choose me. At the end of the day, I gave her my all. There's nothing else I can do.

24

MAEVE

I LOVE MY CHILDREN. I do. But sometimes at the end of the day, when my energy is depleted and I'm on my last thread, I just wish they could put themselves to bed. It doesn't help that Collin's teething and probably won't sleep through the night.

I'm about to lose my shit. I haven't had a moment to myself since Alex returned last week. While I appreciate the intention behind him taking a break from work to focus on our family, it's stifling having him home twenty-four-seven. I can't even remember a time when he was home this many days in a row. It has me on edge. I feel as though I can't even think. My to-do list piles higher than the dishes in the sink, and the worst part, Alex doesn't even notice. Or maybe he does but he's comfortable watching me flounder.

If Rainer were here, he would take one look at me and take over. I would be able to recharge because he would do everything that needed to be done. I wouldn't have to ask. I wouldn't have to make a list. I wouldn't have to run myself into the ground before he would notice.

But Rainer isn't here, and I gave Alex a second chance. I've regretted that decision every day, and I'm angry with myself because I should have known better. Giving up my best friend of two decades was never the answer.

"I need to get Lulu to bed, can you hold Collin?" I exhale a frustrated sigh as Collin pulls at my shirt and whines.

Alex barely glances at us from his place in front of the television. "There're two innings left in the game." He reaches over to ruffle Ari's hair. "We're watching the game together, aren't we, big guy?"

Ari beams at his daddy. "Go D-backs!"

Alex laughs, then glances over to where I'm still standing near the hallway. He shrugs before returning his stare to the television. "If you give Collin to me, he's just gonna cry."

He's probably right. Collin would cry if I gave him to Alex. But I'm touched out, sleep deprived, and fucking exhausted.

"Fine." I huff and turn back to the kids' rooms.

Lulu is a handful tonight. She's upset that Ari gets to stay up, and drags out every step to bedtime. When she's finally tucked in bed, I settle into the rocker and attempt to soothe Collin. He fusses and flops for what feels like an hour, but eventually gives in to the pull of sleep.

His little eyelids flutter with each rock, and his body sags, relaxing into my arms with his full weight. He's getting so big. Too big. And I wish I could turn back the clock. He won't be my baby much longer.

Before I get up to set him in his crib, I make a mental list of all the things that need to be done before I collapse on the bed. Switch the laundry, wash the dishes, pack Ari's lunch for school, and pick up the toys.

If Rainer were here, he'd have those tasks done already, and without me having to ask. Because he pays attention. Because he doesn't like to see me worn out and at my wits' end. He'd have a decaf coffee brewed and a game to play set up on the table waiting for me.

God, I miss him. I wish he were here. I wish I hadn't let Alex back in.

Guilt sours my longing.

I shouldn't want Rainer when I'm married to Alex. I've never been like this. Never lusted after a man when I was unavailable. I'm loyal to a fault. Or at least I was.

Now that I've had Rainer—all of him—I can't help but think about him. It's not just that he's kind or a good listener or helpful around the house. It's not the way he made me feel more beautiful and more cherished than I ever had. Hell, it's not even how good the sex was, and it was really fucking good. It's that he and I share the kind of connection that is so rare, and so aligned, the hard days felt easier when we tackled them together.

Easy day.

There haven't been any easy days since I asked him to leave.

God, what is wrong with me? Why can't I stop thinking about Rainer? Can't stop comparing him and Alex and noticing all the ways my husband falls short?

I told Alex he could have a second chance. I have to give him an opportunity to do that. For fuck's sake, I'm carrying his child. My nostrils sting. Tears fill my eyes. A sob tries to escape my lips.

I glance across the dimly lit room. Lulu is sleeping, thank God. I don't want her to see me like this.

I wipe beneath my eyes, catching the tears before they fall. I force myself to breathe, calming the impulse to cry. I can't do this right now. I don't have the time or energy to fall apart. Placing Collin down in his crib, I quietly step out of the room and pull the door shut behind me.

The familiar narration to Ari's favorite cartoon greets my ears as I walk to the living room. I wonder how long the game's been over, and why Alex hasn't started putting Ari to bed. The exhaustion from the day sits heavy on my shoulders along with the guilt eating me up from inside.

"Hey," I say.

Alex jumps at my voice. He swipes across his phone screen, minimizing whatever he was looking at. "Hey."

There's something in his reaction that makes me pause. "Everything good?"

"Yeah, everything's great." He smiles and sets his phone down, then knocks Ari's shoulder lightly with his fist. "Isn't it, bud? D-backs pulled out a win."

Ari ignores him, completely entranced in his show.

Alex reaches for the remote and turns off the television. "We gotta get you to bed, big guy."

"I wanna stay up with you," Ari whines.

"Daddy's going to bed too. Come on, let's go brush those teeth." Alex stands off the sofa. "I'll get him to bed and clean up. Why don't you get a shower? Take a minute to yourself to wind down."

"Thanks." I feel bad for all my negative thoughts. Alex might not be as efficient or intuitive as Rainer, but he does care. He's making an effort.

"Night, Mama!" Ari wraps his arms around my waist.

"Night, Ari. I love you. Sleep tight."

As they head down the hall into the bathroom, I turn toward my bedroom door, but something pulls my attention back to Alex's phone. I can't explain why, but I need to know what he was looking at when I walked in.

Listen to your gut. If something seems off, it probably is. The words of advice that Bernadette's friend Mimi offered, ring in my ears.

Picking up the device, I type in the chain of numbers to unlock the screen. Only, they don't work. Weird. He's used my birthday as his code for as long as I can remember. Suspicion coils in my gut. *What is he hiding?*

I think of other significant dates and type them in, my fingers shaking as my stomach fills with dread.

His birthday. Fail.

Our anniversary. Nope.

A warning pops onto the screen. *Shit.* I only have a few tries to guess correctly before it's locked up. If that happens, I'll have to explain myself.

I inhale a deep breath. Alex's voice is muffled as he helps our five-year-old get ready for bed. The affectionate tone of their voices almost makes me abandon my spur-of-the-moment investigation. This is stupid. What do I think I will find on his phone?

I surprised him. That's all. It doesn't mean he's hiding something. If he was, why would he leave his phone behind?

Fuck it.

Right or wrong, I glance down the hall to make sure he's still helping Ari, then I punch in the date to our firstborn's birthday.

The screen unlocks. *Thank fuck.*

I swipe to see the apps that Alex left open. I briefly scan his text messages, finding nothing out of the ordinary. YouTube is pulled up, paused halfway through a fishing video. Netflix, with the last played being one of his favorite comedy shows. Google. I check the history.

Nothing strikes concern.

My nervous system begins to calm. The panicked alarm dissipates and I scroll through the screens as guilt seeps into my thoughts. My imagination ran wild. Nothing else. Or maybe I'm looking for a reason to push Alex away? Fuck. If we're going to have any chance of repairing our marriage, I need to trust him.

That's when I notice something out of the ordinary. There's an icon I don't recognize. It's a texting app. One I've never seen him use.

The hairs on the back of my neck rise and I hold my breath as I tap on the app. It loads and I click on the most recent text exchange.

> A: I'd have my head between your thighs so I could eat that pussy.

What the actual fuck?

> E: What would you do to me if you were in my bed right now?

> A: I need you too, baby. And I'll be back as soon as I can.

> E: I need you.

My stomach twists and bile sours my throat as I read message after message. I can't believe what my eyes are seeing. *My husband is having an affair.*

I try to give everyone the benefit of the doubt, but the evidence is damning. He's in a relationship with another woman, and that motherfucker had the nerve to guilt me into inviting him back into our lives?

I think I might be sick.

My knees buckle, and I sink onto the sofa, unable to stop myself from reading every line of betrayal. The messages go back as far as six months, and they keep going. Anger builds in my chest. His infidelity goes long beyond the time he was away. It goes beyond anything I could have imagined. In addition to the texts, there are nudes. She's pretty. Beautiful, even. Thankfully, I don't recognize this woman. At least I don't think she's someone I've met before. That would be worse, I think. *Fuck.* Not that any of that matters. It doesn't matter what she looks like or if I know her; I didn't consent to my partner fucking other people.

"Okay, bud, finish reading your book and then we'll get you tucked into your mama's bed." Alex's voice pulls my gaze away from the screen.

Disgust, anger, and betrayal course through my veins as I wait for his footsteps to reach the living room.

He freezes as soon as he notices me holding his phone.

"Who the hell is E?"

His eyes widen. "It's not what you think."

"It's not what I think?" Laughter shakes my chest. Nothing about this is funny, yet I can't seem to stop myself.

"Are you okay?" Alex steps forward with concern.

"Am I okay?" I shoot to my feet and yell. "Am I okay!"

"Maeve, you're gonna wake the kids," he scolds.

"Oh, you're worried about the kids?" I laugh again, mania filling my chest. "That's fucking hilarious!"

"Maeve. Language," he says through gritted teeth.

"I just need to get one thing clear. Tell me if I got this right." I hold the phone in my hand, shaking it in the air and using all my self-control not to chuck it at his stupid face. "You had the audacity to come into this home and ask for a second chance after you abandoned me and your children for over a month—a month in which you never once called or checked in or made sure we were okay. And you had the nerve to do all of that while you were texting your side piece and making plans for the next time you could get away? Alex, what the actual fuck?"

"Maeve, I'm sorry. Okay?" He shakes his head. "What do you want me to say?"

"I want you to be faithful. I want you to give a fuck! About me, about the kids, about our unborn child!" I scream.

"I messed up, okay?" His eyes fill with tears as his gaze meets mine. "I'm sorry."

"Are you? Or are you sorry for getting caught? Jesus. Why

come back at all?" Why fuck up my life? "Why pay our rent for the year?"

"What are you talking about?"

"The rent." At his blank expression I clarify, "Someone paid it through the year."

"Well, that wasn't me. I don't know what kinda money you think I'm making, but I sure don't have enough to pay four months of rent at a time."

It wasn't him. Of course it wasn't. *Fuck.* How stupid am I? It was Rainer. It had to be.

"It was him, wasn't it? Your little puppy dog best friend," Alex snarls. "You suck his cock for that?" he scoffs and glares. "I'm not the only one who's been unfaithful. Am I? Hell, is that baby even mine?"

His accusation snaps something inside of me. It's the last straw. I can't take anymore.

"Get the fuck out." A calmness steadies my demand. It's the kind of control that comes before being swept up in the roar of a storm.

"Excuse me?"

"Get! The fuck. Out!" I scream, pointing at the door.

"This is my house."

My body shakes. "So help me God, get the fuck out of this house before I call my brothers and ask them to physically remove you."

"Maeve. Calm down. You just need some time and then we can talk about this rationally."

"I don't ever want to see your face."

"Yeah, well yours isn't my favorite right now either."

"Get the fuck out!" I shout so loudly my ears ring.

Collin cries first. Then Lulu. Ari's worried face stares back at us from the end of the hallway.

Alex's face screws up in anger, but he doesn't say another

word. He stomps to the door, shoves his feet in his boots, then storms back to the counter to grab his keys and wallet. He slams the door on his way out.

My body flinches at the sound.

The roar of the diesel engine breaks through the night a few seconds later.

"Mama?" The fear in Ari's voice pulls my sanity back into my body. "Did Daddy leave?"

"Daddy can't stay here tonight." The adrenaline dump diffuses my remaining strength. I drop down to the sofa and hold my arms out for Ari. He runs into my embrace.

"Did Daddy do something bad?"

Oh, sweetheart. He's done something very bad. Something we're never coming back from. I hold Ari tightly, or maybe he holds on to me. I need to calm down so I can check in on Lulu and Collin, but it's impossible. Tears fill my eyes and my body trembles. All the emotion I've kept inside this last week releases like a flood from a broken dam.

My phone rings from the kitchen table, but I ignore it. Whoever it is will have to wait. If it's Alex, I might lose my mind. If it's anyone else, I won't be able to speak through my sobs. The tiny humans under this roof need me most, and I have to pull myself together. Because if I don't, there's no one else, and that's a lot of fucking pressure for someone whose entire world's been knocked off course.

25

MAEVE

MY BROTHER and Sarah are getting married today and it's the last place I want to be. It's not personal; I don't want to attend any weddings. Hell, I don't even want to leave my house. The last few days have been an emotional roller coaster, one I wish I could get off. After I kicked Alex out and dried my tears, I retrieved my phone to discover seven missed calls, first from the facility where my father lives and then from every single one of my siblings and their partners.

As if my life couldn't be more in shambles, Pops fell and broke his hip.

It's no one's fault. Though it's hard to comprehend how a man I'd seen thrown from horses a half dozen times and who I always viewed as tough as nails, could injure himself so greatly by way of a simple accident.

As difficult as it is having him farther away from the family, him being minutes from a major hospital and receiving surgery within the first twenty-four hours is a blessing. I haven't driven up to see him yet, and it breaks my fucking heart. But there hasn't been time. Not with the wedding. Not with the slew of sticker orders coming through, thanks to a semi-viral social media post. But even if there was time, the drive there and back is too much for the kids, and the hospital floor he's on doesn't allow visitors under the age of twelve.

Doesn't lessen the guilt I feel for not being by his side.

And the one person who could hold things down, the same person who would insist I go visit my dad if he knew the situation, is the same man I cannot ask. Not after the hurt I caused him. I have too much respect for him to even ask. Besides, my brothers have assured me Pops is in the best care, and that he's not up for visitors anyway.

Still, I worry.

I read between the lines in our family text thread. I've spoken to the nurses and doctors. This fall has somehow worsened my father's dementia drastically, and he's not recovering from his surgery the way he should be.

I have half a mind to ditch this wedding and drive straight to the hospital, just so I can sit with him. Even if he doesn't know me. Even if we don't talk.

But I won't do that to Sarah and Aiden. I already promised I would do her hair. I'll just have to beg Jackson to stay with my kids tomorrow and push aside the feeling that somehow, I'm letting my father down. Hell, I might be letting everyone down at this point.

I glance down at my stomach and rub my open palm against the prominent bump. As of right now, no one knows I'm pregnant, that is, other than Alex, Rainer, and my father.

But after today, everyone is gonna know.

I've been able to hide under oversized t-shirts and stretchy pants for the last few weeks. But those days are gone. In my bridesmaid gown, there's no hiding this pregnancy. I don't know what happened, but over the past few days my belly decided to fully pop out. I'm just thankful Sarah picked bridesmaid dresses with a high waistline or mine probably wouldn't fit.

I'm anxious, my pulse racing as I pack a few last items before heading to my childhood home to do Sarah's hair and await this afternoon's ceremony. I'm nervous for everyone to know I'm pregnant again. Nervous for the questions to come. Like, where's Alex? Or worse, where's Rainer? There will be rumors and speculation about the paternity of this child. I get it. It's natural to wonder about these things, especially when you're a part of such a close-knit community.

I'd like to think I don't give a fuck, but that's not true. My family holds a legacy in this town, and I've always worked to uphold our good name. We aren't cheaters. We aren't liars. We are good, hard-working people who take care of each other and stand up for what's right.

I am still all of those things.

I'm just feeling a little lost.

A little alone.

What would my mother say if she could see me now? The thought brings tears to my eyes and an ache to my chest. God, I wish she were here. She would know what to do. She'd remind me to hold my head high. She'd silence anyone with a glare who dare imply I'm doing anything other than my best.

I miss her.

I also miss my best friend.

All of this would be easier to bear with Rainer at my side.

Fuck.

In the days since kicking Alex out, I have picked up my phone to call Rainer or text him so many times I've lost count. But each time, I stop myself.

I want to see him. I want to tell him what happened. But after the pain I caused, I don't deserve his friendship. I wouldn't be surprised if he never wants to see me again. And I don't blame him. I fucked up. I should have never allowed Alex back into my home. But I did, and now I have to live with the consequences.

If Rainer's at the ceremony today, I don't know that I'll be able to stop myself from begging for a second chance. At the very least, I owe him an apology. But part of me knows he won't come. He's done with me. He laid his heart on the line and I didn't treasure it the way I should have.

He probably hates me.

Hell, he wouldn't be the only one.

I kinda hate myself.

The doorbell rings, and a second later Lulu calls my name. Collin cries from his bedroom, and Ari comes to my doorway. "Mama, your friend Jamie is here. Can I open the door?"

I scan my room to make sure I haven't missed anything, then lift my duffle bag onto my shoulder. "Let's make sure it's her before we open the door."

His wide eyes meet mine and he nods. I had a long talk with both him and Lulu about safety. I don't believe Alex would do anything to hurt them or try and take the kids without my permission, but when it comes to their safety, I can't be too careful.

"Mama!" Lulu squeals when I walk into the living room. "Pretty dress!"

"Thank you." The first genuine smile I've had in days sneaks onto my face. I check the porch through the window and nod for Ari to open the door. Standing back, my smile pressed in place, I wait for my friend's reaction.

"Hi, Miss Jamie."

"Well, hello there, Ari. You ready to have fun today?" She steps into the house. "Hey, Maeve." Her smile falters as her mouth falls open. "Oh my God, you're pregnant!"

Of all the ways I anticipated her reaction, blurting her observation was not one of them.

"You're gonna have another baby?" Ari gasps. "I thought your belly was getting big, but you said it wasn't polite to comment on other people's bodies."

"Thank you, son." In spite of everything, I chuckle.

"Sorry." Jamie winces.

"It's okay. They would have figured it out sooner than later."

"Congratulations." She pulls me into a quick hug. "We have so much to talk about, but that's gonna have to wait. Go. Have a great time. I've got this." She and the rest of my book club besties know all about Alex. I caught them up in the group chat while waiting to hear updates about Pops's hip surgery, but there's still so much to tell her. She's right, though. It will have to wait.

"Thank you again for agreeing to be here today." I had always planned to bring the kids to the wedding, but there is no way I could wrangle them on my own while being in the ceremony. Jamie was kind enough to volunteer to watch them today. I bend down to give Lulu a kiss, then walk to Ari and do the same. "Be good for Miss Jamie. I love you both."

"Love you, Mama!" they say back.

"Come on. Why don't we get your little brother up?" Jamie says to Ari and Lulu as I step out and lock the door.

On the drive to the ranch, I make my daily call to the hospital. They're probably sick of me by now, but I can't help it. If I can't be there with Pops, I need to know how he's doing, even if the status hasn't changed. "I'm calling to check on my father, Tim Wilder. He's in room 305. I'm his daughter, Maeve Adler." I say after the receptionist to his floor answers.

"Sure thing. Give me a minute to track down his nurse and get an update for you."

I wait for what feels longer than the few minutes I sit on hold.

"Ma'am?"

"Yes, I'm here."

"The doctor on duty hasn't made his rounds for the day, but your father is stable. He's still refusing to eat."

My heart falls. "Okay." I reach for one of the tissues I tucked inside my bra and dab beneath my lashes before I ruin my eyeliner. "Thank you."

"Of course. I will personally call if there's any change."

He's a strong person, but his dementia has created countless challenges when it comes to his recovery and rehabilitation. The longer he refuses food, the weaker he gets, even with the feeding tube. He needs to get up and start moving. He needs to fight.

I thank her again and end the call, offering up a prayer for a miracle. I wish I could talk to Rainer. He would reassure me that my father is going to make a full recovery. He would help me face today with confidence.

Pulling onto the familiar gravel road, I drive until I reach the ranch. It's a beautiful October day, the sun shining high in the sky and not a cloud in sight. It really is the perfect day for a wedding.

I consider how long it took Aiden and Sarah to find each other again. Maybe, just maybe, it's not too late for me and Rainer. I love him, and I know he loves me. But it takes more than love to make a relationship work. I only hope it doesn't take us decades to figure it out.

26

RAINER

IT'S crazy that a week ago I believed Maeve and I would be attending her brother's wedding today. As a real couple. Now, I can't even imagine going to the ceremony or pasting on a fake smile for the reception. The last thing I want is to witness her and Alex together again.

I hope she's happy. I do.

But I also hope he falls off a cliff.

Or better yet, that he leaves again. For good this time.

I'm not proud of the fact I am praying on the downfall of someone else's marriage. Or that I fell in love with someone else's wife. Though that's nothing new. What changed is she fell for me too. And she deserves better than what he can provide. She deserves to be loved fully and completely, the way I love her.

My plan is to hole up in my house for most of the day, avoiding the wedding festivities and everyone who will be there, but I'm in desperate need of groceries. Our local store is the gathering space, especially on a Saturday. Townies go there to socialize as much as to replenish their cupboards. I check the clock, estimating that everyone who knows the Wilders will have done their shopping earlier and are already on their way to the ranch for the ceremony.

My misstep is not taking into account that this would also be the perfect place to pit stop if you needed a last-minute gift. As soon as I fetch an empty cart from the parking lot and walk inside the sliding double doors, I am greeted by two of Maeve's book club friends, Liv and Rosalie.

"Rainer! Hey!" Rosalie's eyes widen as she takes in my appearance. She's dressed in a stylish black dress and cowboy boots so shiny they've probably never seen dirt.

"Hi." I lift my hand and try to smile.

Liv frowns, the flowy sleeves of her dress waving as her hands motion to my t-shirt and jeans. "You aren't going to the wedding?"

I rock back on my heels, wishing to the heavens I had stayed home a little longer so I could avoid this very thing. "I don't think that's a good idea."

"Really?" Liv glances at Rosalie and then back at me. "I'm surprised you'd let Maeve go alone."

Shit. I'm shocked they don't know. It's not like Maeve to keep things from her friends. "Um, she's with Alex now."

"Uh, no she's not." Rosalie laughs. "She kicked his cheating ass to the curb over a week ago."

"She didn't tell you?" Liv asks, but my stunned expression is the only answer she gets. "Fuck. I guess with her dad being rushed to the hospital and the stickers going viral . . . sorry, we shouldn't have said anything. I assumed you knew."

I don't know what to grab onto first. Alex cheated? Pops is in the hospital? "Is her dad gonna be okay?"

"I don't think they know yet. He had surgery a few days ago but he's not recovering well. Sarah even considered pushing the wedding back, but Aiden wouldn't let her."

"Shit." The desire to find Maeve is so strong, I almost leave without saying another word. "I've got to go." I abandon my grocery cart. "Thank you," I call over my shoulder and jog to my truck.

My heart pounds in my own ears as I turn the key in the ignition and the engine roars to life. I check the clock on the dash and mentally calculate how long it will take to drive back to my house, get ready, and get to the ranch. Fuck. I might miss the ceremony, but there's no way in hell I am going to keep my distance or wait for her to call. I want to be there for her. I *need* to be. Worry twists my gut, just thinking of what she's going through and how alone she must feel. Maeve needs me, and I can't turn off a lifetime of being her friend. I need to be with her. No matter what happened between us, I hope we can find a way back to each other, even as friends.

Because as much as it hurt when she chose Alex over me, it's devastating facing an eternity without her in my life.

27

MAEVE

SARAH IS A BEAUTIFUL BRIDE. I curl and pin her hair the way we practiced a few months ago, and we both shed a few tears when I offer for her to borrow my mother's sapphire earrings. They're a perfect addition to her blue gown. Before we know it, it's time to head to the old barn.

Val drives us in my brother's truck, parking out of sight from the clearing next to the barn where the white folding chairs are already filled with guests. I look for Rainer in the crowd. Even though I doubt he'll come, my heart sinks with disappointment when I don't see him.

Inside the barn, Sarah's parents are waiting. They greet their daughter, then say hello to Val and me. Their eyes widen at my protruding baby bump, but they don't comment, and for that I'm grateful. I'm sure others won't be so polite. I told Val and Sarah earlier, but they weren't as surprised as I expected. However, like the wonderful sisters-in-law I know them to be, they offered nothing but congrats and well wishes.

I pick up my bouquet of wildflowers and line up for the procession, checking out the barn while I wait. The reception will immediately follow the ceremony, and my family has done an incredible job transforming this space. Fairy lights wind around mason jars filled with sunflowers. A catering crew is busy setting up at the far end of the room, and the aroma of food causes my stomach to rumble. There are kegs of beer and bottles of wine in another corner, and a DJ with a massive speaker system sets up near the makeshift dance floor in the center of the room.

A wave of bittersweet longing settles on my shoulders as I think back on all the weddings held in this barn, my own included. That was a happy day, but the memories are soured by what I now know.

I shake off the negative energy, refusing to let intrusive thoughts ruin the rest of the afternoon. I peek my head outside the barn door, to scan the crowd. I look for Rainer. I can't help myself. But I'm not surprised when I don't find him among those waiting.

Still, disappointment wraps around my heart.

Meeting Aiden's gaze, I almost laugh. My older brother cranes his neck as if he can somehow see past me and the half-opened door from his vantage point. "I think your groom is getting impatient."

"That sounds about right." Sarah's mom chuckles. "That man's been waiting for this day for over twenty years."

We line up in order and I start the small procession. Pasting on my bravest smile, I begin to walk down the aisle. My brother Wild plays his acoustic guitar from where they've set up his mic and amp. Murmurs from the crowd lift above the music just enough that I can hear their existence, but I hold my head high and ignore the whispers.

Taking my place to the left of the arch woven with fabric and flowers, I turn and meet the rest of my brothers' stares. Well, Ryan's and Jackson's. Aiden stands at attention in his Army dress blues, next to Sarah's sons. I may have walked right in front of him, but he barely notices. He can't look away from the doorway where Sarah will step through.

Val joins me at my right, offering me a warm smile, and then the music shifts. The guests stand and turn to watch the beautiful bride walk down the aisle, her mother and stepfather accompanying her. The song playing is an original Wild wrote just for Sarah and Aiden, and the lyrics are so perfect that my eyes can't stop from watering.

My heart squeezes almost painfully in my chest, wishing our parents could be here to witness this day. It aches again as Aiden wipes away his own tears, the look of utter devotion on his face unmissable as he meets his bride at the end of the aisle.

Rosalie officiates the ceremony, garnering the attention of everyone in attendance. As she welcomes the crowd and leads the couple through their vows, I allow my gaze to wander back to the guests.

The last person I expect to see sitting in the back row is Rainer. I don't know when he arrived, or what he knows, but when I find him staring back, I can't look away. The rest of the ceremony proceeds, but I don't hear a word. Something could fall from the sky and I'd hardly notice. Because Rainer is here. The wild storm in his eyes calls to my racing heart.

Val nudges my arm, and it's only then I realize the ceremony is over. As much as it pains me, I tear my gaze away from Rainer and focus on putting one foot in front of the other. As soon as the procession leads us back inside the barn, I turn back outside.

Val chuckles, reaching for my hand. "Don't run off yet. We have pictures."

"Right." Fuck. I hate weddings. Rather, I hate how drawn out the formalities of them can be, especially when your heart is burning to have a discussion that's long overdue. But it's not Aiden and Sarah's fault, and they deserve to have everything they desire on their special day. Dutifully, I follow my family out through the other doors to the barn and around to the picturesque sunset that frames our family's ranch.

It's another hour before we're back in the barn for the reception, but I'm directed into the buffet line. My stomach is tight with nerves, anxious to find Rainer, but I can't skip this meal. As it is, I didn't eat enough today, and the baby growing inside me takes priority.

Joyful conversation fills the table while we feast on smoked ribs and comfort dish sides. It's been months since the last time my siblings sat down at the same table, and it's nice to gather for a joyous occasion instead of a funeral. Distracted as I am, I force myself to join in the conversation and not spend every second trying to catch Rainer's gaze across the room. Who knows when we'll all be together again next, especially with Wild's demanding tour schedule.

But once Aiden and Sarah are pulled out to the dance floor for their first dance, I excuse myself from the table to go find Rainer.

Only I'm too late.

He's not here.

He's gone.

Fuck. I missed my chance.

My lungs squeeze painfully. My pulse races. I can't keep up the pretense that everything's fine. Not in front of all these people. Hell, I can't take a full breath. The bodice of my gown feels as if it's three sizes too tight. I need air. Giving in to the panic, I stride through the crowded barn and push outside. The fall night air is cool, filling my lungs with a moment of relief before the stress of the last few months topples like a house of cards.

Lifting the skirt of my dress, I walk around the building, away from the joyous noise and bright lights. I can't take it anymore. I can't pretend I'm happy on the outside when inside everything hurts.

"Hey." Rainer's deep voice catches me by surprise.

"Hey," I whisper, not totally believing he's standing before me. I wouldn't put it past my brain to start hallucinating. "Are you leaving?"

He glances over my shoulder toward the barn. "I'm not sure."

"Oh." *Don't leave!* I want to scream and beg, but I have no right to ask this man for anything. "Rainer," I say.

At the same time he says, "Maeve."

Silence stretches between us, and for the first time it's filled with discomfort. We've always been so close. I hate that I've ruined that. I hate that I'm responsible for losing what always came so easily to us.

Rainer meets my stare, but in the shadows I can't decipher his thoughts. "Do you want me to stay?"

I nod, unable to help myself. "If I say yes, will you?"

"Rosalie and Liv told me about Alex. And your dad." The hurt in his tone slices through my already battered heart. "Why didn't you call me?"

I huff out a humorless laugh. Of all the things I expect him to say, this is not it. He's hurt I didn't come to him? After everything I did? "I can't run to you every time I have a problem."

"Why not?" He takes a step forward, the frown lines on his forehead bathed in the dim light. His eyes search mine as he crowds my body. "Maeve, I'm your person. You call me and I'm there. Always."

"I wasn't sure if that had changed." My eyes fill with tears and I chew at the inside of my cheek, unable to hold his gaze. "I'm sorry. I was a fucking idiot to let Alex back in."

"I'm sorry too."

My gaze whips up. "What are you sorry about?" He has done nothing wrong.

He reaches out, cupping my cheek so I can't look away. "I'm sorry Alex didn't appreciate you the way he should have. I'm sorry he didn't realize what a gift you are, or how lucky he was to have such a committed partner." His thumb rubs away my tears as they fall. "Most of all, I'm sorry he hurt you and I can't take that pain away."

"You are too good to me." The urge to sob hits me square in the chest, but I hold it back. "God, I missed you."

"I missed you too." He swallows hard, pulling his hand back and shoving it into his pocket.

I long for his touch as soon as it's gone. I consider flinging myself into his arms, holding tight and refusing to let him go. But there's still so much to say. So much to apologize for and work out, if that's even something he's open to.

"Maeve." Rosalie's voice cuts through the night. "They're looking for you."

I sigh. "I have to go back in."

"Yeah, go." Rainer nods, taking one step back. "Go."

I hate that we can't finish this conversation, but duty calls. I take several steps toward the barn before turning around. "Rainer?"

He hasn't moved and his gaze is steady as it meets mine. "Yeah?"

"Stay. Please?"

"Okay, I'll stay." He offers me the smallest of smiles, and my heart leaps in response.

Relief floods my veins as I walk away, catching up to where Rosalie waits.

"Are you okay?" she asks.

"Yeah. Why?" I brush off her question and walk a little faster.

"Oh, I don't know." She keeps up with my pace. "Maybe because in all the weeks we've met up for book club, you failed to share you're pregnant again, and your best friend looks like you kicked his puppy."

"Rainer doesn't have a dog." I swallow hard.

"Oh, okay." She laughs, raising her brows. "I'm letting this go.

At least for now. But if you need to vent or scream or cry or whatever, I'm here. And always a phone call away." She reaches for my arm and we both stop before entering the barn. "Maeve, I know what it's like for your entire world to fall apart. And I know what it's like to feel totally alone or that somehow sharing what you're going through is a burden to others. But you aren't. You don't need to carry all of this alone. We were all giving you your space because of everything going on with your dad, but if I had known it was more . . ."

"You would have shown up on my doorstep with casseroles?"

"Bernadette would, but come on." Rosalie rolls her eyes. "You know I don't cook. It would be takeout from the diner."

"I'm sorry I didn't tell you or the rest of the group." I press my palm against my stomach. "I didn't know how to."

"I get that." She exhales a rush of breath that's almost a laugh. "Boy, do I get that. But you don't owe anyone an explanation. Just let us be here for you."

"Be patient with us, folks, we're still tracking down the matron of honor, then we'll get started with our speeches," the DJ says from inside.

"Shit." Rosalie winces. "We better get you inside. Unless you need a minute? I can stall them."

I appreciate the offer, but it will only put off the inevitable. "No, that's okay. Let's get this over with."

"That's the wedding spirit," she says, and we both laugh, rejoining the party. "Found her! Told you all to check the restrooms," she announces as we make our way through the guests, narrowing her gaze at the concerned stares from my brothers. "Pregnancy equals squished bladder."

I flash her an appreciative smile as I join my family at the front of the room. We all take turns, Ryan and Jackson roasting our brother, then Wild offering a speech that brings tears to everyone's eyes, including my own. When the microphone is passed to me, I decide to ditch what I prepared and speak from the heart.

"Well, that's just unfair, having to follow you." I shoot my brother a mock glare and earn a few laughs. My gaze moves to Sarah. "I want to apologize. I won't be as funny or as eloquent as my brothers, yet somehow, I've still found a way to become the center of attention at my own brother's wedding." I flash her a grin. "It's a talent that comes with being the only girl in a family with four brothers." I turn to the crowd, addressing the elephant in the room. "I basically planned the inception of this child around their wedding." My stretch of the truth lands as intended, and the chuckles throughout the room lighten my anxiety.

"Growing up with four brothers, there isn't a lot of tenderness and affection. There's wrestling and competition, though." I can't help but smile as childhood memories come together in my mind like shapes in a kaleidoscope. "My first introduction to marriage and to the meaning of love, came from our parents. They taught us the power of hard work, and that at the end of the day nothing is more important than family. But my second examples of love were Ryan and Val, and you and Aiden. I was just a kid, but Lord, did I idolize y'all. That's when I learned there was more to a relationship than hard work. It took devotion, loyalty, and commitment. It also involved fun. Yeah, I caught the two of you making out in this very barn on more than one occasion." I bug out my eyes, earning more laughter. "*Just* kissing. Thankfully."

Aiden and Sarah share knowing smiles, and I'm struck by the way they still look at each other the way they did back then.

"But that's how I know y'all are going to make it through anything life throws your way. It's not the time or the years you spent together and apart. It's not even the way my brother lights up the second you walk into the room, or the way you reach for his hand without even thinking about it." I grin, glancing to where their hands are joined this very moment.

"But the reason everyone in this room knows the two of you share a bond that can never be broken is because we are looking at two best friends. You were meant for each other, and even when life tried to pull you apart, it couldn't because nothing compares to that bond." Emotion tightens in my chest. "A person who knows you better than you know yourself. A person who holds up a mirror, even when it's painful."

I've done a spectacular job pretending Rainer isn't in this room. But my eyes can't help but search for his, and like a magnet unable to turn anywhere else, when I find him staring I can't look away. "A person who loves you for everything you are, never expecting anything in return. Loving you, because you are their person and they couldn't stop even if they tried." I clear my throat and lift up my glass, turning back to my brother and his bride. "To Aiden and Sarah. May you spend the rest of your days loving your best friend."

I hand the mic back to the DJ as everyone in the room echoes the sentiment, and make my way over to the happy couple.

"I love you, little sister." Aiden pulls me into a hug.

"Love you too." I step out of his embrace to hug Sarah. "And thank God you are officially family because I need another sister to balance out all this testosterone. Love you."

"I love you too." She squeezes me tight, then pulls back. "Now maybe you can find a happily ever after with your best friend?" She glances briefly to where Rainer stands across the room before meeting my eyes.

"Maybe." I force a laugh. "But I think I've drawn enough gossip during your wedding already, maybe we just focus on you and Aiden."

"Let them talk." Sarah shrugs. "I just want to see you happy."

I nod, blinking back emotion. "I want that too."

"Okay, let's heat things up on this dance floor, shall we?" the

DJ says over the speakers. "Can I get all the couples out here for our next song, including our bride and groom?"

"That's us, babe." Aiden holds out his hand.

Sarah beams, letting him pull her out to the dance floor.

I look on as more and more couples join them. My pulse thrills as Rainer makes his way around the periphery to where I stand.

"Shall we?" He holds his hand out when only a few feet separate us.

"That depends." What will everyone think? Hell, why do I care? Everyone in town is already making their assumptions. "Are we a real couple?"

"Maeve." He takes a step forward, reaching for my hand while his other slides over my hip. Goosebumps race across my skin and my breath catches as he moves his lips to the shell of my ear. "There's nothing fake between you and me."

It's as if his words strike a match, lighting me up from the inside and warming my body as we sway to the music. It feels so good to be in his strong arms. To let him lead. To know that no matter what I do, he is here for me, a steady partner who always lifts me up.

"How are you feeling?"

I answer his question honestly. "Better now."

"How are the kids?" He pulls back enough to meet my gaze. "I've missed them."

"They're doing okay. Jamie is watching them tonight."

"Okay, folks," the DJ interrupts, the music lowering for his brief interjection. "If you're out there dancing and you've been together one year or more, you keep dancing. Everyone else, it's your time to be excused."

"I guess that's us," Rainer says.

"Yeah, I guess so." We were barely together for a few weeks, yet that doesn't seem to encompass the magnitude of our relationship.

Rainer holds my hand and leads us off to the side. He pulls out a chair at one of the tables, and I take a seat. He scoots his chair next to mine and we watch as the crowd on the dance floor gets smaller and smaller until only four couples remain.

"Fifty years. Wow, folks. How beautiful is that?" the DJ says.

I've attended dozens of weddings, and this tradition has always been one of my favorites. I always imagined being one of those couples still on the dance floor, swaying in my husband's arms. Imagined being more in love than the day we met while others looked on. That maybe one day we would be the final couple left, celebrating forty or even fifty years together, a testament to true commitment and the power of love.

But that won't happen.

Not now.

Tears prick my eyes, but I refuse to let my smile drop.

I don't want to be with Alex, but this is just one of many little things I have to grieve. I'm thirty-two and about to be divorced. The future I envisioned, the one I thought I had, is gone.

I love Rainer, but there's no guarantee that will result in marriage. What we have is too new, and after the betrayal I've experienced, it's not as if I'm clamoring to race down the aisle. But we only get so many years on this earth, and my chance of celebrating a fiftieth wedding anniversary with anyone is almost basically impossible. It's silly, really, but letting that vision for myself go, hurts so deeply.

"Hey, you okay?" Rainer's voice cuts through my thoughts.

"Yeah." I nod, even though I'm anything but. I blink back my tears and shove to my feet. "I'm going to use the restroom."

I turn away from Rainer and practically power walk to the back of the barn before he or anyone else catches sight of the first tear to fall. And it's a good thing I do, because once they start flowing, I can't make them stop.

28

RAINER

MAEVE BEELINES out the back door of the barn before I have a chance to catch up. Not wanting to draw attention, I wait until I'm outside before calling after her retreating form. "Maeve!"

She doesn't stop or slow down, but I close the space between us with a jog to block her path. My soul squeezes almost painfully at the tears streaming down her beautiful face. "Hey, what's wrong?" We were having a good time. At least I was. I don't know what shifted, but I want to make it right.

"It's nothing." She sniffles. "Just give me a minute."

"Maeve. It's not nothing if it makes you feel bad. Tell me."

"It's just that I realized, I'll never get that." She throws her hands up and motions toward the barn. "Those couples on the dance floor, the ones who were still there after the DJ called forty years or more." She inhales a sharp breath and looks up at the night sky. "I always thought I would be one of those couples."

Relief chases away my early concern, and in its place comes empathy. I understand all too well what it's like to grieve the loss of the life you always imagined. "This might not make you feel any better, but tonight I got to live one of my dreams."

"What's that?"

"Every wedding I've ever been at when they do that couple dance?" I crowd her personal space and press my lips to the corner of her mouth. "I've always wished I could be out there with you."

"That does make me feel a little better." Her lips lift with the hint of a smile.

I wrap my hands around her waist and tug her closer. "Sure, we don't have a twenty-plus-year marriage, but you have been my best friend since I was eight years old. I think that's more significant than anything. You will always be my best friend first. Anything else you give me, like tonight, is icing on the cake."

"Rainer." Her gaze drifts to my mouth.

"Yeah?"

"I don't know what I did to deserve you." She presses a kiss to my lips. Her hands rest on my shoulders, and the heat of her body pressed against mine sends a thrill down my spine. I don't think I'll ever get over this. Kissing her. Holding her. It's a fucking dream come to life.

Her lips move, gentle and hesitating, almost as if she's unsure about taking this kiss any deeper. Desire thrums through my veins, but I let her set the pace, and when she pulls away, I try not to be disappointed.

"I'm really happy you're here, and that you still want to be my best friend." She meets my stare. "I know that I hurt you, and I don't think there's any way I can ever take that back. But if you'll let me, I want to show you how good we can be together. I'm a mess, and being pregnant with my soon-to-be ex-husband's child is probably not the best time to start a relationship." She chuckles wryly. "But I don't want to waste another day. I want to be with you, real and honest and out in the open this time."

"That's all I've ever wanted." I can't hold back my smile. "Easy days with you."

"Easy days with you." She presses a kiss to my lips. "I want that too."

God, she feels so good in my arms. As if we were made for each other and the universe finally got the memo. We're right where we belong, and I'm never letting her go.

Her hands play with the collar of my dress shirt. "How do you think my brothers will react when we tell them we're together?" She glances over to the barn.

"About that . . ." Quiet laughter rattles my chest. "I don't think we were as sneaky as we thought. They already know. Or at least, they know enough. Your brothers sort of threatened me on the cattle drive."

She narrows her gaze. "They did not."

I laugh. "They did. Though, I don't think they were serious. At least not all of them."

"I guess it doesn't matter how old I am, I'll always be their sister who needs protecting." She sighs. "I'm sorry."

"I'm not." I shake my head. "I want everything when it comes to you. Big brother warnings about breaking your heart and all."

She lowers her gaze to my lips as my fingers rub languid circles at the small of her back. The silky fabric is the only barrier between my hands and her skin. I close my eyes and imagine stripping it off. Fuck, I want her. I hold back a frustrated groan. It's been too many days without her touch, her taste, her love.

"So." Maeve leans forward and presses a kiss against my skin before she whispers at the shell of my ear, "Crazy idea." It's the gentlest of touches, almost teasing, and my body responds, roaring to attention with lust.

It takes all my willpower to not drag her somewhere more private. "I'm listening."

"Why don't we go back to your place?"

She doesn't need to ask twice. I'm down for that. "How much longer do you have to stay? Any more bridesmaid duties?"

"The only thing they have left is to cut the cake and I'm not needed for that." She grins, taking a step back and reaching for my hand. "So, what do you say? Should we blow this pop stand?"

"You don't want dessert?"

"Only if I get to have you."

"Fuck." I tug her arm, pulling her to my side. "Let's go."

Her laughter rings through the night air as we practically race to my truck, and it's the most delightful sound. Doesn't matter that we're grown adults, I feel like a fucking teenager, sneaking away from the party to be with my girl. All the challenges that existed a few hours ago haven't lessened, but somehow when I'm with Maeve they feel a whole hell of a lot lighter.

29

MAEVE

I HAVE NEVER BEEN MORE thankful Rainer's house is only a fifteen-minute drive from the ranch. The desire to be with him, to strip away all our clothes and defenses, is all consuming. I want to feel his body over mine, his strong arms braced above my shoulders as he thrusts inside me. *Fuck*. My cheeks are flushed and my body is warm all over as Rainer pulls into the drive.

"Wait there," he demands, exiting his door and walking around the front to come around to open my door. This man. Chivalrous down to his core, yet I never feel caged in or stifled by his actions. Only cherished.

"Thank you." I hold on to his shoulder as I step down, delighting in the way his arms wrap around my waist. The heat in his gaze is intense, and my entire body tightens with need. I need him. Now. If he doesn't take me inside, his neighbors are about to get quite the show.

"Come on," he practically growls, pulling me to his front door. He unlocks it, pushing it open and allowing me to pass through. He's right behind me, his body my shadow. As soon as we cross the threshold, he tugs my arm, closing the door and whirling around to press my back against the hard wood. He captures my mouth, along with my gasp of breath.

Our hands move with urgency, tugging at buttons and zippers, yanking away fabric until we're both breathing heavily and clad only in our underwear.

He drops to his knees, his hands wide as they palm my stomach. "She's growing," he whispers reverently, looking up at me from his place on the floor.

"Yeah." I nod.

"You are amazing, you know that?" He caresses my skin and presses a kiss to my baby bump, then another and another, lower and lower until he's between my legs. "Fucking incredible." He hooks his fingers into the waistband of my panties and drags them down my legs as if he has all the time in the world.

"Rainer." I hear the neediness in my own voice, but I'm not embarrassed. I don't feel one ounce of shame for the way I need this man. My legs tremble as the scruff of his beard brushes against my inner thighs.

"I got you, baby." His words are a promise, because a second later his mouth is on my center. Licking, sucking, finding the place and pace that make me want to fall apart. I press my head back into the door, my fingers weaving into his hair and holding him there.

"Fingers," I beg. "Add your fingers."

He pulls his face away. "I don't want to hurt you or the baby."

"You won't." I pull him back to where I'm an aching, wet mess. "I promise. Please."

"You like it when I eat this pussy?" The rumble of his voice sends a shiver up my spine.

"Yes." I tug at his short locks. "I fucking love it." My breaths come faster as he slides several fingers inside me. When he pumps them and flicks my clit with his tongue, I almost groan in relief. "Yes. There. More of that. Don't stop. Faster. Don't be gentle." Encouragement and direction tumble past my lips.

He moans against my body, his ministrations increasing in pressure and pace. *That's it. Right there.* I'm so keyed up, so fucking in love. It won't take much more to push me over the edge.

Squeezing my eyes shut and focusing on the sensations, I begin to rock my hips against his mouth. Our shallow breaths. The smack of his lips. Throaty moans. His fingers digging into my thigh. They overwhelm me, coming together with my body's most natural response.

"Yes. Yes. Yes." I fall over the edge. Soaring, crashing, riding the wave of my orgasm. A shiver runs through my entire body and my legs almost give out. It's not until I'm catching my breath that I realize my fingers are still holding Rainer against my body.

Not that he complains. His mouth licks and kisses, lapping up the evidence of my orgasm. The sight turns me on, and when he draws his fingers out, my body aches for him to replace them with his cock.

His satisfied smirk meets my stare as he rests back on his heels. "I could do that every day."

"Every single day?"

"Every. Single. Day." He licks his lips, then pushes off the floor and pulls me into his arms. His beard glistens in the dim light and I smell myself on him. "I have a perfect record. In case you're keeping count."

I can't help but laugh. "You're awfully smug."

"I'm just saying, for someone who apparently has a difficult time reaching orgasm, I'm feeling like a stud."

He might very well be, but I also have my suspicions about this topic. "I hate to break it to you, cowboy. But it's not all you."

"I beg to differ. Pretty sure it was my mouth on your clit and my fingers in your pussy that made you come." Fuck. When he talks like that, I want to push him down on his sofa and ride his face.

"It's also my elevated hormones. Second-trimester horniness."

"Is that the technical term?"

"It should be." I laugh.

"I don't mind getting a little help from Mother Nature." He takes my hand in his and leads me to his bedroom.

"I just don't want you to get too cocky. The job might get a little harder as time goes on." In his bedroom, I release his hand and climb onto his bed, scooting back on the mattress and lying back to rest on my forearms.

"I'm up for the challenge." He shoves his boxer briefs to the floor, his erect penis bobbing to attention. "And I love the sound of us being together for the long haul."

A slow smile takes over my face as he approaches the bed. "I think it's safe to say, you're never getting rid of me now."

"Because of my mad oral skills?" He crawls over my body.

"Because of your heart." I press my palm against the center of his chest before meeting his stare. "Your prowess in the bedroom doesn't hurt, though."

"That so?" The playful lift of his brows pushes a giggle past my lips, but he swallows it up. His mouth slanting with mine as he lines himself up to my center and pushes inside. Inch by inch, he works himself into the hilt. Each powerful thrust is controlled, and I wrap my legs around the back of his, wanting to keep him close. Needing to stay connected.

I brush my fingers through his chest hair, finding his nipples and brushing them with my thumbs.

He sucks in a breath.

"Do you like that?" I ask, delighted to find another pleasure spot on this man's body.

"Yeah." He rocks his hips forward.

"What about this?" I lift my head and brush my tongue against his pert nipple.

"Fuck, Maeve," he groans in a rush. "Do that again and you'll make me come."

I like watching him unravel. Even more so, I love being in control of his undoing. It's only fair after the way he worked my body over. "Like this?" This time when I brush my lips across his sensitive skin, I suck.

"Fuck." A guttural sound presses past Rainer's parted lips. His body tenses, and his hips thrust forward in one powerful movement, filling me so right, I forget to breathe. His body sags in relief, the pulsing of his cock inside of me coinciding with the spasms that ripple through him. He only stays on top of my body for a short moment before he lifts his weight off and rolls to the side.

I turn to face him, running my fingers down his arm until I find his hand.

"You know"—he threads our fingers together—"I would have lasted longer if you hadn't done that."

"Totally worth it." And it was. I think I'm going to love discovering all the little ways to drive this man wild in the bedroom.

"Do you need anything? Water? Snacks?"

"Rainer." I can't hold in my smile. I love the way he cares for me, and his concern is sweet, even if it is a little over the top. "I'm fine. It was sex, not a marathon."

"I just want to make sure you're comfortable."

"I'm always comfortable when I'm with you." That's why I've been able to orgasm. Because with him there's no pressure. No expectations or hurt egos. I'm not as stressed either. With him I don't carry the mental load of raising kids and running a household on my own. I'm sure that plays a part. No doubt I won't always come, but when I don't, I can't see him punishing me with the silent treatment or accusing me of taking care of my needs without him.

"You probably can't stay here all night," Rainer says, interrupting my thoughts.

"Definitely not." I sigh. Though, I wish I could. "Jamie's watching the kids, but I didn't plan to be gone overnight."

He raises his head and cranes his neck to look at the clock. "I should drive you home."

I change back into my dress and gather my things while Rainer changes into a pair of jeans and a shirt. He looked amazing in his suit, but I quite prefer this look on him. My cowboy. The drive to the house goes by too quickly, and before I know it, he's getting out of his seat and coming around to help me down.

My feet slow as we approach the porch steps. I'm not ready to say goodnight. I don't want him to leave. "Do you want to come inside?"

He glances at the house. Jamie is peeking, not so stealthily, from behind the curtains. He grins before meeting my gaze. "I don't know, is that a good idea?"

"Not to sleep on the couch this time."

"You want to play a board game, don't you?"

I tip my head back, my laughter drifting into the night air. Taking a step forward, I loop my arms around his shoulders and lean into his body. "I want to know what it feels like to fall asleep next to you, and wake up with you the next morning. And then I want to do it again, every single night. If you'll let me."

"I want that too. Fuck, that's all I want." His brows furrow as he searches my face. "But if you need more time, we don't have to rush."

"I'm done with slow. I don't need time. I don't need to be on my own, or to see other people. I already know it's you I belong with."

"It's about damn time." His lips lift in a grin before pressing against mine. "I've always known."

I pull back and narrow my gaze. "You're going to remind me of that often, aren't you?"

"Damn straight." He winks. "Now, come on, let's go relieve Jamie for the night and get you changed into something more comfortable. We've got a cutthroat game of Clue calling our names."

30

RAINER

THERE IS nothing more perfect than waking up next to Maeve. Okay, maybe the only way this gets better is when we're in a place we both call home. But Rome wasn't built in a day. I'm a patient man. We've fast-tracked so many elements to our relationship, and I'm confident that when she's ready, we'll settle into a bigger place together. There's no rush. Besides, I paid the rent through the end of the year. There's change on the horizon, and the kids have been through enough already; I'm not looking to upend everything steady in their lives.

I'm proud to be one of their constants. It's not as if I'm a new guy they've never met. I've changed diapers. I've cut food into bite-size pieces, dressed up like a princess for tea parties, and rocked each one of them back to sleep when they were babies. I've dried tears and answered hard questions. I've been in this with Maeve from the beginning. Been the best friend I could be. I've always wanted to raise a big family with Maeve, and now I get to do that fully. She's made me the luckiest man on earth.

"Hey." She blinks her eyes open and yawns, stretching out

next to me on the bed. Her brow furrows, her voice low. "Are they still asleep?"

"Yeah." I nod. I was surprised too. Jamie either wore them out or slipped them cold medicine. I'm certain it's the first option. "I checked on everyone when I made coffee."

"You made coffee?" Maeve perks up.

"I did." I grin, leaning forward to brush my lips against hers. "I know it's your favorite way to wake up."

"Second favorite."

"Oh?"

Her hand runs along my chest. "I like having you here in my bed."

"Funny. I was thinking the same thing." I push up on my elbow and roll her to her back, capturing her lips in a kiss that steals both our breaths.

"Mama!" Lulu's sweet but demanding voice calls through the closed door. She jiggles the knob from the other side.

Maeve glances at my lips with longing. "Let's continue this later."

I smile and push off the bed, moving to unlock the door before Lulu breaks through, or more likely, before she wakes her brothers.

"Mama!" She beams when the door opens. She races to the bed and climbs into her mother's arms, tackling her with a hug. It's only then she notices me standing by the door. "Rain Rain?"

"Hey, girlie." I walk to the bed and pick her up. Hugging her to my chest, I meet Maeve's stare and ask, "Do you have any plans for the day?"

"No." She bites at her lower lip, her gaze drifting where her hands rub together.

"You want to visit your dad?" I ask, setting Lulu back down on her feet.

"That obvious?" Her smile is sad.

"I just know you, and I know your heart."

She gets out of bed and starts pulling the covers into place. "It's almost three hours round trip, and they won't let children inside."

I move to the other side of the bed and help her make it. "I know."

Her gaze snaps to mine. "You know?"

"I called Ryan before you woke up."

"Oh?"

"And I bribed Riley to come babysit." I toss one of the pillows over to her side, then smooth out the top blanket. "She'll be here at ten."

"You arranged for a sitter so we could visit my dad?" Maeve doesn't move. Her eyes get that misty look that fucking kills me. I'm sure she's extra emotional because of the pregnancy hormones, but she's been through more than anyone should have to go through while growing a human.

"I don't want you to have to go alone." I walk around the bed and slide my hands around her waist. I hate the pain etched on her face. I want to see her smile again. "Besides, I think you kind of like being a passenger, princess."

"Rainer." She huffs out a soft laugh.

"Yeah?"

Her fingers rub along my beard as she cups my face in her hands. "I love you so much. You know that, right?" She presses a kiss to my lips.

"I think you should remind me again."

"How about I remind you every damn day?"

I kiss her back. "Deal."

FROM MY CALL WITH RYAN, I knew things were bad, but nothing really prepares you for seeing someone on death's door.

Especially when only weeks ago Mr. Wilder was perfectly healthy.

We've been in his room for over an hour, and as hard as it is to see Pops so sick, it's harder witnessing the toll it takes on Maeve. He's not eating, and because of that, his strength is too low to rehab his surgery. Everything is exacerbated by his dementia. He doesn't understand where he is or that he's running on borrowed time.

"I'm going to see if I can speak with his doctors." Maeve pushes to her feet.

"Want me to come?" I move to join her.

"Stay here with Pops . . . in case he wakes up?"

"Of course." I wish I could do more to ease her worries, but I am happy to stay if that's what she needs. "Come get me if you need anything."

"I will." She nods before slipping out the door.

I sit in silence, watching the soft fall of Mr. Wilder's chest with each exhale. He's slept most of the time we've been here, and that only adds to the worry I have for his recovery.

He can't leave us. Not yet.

There's something I need to tell him.

"Hey, Mr. Wilder. Sir." I clear the emotion from my throat, speaking out loud in hopes he somehow hears my words. "I know you've had a rough go of everything lately. But I need you to hold on a little longer. I need you to stay and fight. You have another grandkid on the way, and Maeve, she might be tough and independent and whip smart, but she still needs her daddy. We all need you."

I watch the green light dip and rise rhythmically on the digital screen monitoring his heart rate. Growing up, I was terrified of this man. He was larger than life. Stern and tolerated zero bullshit. It's humbling seeing him this way. Without the spitfire in his tone and serious stare, he appears so frail. A shadow of his former self.

But he didn't end up like this overnight. It was a slow and painful process, his dementia stealing pieces of his memories and independence. Stealing moments with his children. No one's fault, and yet so much heartache. So much worry.

I try not to think about what will happen if he doesn't pull through this. The decisions Maeve and her brothers will be forced to make. They've already lost so much, it doesn't seem fair. A panic stirs in my chest, for all the things I want to tell him, and ask him, before it's too late.

"And, Mr. Wilder, I want you to know that no matter what happens, I'm going to take care of Maeve. She won't want for anything. I will provide for her and the kids, and I will love them with my whole damn heart. I promise to always make her days easier. And I will make sure she always has time for the things that bring her joy. The things she loves just for herself, like riding horses and creating stickers, and sunrises with yoga, and whatever else she wants to try. I won't let her forget who she is or hold her back from growing."

Emotion presses heavy on the center of my chest and I blink back tears as they fill my eyes. "And you don't have to answer me, because, well, it won't happen tomorrow, but when the time's right, you should know I intend to ask your daughter to marry me. I hope when that day comes that I have your blessing. Because I respect the hell out of you, and Maeve is the greatest gift in my life. You probably already know this, but you helped raise one of the kindest, most hard-working, beautiful humans I've had the pleasure to know. She's an incredible mother, and my best friend. My world would be bare without her, and I'm forever grateful you welcomed me into your home all those years ago, and that I had the opportunity to spend so many hours with your family on the ranch. I wouldn't be the man I am today without that."

The creak of the door opening straightens my spine.

"Hey." I scrub a hand over my beard and blow out a ragged

breath, turning in my chair to meet Maeve's stare. "Did you find his doctor?"

"Yeah." She nods, blinking rapidly, though a few tears escape anyway. "It's not great."

"Oh, baby." I push to my feet and close the short distance, pulling her into my arms. "I'm sorry."

"I just wish he would fight. You know?" She sniffles into my shoulder. "Because I'm not ready to say goodbye."

"I know." Fuck. I wish I could take this pain from her. I rub her back until she pulls out of my embrace.

"Can we sit with him a little longer?"

"We'll stay as long as you want."

She takes a seat and I drag my chair closer so I can hold her hand. We sit in silence, the occasional beep of medical monitoring breaking up the passing seconds. There's nothing to discuss, no conversation to lighten the gravity of this situation. Still, I want to make it better for Maeve. An idea pops into my mind. I squeeze her hand. "Are you okay for a few minutes on your own?"

"Yeah."

"Just give me a few minutes." I flash her a reassuring smile before I walk out of the room. Hustling through the hospital and down to my truck, I dig around the glove box, grinning when I find what I came for. I make my way back inside and through security, retracing my steps back to Mr. Wilder's room.

Maeve lifts her gaze as I push open the door. "That was fast."

"Told you." I wink, taking a seat and orienting my chair so we're facing each other. I produce the deck of cards with a hesitant smile. "I thought we could play."

"Yeah?" She glances at her father's resting form. "He would like that."

"Maybe listening to his daughter lose will put some fire in him."

"Lose?" She gasps. "You're kidding, right? Pops taught me everything I know."

"Yeah, well, you're not the only one with a father who loves cards." I chuckle, shuffling the deck. "What are we playing?"

"Texas Hold 'Em." She relaxes her shoulders for the first time since stepping foot in this hospital room. For the next several hours I distract her with a healthy dose of competition. It's the perfect way to pass the time, and I'm happy to give Maeve this time with her father, even if he's not awake for most of it.

When the sun hangs low in the sky outside the hospital windows, I put the cards away while Maeve shares an emotional goodbye with her father. All I can do is hold her hand as we walk out of the hospital together, that and pray Pops pulls through.

"Let's go home," I say as we reach the truck. I unlock her door and help steady her as she climbs inside.

"Rainer?" Her eyes meet mine, and it breaks my heart to see the weariness in them. This has been a long, stressful day. "Where is home?" Her chin trembles, a tear escaping down her cheek. "You paid my rent, didn't you?"

I nod, but I want her to know it doesn't matter. I'll live wherever she wants. On her family's ranch, my house, her rental, or someplace new. "Home is where ever you want to be." I lean inside the cab and press a soft kiss to her lips, then shake my head, correcting myself. "My home is wherever you are. It always has been. It always will be."

EPILOGUE
RAINER

Four months later

"OKAY, on the count of three I want you to give me another big push," the doctor says from his position between Maeve's legs.

"You can do this, sweetheart. You are so strong. You're almost there," I encourage her, my body tense and anticipation high.

Maeve lets loose a guttural groan, pushing at the doctor's command as myself and a nurse help by supporting her legs. We've been at this for what feels like an eternity, but is likely only an hour. I've always held a great amount of respect for Maeve, but the experience of being in this room as she gives birth leaves me utterly amazed.

"There's the head," the doctor says cheerfully. "I know you're tired but give us one more big push and you get to meet your daughter."

Maeve bears down harder, her hand squeezing mine until I'm certain she's cut off circulation to all of our fingers.

I watch in awe as our daughter is pulled from between her legs.

"Congratulations mom and dad." One of the nurses holds up the baby for Maeve to see better. "Meet your new baby girl."

Maeve smiles, a bubble of laughter mixing with her tears. I wipe the sweat from her brow and then kiss her forehead. "You did it. You are amazing. I love you so much."

"Would you like to do the honors?" the doctor asks as the umbilical cord is clamped and a pair of scissors are procured by the nurse.

Emotion overcomes me as I partake in a ritual I've only seen on television up until now. It's an honor to be in this room, and be a part of this child's birth. It doesn't matter that biologically she's not mine, because with every beat of my heart I promise to always protect her and love her as if I were the one to help create her.

There is a rush of movement around the room as the baby is weighed and examined. Within minutes, the nurses place our daughter on Maeve's chest for skin to skin contact, and the memory of this moment is branded on my soul.

She's so tiny, and I feel the urge to count her little fingers and stare into her wide eyes, wondering if they'll be the same shade of brown as her mama's. Will she look like Lulu when she's older? Or will she favor her brothers?

"She's perfect," Maeve whispers.

"She is. Just like you."

Maeve glances up at me. "Will you take a few pictures and text them to the family?"

"You don't want to make them wait?" I chuckle with a grin as I pull out my phone. I stand back, tapping the screen and capturing this perfect moment for everyone to see. "I'm pretty sure they're all on their way by now." I texted them when it was time to push.

"Ryan and Val are bringing the kids?"

"They should be here within the hour." I set my phone down.

"Oh, good." There's relief in her smile. "I can't wait for them to meet her."

"Me too."

"What about Alex?" Her eyes lower to the baby. It hasn't been easy for any of us, but we are all doing our best to handle this situation with maturity and grace. Maeve has allowed Alex weekly visitations with the kids. Sometimes he shows up, others he doesn't. His communication still sucks.

We each have our feelings on the matter, but the most difficult of them all is witnessing the disappointment on Ari's face when Alex doesn't show. Lulu and Collin are too young to pay much attention to what day it is or how long it's been since they've talked to their dad. I wish I could make it all better, or take away the pain he's caused his own family, but I can't. All I can do is continue to show up, and to love and care for them the way they deserve.

"Let me check." Retrieving my phone again, I'm surprised at the message I find from Alex. "He's here. He wants to meet her."

Maeve's eyes are full of tears as they meet mine.

"Do you want me to go get him?" I swallow my pride and ask.

Maeve nods. "Yes. Please."

"Okay. I'll be right back." I press another kiss to her forehead and then lean down to brush my lips against the warm skin of our baby. "Welcome to the world, sweet girl. We're so glad you're here."

"Rainer." Maeve reaches for my hand before I move away.

I hold it and give it a squeeze.

"Thank you."

"You don't have to thank me. I'm right where I want to be."

She releases my hand and I walk out into the hallway, weaving my way through the space until I reach the waiting area. Alex is there, pacing, his eyes full of worry until they meet mine. "Is she okay?"

I don't know if he means the baby or Maeve, but the answer is the same. "Everyone is healthy and doing great. Would you like to come back and meet her?"

Alex glances around the room before lifting his gaze to mine. "Only if it's okay with Maeve."

"Yeah, it is. Come on back." I lead the way back to the room, Alex following closely behind. We don't talk, almost as if we're both acutely aware of the other's role in this unconventional family.

When we reach the room, I hold the door open for him.

He hesitates a moment before entering, but as soon as his eyes fall on the baby girl snuggled on Maeve's chest, he approaches the bed. "Oh, Maeve. She's beautiful."

Maeve smiles, her gaze transfixed on the baby. "She really is."

"Did you pick out a name?" His gaze darts to mine before returning to Maeve's.

"Cassandra. Cassie for short."

"After your mom." He smiles.

"Yes."

"It suits her." Alex shoves his hands into the pockets of his jeans and rocks back on his heels. "When are the kids coming to meet her?"

"They're on their way." Maeve glances at me. "Along with the rest of my family."

Alex nods, biting the inside of his cheek. "I should go."

"You don't have to," Maeve says.

"You're welcome to stay a while," I add when his gaze drifts to mine. As much as I don't really want him to be here, this isn't about what I want. We all have to find a way to coexist, because it's what's best for the children.

"I've got a job that starts tomorrow." He drops his gaze to the floor. "But thanks for letting me meet her."

"Of course." Maeve stares at Cassie, her smile sad. "I would never keep you from knowing your daughter."

Alex's jaw works back and forth. He sniffles as if he's about to cry. "I should go. Y'all take care." He dips his chin and turns to leave the room. He pauses at my side, not lifting his stare from the floor as his voice drops. "Take good care of them."

"Always." As if I would do anything else.

Shortly after Alex's departure, we're moved to another room where Maeve and the baby will stay for the duration of their visit. I eye the small sofa in the corner, my bed for the next few nights. Not that I'm complaining.

"I saw that." Maeve chuckles, her eyes heavy with exhaustion.

"Just admiring my accommodations." I rock the tiny bundle of joy in my arms.

"You can go back to the house with the big kids tonight." Her lips curve with a smile as she watches me holding Cassie. "I've done this several times. We'll be fine on our own, and I can always page a nurse."

"You know I love sleeping on sofas," I coo softly as Cassie begins to fuss.

"That one seems a bit small, even for you."

"You calling me short?" I grin.

"No." She shakes her head. "You're just right."

My phone vibrates from its place in my back pocket. I move closer to the hospital bed and turn to the side. "I just got a text. Can you check to see if it's the kids?"

"If this is a ploy to get me to touch your butt, you could just ask," she teases as she pulls out my phone. She swipes across the screen, her smile beaming as it lifts to mine. "They're here!"

"Where should I put her? In her bassinet?"

"No." Maeve adjusts herself in the bed, sitting up and shoving a few pillows around her body. When she's done, she lifts her hands. "Give her to me."

"Okay, sweet girl." I hand her off. "Time to go back to your mama." Maeve and I share smiles full of excitement before I walk out of the room to retrieve our family. Everyone is in the waiting room this time, and I almost laugh. Between the gifts, the bags of takeout food, and the sheer number of people, they take up the entire room.

"There he is!" Aiden nods. "The proud papa."

I'm enveloped in hugs and congratulations from Maeve's brothers, their partners, Maeve's kids, and all the nieces and nephews.

"I wanna hold my baby," Lulu demands, her arms folding over her chest.

"Cassie is not your baby," Riley says. "She's your sister, like Tess is my sister, and you have to be very gentle with her."

"She's my baby," Lulu mutters, her chin lifting in defiance.

"Hey, girlie." I scoop her off the floor. "Let's go see your mama and Cassie."

Ari walks at my side, Ryan following behind with Collin on his shoulders. The nurses stop and stare at our group as we make our way to the recovery room. I have no doubt they'll kick almost everyone out soon enough. But as long as everyone gets a chance to see the baby first, we'll be just fine.

"Hi, Ari. Hi, Lulu." Maeve beams from her bed as we enter the room. "Collin." She laughs. "Everyone. Thanks for coming."

"Of course." Aiden grins. "Couldn't pass up a chance to meet the latest addition to the Wilder clan."

"Mama." Lulu's sour face breaks long enough to scramble down from my hold and race to the edge of the bed. "My baby?" Her eyes are wide with wonder as they dart between her swaddled sister and her mother's face.

"This is baby Cassie. Isn't she cute?"

"That's her baby," someone whispers from the back, causing most of the room to erupt in laughter.

Lulu moves closer, patting her sister and pushing up on her tiptoes to press a kiss to Cassie's knit beanie.

Ari is more cautious in his approach, observing with worried eyes before moving to his mother's side. His little face lights up with a smile as soon as he takes in his new sister, and it's the most heart-warming sight.

I take Collin from Ryan's arms and bring him over, pulling him in my lap as we sit on the chair next to the bed. Questions fire off faster than we can answer them, both from the kids and from Maeve's family.

How long will we be in the hospital?

When was the last time we ate?

Are we hungry?

Who does she look like more, Ari, Lulu, or Collin?

Why can't she talk?

The last question coming from Lulu when Cassie begins to fuss. It's chaotic, and loud, and so full of love. My chest fills with pride, for this family and this life we've created. We might have gotten a rocky start, but it was all worth it in the end, because it led us here. Sometimes a wild crush leads to heartache. Sometimes it leads to the best damn decision of your life. There's no room for regret, not when you have everything you've ever wanted.

BONUS EPILOGUE
MAEVE

Five months later

"Is this one ready, Mama?" Ari points to one of the cucumbers in our garden.

"Yeah." I nod. "You may pick that one and put it in the basket."

"I pick?" Collin runs toward us, his hearing better than any two-year-old's should be. He practically tumbles to a stop at the end of the row, narrowly missing my tomato plants. Honestly, it'll be a miracle if they survive the elements—my children and Mother Nature.

"Storm's coming," Rainer calls from across the yard. Shirtless and with his tool belt slung low on his hips, he is the most attractive man I've ever seen, and he's all mine. "Hey," he shouts. "My eyes are up here."

I bite back a laugh as my gaze lifts. "I'm just appreciating the view, and all your hard work."

"Yeah?" He chuckles.

"Rainer." Lulu tugs on his arm. She's sporting her own toolbelt, one made up of plastic toys. She's been following him around all day, his shadow as he puts the final touches on our chicken coop.

"What's up, girlie?" He bends down to meet her at her level.

"How much longer till we get baby chicks?"

He appraises his work. "If we work hard, maybe by the end of next week."

Her eyes are wide with excitement. "Ari! Ari, did you hear that?" She races toward her older brother. "It's almost time for baby chicks!"

A flash from the sky, followed by a crack of thunder, ends our outdoor fun. I share a look with Rainer, and we quickly pack up our tools and the children, making our way inside right before fat drops begin to fall.

"Take off your shoes before you go in the house!" I call to the children as they race inside the mud room.

Another roll of thunder rattles the house.

Rainer comes to my side, glancing down at the video monitor in my hand. "She's sleeping through all this?"

"You know she is." I chuckle. I don't know how we got so damn lucky, but Cassie is the easiest baby. She's perpetually happy, has been sleeping through the night since she was three weeks old, and naps a solid three hours every afternoon. It's almost as if the universe knew I couldn't handle any more stress. The only down-side about her being so good? I'm tempted to have another.

"What are you thinking about?" Rainer studies my face, taking the basket of vegetables from my arm and setting the baby monitor on top of today's haul.

I almost don't want to admit it, but this is my best friend. I can't keep anything from him. "I was just thinking about how Cassie makes me want to have another one."

"Really?" His brows lift in shock.

"I mean, what's one more when you already have four?"

"Our own basketball team." He nods. "I dig it."

"Really?" Now it's my turn to be surprised. "You would be open to that?"

"Making a baby with you?" He wraps his arms around my waist, his gaze roving down my body appreciatively. "We can practice later."

"Later?" I shrug. "Why not now?"

"Kids! Movie time!" Rainer calls over my shoulder.

"Can we make popcorn?" Lulu yells from inside the house.

"You can have whatever you want!" He laughs.

I shake my head. "You do realize she has you wrapped around her finger?"

"So? I like it that way." He presses a kiss to my mouth, then nods toward the house. "Now, you promised me an afternoon delight. I'll get the little monsters settled, you go upstairs and take a few minutes to decompress. Maybe even start without me." He nibbles on my neck. "As long as you wait for me to finish."

I meet his grin with one of my own. Everything this man does, he does it to make my life better. Like buying us a house with room for chickens and horses. Or raising my children as if they were his own. Or holding things down so I can coach young breakaway ropers twice a week. And yes, even buying me new vibrators so that I'm able to climax easier when we're rushed for time.

Sure, we're going about this family thing a little unconventionally. We're still not married. But I don't need a band around my finger to declare my love. Anyone who steps in this house we share knows within an instant how hard we love, and that the best things in life are free. Rainer is my person, and we belong together. Everything else can be figured out.

ACKNOWLEDGMENTS

Writing is a solitary act, but I couldn't do this without the support of the people who love and support me. I'm incredibly grateful for the individuals who keep me happy, healthy, and sane as I attempt to meet deadlines and navigate life when the world feels like it's on fire.

To my best friends—Kerry and Viv for cheering me through missed deadlines and reminding me I deserve good things, especially when I doubt myself. For reading my work when it's messy and giving me valuable feedback. I love you both!

To my children, Abby, JD, and Gianna. You are my reasons—the motivation in everything I do. You bring so much joy to my life, and I'll never get over the way you support my writing career. I love you.

To my author friends, thank you for the support and camaraderie. Marley, thank you for listening to my countless messages. Ginger, we just get each other and being understood is one of the best gifts. AJ, thank you for the conversations and writing dates.

I also want to thank Debbie and Eddie for creating the best community to workout in Chandler, Arizona. To the many FLO instructors who remind me that I'm strong and capable, I appreciate you more than words can express.

To my PA, Debra, you are an incredible human. Not only for what you do for me, but for all the ways you support others while navigating life.

Shauna, thank you for working with me as I slogged my way to the finish line on this book. You are professional, talented, and I look forward to the next time we get to work together.

Laura and Melissa, thank you for sharing your gift of being able to catch all the errors that make it through edits. I appreciate you both so much!

To Jane Ashley for another cowboy! I don't know where you find these guys, but they make the best covers.

Kim Wilson, I love what you've created for this series and I'm absolutely in love with the color palette and design for Wild Crush. Thank you and I can't wait to work together again in a few months!

I also want to thank my audiobook team, Dani from Elysian Nightfall Studios for editing and mastering and Brittney from Lady Bee Media for proofing. Erin and Rob, thank you for voicing Maeve and Rainer's story. You both captured these characters perfectly and it's another fantastic edition to the Wilder Valley series.

Thanks to Shauna and Becca from The Author Agency for being such an amazing support, and for helping this book reach new readers. I am forever appreciative of your genuine spirit and hard work.

Thank you to my ARC team and each and every book blogger, bookstagrammer, and booktoker who spent their time reading and recommending this book. I am overwhelmed by your support!

Most of all, I appreciate and thank *you*—the reader who decided to pick up this book. I hope my words gave you a beautiful escape. You are the reason I get to do what I love while supporting my family. Thank you!

ALSO BY KACEY SHEA

Wilder Valley

Wild Hearts

Wild Mistake

Wild Love

Wild Crush

Wild Kiss

Standalones

One Good Thing

The Perfect Comeback

Firefighters

Caught in the Flames

One Hot Night

Caught in the Lies

Caught in the Chase

Caught in Us

Rock Stars

Detour

Derail

Hinder

Replay

ABOUT THE AUTHOR

Kacey Shea is a USA Today bestselling author of steamy contemporary romance. She enjoys writing strong and smart heroines, heroes with hearts of gold, and stories that deliver a satisfying, well-earned happily ever after.

When she's not writing you will find her hanging with her children, drinking iced tea by the gallon, or planning her next escape from the Arizona heat.

Sign up for Kacey's newsletter here to receive a free book, access to exclusive bonus content, and never miss a new release!

Do you use BookBub? Follow me to receive an alert for future new releases!

For more information
www.kaceysheabooks.com
info@kaceysheabooks.com

Made in the USA
Middletown, DE
09 July 2024

57089647R00158